The earth is an eco-system. It possesses a collective memory. Everything that happens, no matter how insignificant it may seem, affects in some way at some time the existence of everything else within that system.

**Eco-Fiction** raises important questions about man's place in the system:

- Will man continue to ignore the warnings of the environment and destroy his source of life?
- Will he follow the herd into the slaughter-house?

The earth as an eco-system will continue into infinity—with or without man.

**Eco-Fiction** brings together the finest environmental fiction of the nineteenth and twentieth centuries.

**ECO-FICTION**
is an original Washington Square Press edition.

# ECO-FICTION

Edited by
## John Stadler

WSP
ｎWASHINGTON SQUARE PRESS · NEW YORK

ECO-FICTION

*Washington Square Press* edition published April, 1971

L

Published by Washington Square Press,
a division of Simon & Schuster, Inc., 630 Fifth Avenue, New York, N.Y.

WASHINGTON SQUARE PRESS editions are distributed in the
U.S. by Simon & Schuster, Inc., 630 Fifth Avenue, New
York, N.Y. 10020 and in Canada by Simon & Schuster
of Canada, Ltd., Richmond Hill, Ontario, Canada.

# ACKNOWLEDGMENTS

JAMES AGEE

"A Mother's Tale" by James Agee, copyright, 1952, by the
James Agee Trust. Reprinted by permission of Grosset &
Dunlap, Inc.

ISAAC ASIMOV

"It's Such a Beautiful Day" by Isaac Asimov, copyright,
1954, by Ballantine Books, Inc. Reprinted by permission
of the author.

J. G. BALLARD

The Subliminal Man" by J. C. Ballard, copyright, ©, 1964,
by J. G. Ballard. Reprinted by permission of the author
and the author's agents, Scott Meredith Literary Agency,
Inc.

# CONTENTS

PREFACE ....................................................................... ix

Ray Bradbury
   A SOUND OF THUNDER ..................................... 1

John Steinbeck
   THE TURTLE ...................................................... 14

Edgar Allan Poe
   THE CONVERSATION OF EIROS AND CHARMION 17

A. E. Coppard
   THE FAIR YOUNG WILLOWY TREE ................... 24

James Agee
   A MOTHER'S TALE ............................................ 32

Robert M. Coates
   THE LAW .......................................................... 54

Daphne du Maurier
   THE BIRDS ........................................................ 59

Robley Wilson, Jr.
   A STAY AT THE OCEAN ................................... 85

E. B. White
   THE SUPREMACY OF URUGUAY ....................... 100

J. F. Powers
   LOOK HOW THE FISH LIVE ............................. 104

Kurt Vonnegut, Jr.
   TOMORROW AND TOMORROW AND TOMORROW 119

Sarah Orne Jewett
   A WHITE HERON ............................................. 134

Frank Herbert
THE MARY CELESTE MOVE ............................. 145

Saki (H. H. Munro)
THE TOYS OF PEACE ........................................ 153

J. G. Ballard
THE SUBLIMINAL MAN ................................... 159

Steven Schrader
THE COHEN DOG EXCLUSION ACT .................... 178

Isaac Asimov
IT'S SUCH A BEAUTIFUL DAY ............................ 183

William Saroyan
THE HUMMINGBIRD THAT LIVED THROUGH
WINTER ........................................................... 207

# PREFACE

Someone inadvertently steps on a butterfly. A man cuts down a willow tree whose branches are reaching too close to a string of telegraph lines. A young man waits for his grandfather's death; when it comes he will inherit his bed and have children himself. A father drives out onto the ocean floor in search of the lost tide. Another man wonders why he buys a carton of cigarettes every day. A child takes the wrong door to school. An old man and a young boy care for a hummingbird. Each of these actions changes the environment. Each changes the course of history.

Scientists speculate upon the consequences of man's interference with the natural world in which he lives. And they sound the alarm at our irresponsible destruction. But, as we shall see, men rarely listen to these warnings—or, if they listen, they even more rarely act. Is it possible that men will be moved by the artist, the short-story writer?

*Eco-Fiction* is not a collection of science-fiction stories, though some are included. Nor is it a collection of nature stories, though they too appear. It is a collection which seeks to make the reader think about his relationship with his natural environment. These are stories about ecology (though that may have been far from some of the writers' intents) to entertain, instruct and disturb the reader.

Every day we witness (and join in) the unthinking actions men take which interfere, sometimes with disastrous consequences, with the natural actions of the environment. We use various pesticides on our farms which sometimes leave dead birds along with bigger tomatoes. We toss the refuse from our industries into our lakes and fling it into our air. We keep our clothes and dishes clean with solutions which spoil our drinking water and despoil our swimming water. We sail along our highways dropping cans and bottles on their surfaces and spreading foul air all about. We commit gradual suicide with our cigarettes.

Yet we want a clean environment, a balanced ecology, a stable population. The dimensions of the problem can be simply stated: it is a simple matter of life—or death. We live in one eco-system, on one planet; each of our actions affects that life system. Our spaceship cannot function if we expect the other fellow to conserve its raw materials, control its population, keep its air and waters clean.

It is, of course, impossible for us to view our every action in terms of its relevance to the environment, but it is possible to understand the importance of our actions in relation to our environment. The importance of our learning cannot be overstated; if we do not learn, we have little hope.

Beyond entertaining the reader, which I hope this collection will do, I hope this anthology will encourage some serious thinking. I have been struck by some repeated themes. The first is that men do not listen to warnings. The second is that even if men hear the warnings, they do not heed them; we do nothing. The third is that we should not let ourselves be paralyzed into idleness by the vastness and complexity of our ecological problems. Ecological catastrophes seem to begin in small, simple, controllable actions. The last theme is that solutions, like the problems themselves, may have their beginnings in the small and simple acts of individual men.

JOHN STADLER

# ECO-FICTION

Ray Bradbury

# A SOUND OF THUNDER

*With the realization of the importance of even our smallest acts, we may come to perceive our tremendous impact upon our environment—the only world we have.*

———◆•◆◆———

The sign on the wall seemed to quaver under a film of sliding warm water. Eckels felt his eyelids blink over his stare, and the sign burned in this momentary darkness:

TIME SAFARI, INC.
SAFARIS TO ANY YEAR IN THE PAST.
YOU NAME THE ANIMAL.
WE TAKE YOU THERE.
YOU SHOOT IT.

A warm phlegm gathered in Eckels' throat; he swallowed and pushed it down. The muscles around his mouth formed a smile as he put his hand slowly out upon the air, and in that hand waved a check for ten thousand dollars to the man behind the desk.

"Does this safari guarantee I come back alive?"

"We guarantee nothing," said the official, "except the dinosaurs." He turned. "This is Mr. Travis, your Safari Guide in the Past. He'll tell you what and where to shoot. If he says no shooting, no shooting. If you disobey instructions, there's a stiff penalty of another ten thousand dollars, plus possible government action, on your return."

1

Eckels glanced across the vast office at a mass and tangle, a snaking and humming of wires and steel boxes, at an aurora that flickered now orange, now silver, now blue. There was a sound like a gigantic bonfire burning all of Time, all the years and all the parchment calendars, all the hours piled high and set aflame.

A touch of the hand and this burning would, on the instant, beautifully reverse itself. Eckels remembered the wording in the advertisements to the letter. Out of chars and ashes, out of dust and coals, like golden salamanders, the old years, the green years, might leap; roses sweeten the air, white hair turn Irish-black, wrinkles vanish; all, everything fly back to seed, flee death, rush down to their beginnings, suns rise in western skies and set in glorious easts, moons eat themselves opposite to the custom, all and everything cupping one in another like Chinese boxes, rabbits into hats, all and everything returning to the fresh death, the seed death, the green death, to the time before the beginning. A touch of a hand might do it, the merest touch of a hand.

"Unbelievable." Eckels breathed, the light of the Machine on his thin face. "A real Time Machine." He shook his head. "Makes you think. If the election had gone badly yesterday, I might be here now running away from the results. Thank God Keith won. He'll make a fine President of the United States."

"Yes," said the man behind the desk. "We're lucky. If Deutscher had gotten in, we'd have the worst kind of dictatorship. There's an anti-everything man for you, a militarist, anti-Christ, anti-human, anti-intellectual. People called us up, you know, joking but not joking. Said if Deutscher became President they wanted to go live in 1492. Of course it's not our business to conduct escapes, but to form safaris. Anyway, Keith's President now. All you got to worry about is—"

"Shooting my dinosaur," Eckels finished it for him.

"A *Tyrannosaurus rex*. The Tyrant Lizard, the most incredible monster in history. Sign this release. Anything happens to you, we're not responsible. Those dinosaurs are hungry."

Eckels flushed angrily. "Trying to scare me!"

"Frankly, yes. We don't want anyone going who'll panic

at the first shot. Six Safari leaders were killed last year, and a dozen hunters. We're here to give you the severest thrill a *real* hunter ever asked for. Traveling you back sixty million years to bag the biggest game in all of Time. Your personal check's still there. Tear it up."

Mr. Eckels looked at the check. His fingers twitched.

"Good luck," said the man behind the desk. "Mr. Travis, he's all yours."

They moved silently across the room, taking their guns with them, toward the Machine, toward the silver metal and the roaring light.

First a day and then a night and then a day and then a night, then it was day-night-day-night-day. A week, a month, a year, a decade! A.D. 2055. A.D. 2019. 1999! 1957! Gone! The Machine roared.

They put on their oxygen helmets and tested the intercoms.

Eckels swayed on the padded seat, his face pale, his jaw stiff. He felt the trembling in his arms and he looked down and found his hands tight on the new rifle. There were four other men in the Machine. Travis, the Safari Leader, his assistant, Lesperance, and two other hunters, Billings and Kramer. They sat looking at each other, and the years blazed around them.

"Can these guns get a dinosaur cold?" Eckels felt his mouth saying.

"If you hit them right," said Travis on the helmet radio. "Some dinosaurs have two brains, one in the head, another far down the spinal column. We stay away from those. That's stretching luck. Put your first two shots into the eyes, if you can, blind them, and go back into the brain."

The Machine howled. Time was a film run backward. Suns fled and ten million moons fled after them. "Think," said Eckels. "Every hunter that ever lived would envy us today. This makes Africa seem like Illinois."

The Machine slowed; its scream fell to a murmur. The Machine stopped.

The sun stopped in the sky.

The fog that had enveloped the Machine blew away and they were in an old time, a very old time indeed, three hunters and two Safari Heads with their blue metal guns across their knees.

"Christ isn't born yet," said Travis. "Moses has not gone to the mountain to talk with God. The Pyramids are still in the earth, waiting to be cut out and put up. *Remember* that. Alexander, Caesar, Napoleon, Hitler—none of them exists."

The man nodded.

"That"—Mr. Travis pointed—"is the jungle of sixty million, two thousand and fifty-five years before President Keith."

He indicated a metal path that struck off into green wilderness, over streaming swamp, among giant ferns and palms.

"And that," he said, "is the Path, laid by Time Safari for your use. It floats six inches above the earth. Doesn't touch so much as one grass blade, flower or tree. It's an anti-gravity metal. Its purpose is to keep you from touching this world of the past in any way. Stay on the Path. Don't go off it. I repeat, *don't go off*. For *any* reason! If you fall off, there's a penalty. And don't shoot any animal we don't okay."

"Why?" asked Eckels.

They sat in the ancient wilderness. Far birds' cries blew on a wind, and the smell of tar and an old salt sea, moist grasses, and flowers the color of blood.

"We don't want to change the Future. We don't belong here in the Past. The government doesn't *like* us here. We have to pay big graft to keep our franchise. A Time Machine is finicky business. Not knowing it, we might kill an important animal, a small bird, a roach, a flower even, thus destroying an important link in a growing species."

"That's not clear," said Eckels.

"All right," Travis continued, "say we accidentally kill one mouse here. That means all the future families of this one particular mouse are destroyed, right?"

"Right."

"And all the families of the families of the families of that one mouse! With a stamp of your foot, you annihilate first one, then a dozen, then a thousand, a million, a *billion* possible mice!"

"So they're dead," said Eckels. "So what?"

"So what?" Travis snorted quietly. "Well, what about the foxes that'll need those mice to survive? For want of ten mice, a fox dies. For want of ten foxes, a lion starves. For want of a lion, all manner of insects, vultures, infinite billions of life forms are thrown into chaos and destruction. Eventually it all boils down to this: fifty-nine million years later, a caveman, one of a dozen on the *entire world,* goes hunting wild boar or saber-toothed tiger for food. But you, friend, have *stepped* on all the tigers in that region. By stepping on *one* single mouse. So the caveman starves. And the caveman, please note, is not just *any* expendable man, no! He is an *entire future nation.* From his loins would have sprung ten sons. From *their* loins one hundred sons, and thus onward to a civilization. Destroy this one man, and you destroy a race, a people, an entire history of life. It is comparable to slaying some of Adam's grandchildren. The stomp of your foot, on one mouse, could start an earthquake, the effects of which could shake our earth and destinies down through Time to their very foundations. With the death of that one caveman, a billion others yet unborn are throttled in the womb. Perhaps Rome never rises on its seven hills. Perhaps Europe is forever a dark forest, and only Asia waxes healthy and teeming. Step on a mouse and you crush the pyramids. Step on a mouse and you leave your print, like a Grand Canyon, across Eternity. Queen Elizabeth might never be born, Washington might not cross the Delaware, there might never be a United States at all. So be careful. Stay on the Path. *Never* step off!"

"I see," said Eckels. "Then it wouldn't pay for us even to touch the *grass?*"

"Correct. Crushing certain plants could add up infinitesimally. A little error here would multiply in sixty million years, all out of proportion. Of course maybe our theory is wrong. Maybe Time *can't* be changed by us. Or maybe it can be changed only in little subtle ways. A dead mouse here makes an insect imbalance there, a population disproportion later, a bad harvest further on, a depression, mass starvation, and, finally, a change in *social* temperament in far-flung countries. Something much more subtle, like that. Perhaps only a soft breath, a whisper, a hair, pollen on the air, such a slight, slight change that unless you looked close you wouldn't see it. Who knows? Who really can say he knows? We don't know. We're guessing. But until we do know for certain whether our messing around in Time *can* make a big roar or a little rustle in history, we're being careful. This Machine, this Path, your clothing and bodies, were sterilized, as you know, before the journey. We wear these oxygen helmets so we can't introduce our bacteria into an ancient atmosphere."

"How do we know which animals to shoot?"

"They're marked with red paint," said Travis. "Today, before our journey, we sent Lesperance here back with the Machine. He came to this particular era and followed certain animals."

"Studying them?"

"Right," said Lesperance. "I track them through their entire existence, noting which of them lives longest. Very few. How many times they mate. Not often. Life's short. When I find one that's going to die when a tree falls on him, or one that drowns in a tar pit, I note the exact hour, minute, and second. I shoot a paint bomb. It leaves a red patch on his side. We can't miss it. Then I correlate our arrival in the Past so that we meet the monster not more than two minutes before he would have died anyway. This way, we kill only animals with no future, that are never going to mate again. You see how *careful* we are?"

"But if you came back this morning in Time," said Eckels eagerly, "you must've bumped into *us*, our Safari! How did it turn out? Was it successful? Did all of us get through—alive?"

Travis and Lesperance gave each other a look.

"That'd be a paradox," said the latter. "Time doesn't permit that sort of mess—a man meeting himself. When such occasions threaten, Time steps aside. Like an airplane hitting an air pocket. You felt the Machine jump just before we stopped? That was us passing ourselves on the way back to the Future. We saw nothing. There's no way of telling *if* this expedition was a success, *if we* got our monster, or whether all of us—meaning *you*, Mr. Eckels—got out alive."

Eckels smiled palely.

"Cut that," said Travis sharply. "Everyone on his feet!"

They were ready to leave the Machine.

The jungle was high and the jungle was broad and the jungle was the entire world forever and forever. Sounds like music and sounds like flying tents filled the sky, and those were pterodactyls soaring with cavernous gray wings, gigantic bats of delirium and night fever. Eckels, balanced on the narrow Path, aimed his rifle playfully.

"Stop that!" said Travis. "Don't even aim for fun, blast you! If your guns should go off—"

Eckels flushed. "Where's our *Tyrannosaurus?*"

Lesperance checked his wristwatch. "Up ahead. We'll bisect his trail in sixty seconds. Look for the red paint! Don't shoot till we give the word. Stay on the Path. *Stay on the Path!*"

They moved forward in the wind of morning.

"Strange," murmured Eckels. "Up ahead, sixty million years, Election Day over. Keith made President. Everyone celebrating. And here we are, a million years lost, and they don't exist. The things we worried about for months, a lifetime, not even born or thought of yet."

"Safety catches off, everyone!" ordered Travis. "You, first shot, Eckels. Second, Billings. Third, Kramer."

"I've hunted tiger, wild boar, buffalo, elephant, but now, this is *it*," said Eckels. "I'm shaking like a kid."

"Ah," said Travis.

Everyone stopped.

Travis raised his hand. "Ahead," he whispered. "In the mist. There he is. There's His Royal Majesty now."

The jungle was wide and full of twitterings, rustlings, murmurs and sighs.

Suddenly it all ceased, as if someone had shut a door.

Silence.

A sound of thunder.

Out of the mist, one hundred yards away, came *Tyrannosaurus rex*.

"It," whispered Eckels. "It . . ."

"Sh!"

It came on great oiled, resilient, striding legs. It towered thirty feet above half of the trees, a great evil god, folding its delicate watchmaker's claws close to its oily reptilian chest. Each lower leg was a piston, a thousand pounds of white bone, sunk in thick ropes of muscle, sheathed over in a gleam of pebbled skin like the mail of a terrible warrior.

Each thigh was a ton of meat, ivory and steel mesh. And from the great breathing cage of the upper body those two delicate arms dangled out front, arms with hands which might pick up and examine men like toys, while the snake neck coiled. And the head itself, a ton of sculptured stone, lifted easily upon the sky. Its mouth gaped, exposing a fence of teeth like daggers. Its eyes rolled, ostrich eggs, empty of all expression save hunger. It closed its mouth in a death grin. It ran, its pelvic bones crushing aside trees and bushes, its taloned feet clawing damp earth, leaving prints six inches deep wherever it settled its weight. It ran with a gliding ballet step, far too poised and balanced for its ten tons. It moved into a sunlit arena warily, its beautifully reptilian hands feeling the air.

"Why, why—" Eckels twitched his mouth. "It could reach up and grab the moon."

"Sh!" Travis jerked angrily. "He hasn't seen us yet."

"It can't be killed." Eckels pronounced this verdict quietly, as if there could be no argument. He had weighed the evidence and this was his considered opinion. The rifle in his hands seemed a cap gun. "We were fools to come. This is impossible."

"Shut up!" hissed Travis.

"Nightmare."

"Turn around," commanded Travis. "Walk quietly to the Machine. We'll remit one half your fee."

"I didn't realize it would be this *big*," said Eckels. "I miscalculated, that's all. And now I want out."

"It *sees* us!"

"There's the red paint on its chest!"

The Tyrant Lizard raised itself. Its armored flesh glittered like a thousand green coins. The coins, crusted with slime, steamed. In the slime, tiny insects wriggled, so that the entire body seemed to twitch and undulate, even while the monster itself did not move. It exhaled. The stink of raw flesh blew down the wilderness.

"Get me out of here," said Eckels. "It was never like this before. I was always sure I'd come through alive. I had good guides, good safaris and safety. This time, I figured wrong. I've met my match and admit it. This is too much for me to get hold of."

"Don't run," said Lesperance. "Turn around. Hide in the Machine."

"Yes." Eckels seemed to be numb. He looked at his feet as if trying to make them move. He gave a grunt of helplessness.

"Eckels!"

He took a few steps, blinking, shuffling.

"Not *that* way!"

The Monster, at the first motion, lunged forward with a terrible scream. It covered one hundred yards in six seconds. The rifles jerked up and blazed fire. A windstorm from the beast's mouth engulfed them in the stench of slime and old blood. The Monster roared, teeth glittering with sun.

Eckels, not looking back, walked blindly to the edge of the Path, his gun limp in his arms, stepped off the Path, and walked, not knowing it, in the jungle. His feet sank into green moss. His legs moved him, and he felt alone and remote from the events behind.

The rifles cracked again. Their sound was lost in shriek and lizard thunder. The great level of the reptile's tail swung up, lashed sideways. Trees exploded in clouds of leaf and branch. The Monster twitched its jeweler's hands down to fondle at the men, to twist them in half, to crush them like berries, to cram them into its teeth and its screaming throat. Its boulder-stone eyes leveled with the men. They saw themselves mirrored. They fired at the metallic eyelids and the blazing black irises.

Like a stone idol, like a mountain avalanche, *Tyrannosaurus* fell. Thundering, it clutched trees, pulled them with it. It wrenched and tore the metal Path. The men flung themselves back and away. The body hit, ten tons of cold flesh and stone. The guns fired. The Monster lashed its armored tail, twitched its snake jaws and lay still. A fount of blood spurted from its throat. Somewhere inside, a sac of fluids burst. Sickening gushes drenched the hunters. They stood, red and glistening.

The thunder faded.

The jungle was silent. After the avalanche, a green peace. After the nightmare, morning.

Billings and Kramer sat on the pathway and threw up.

Travis and Lesperance stood with smoking rifles, cursing steadily.

In the Time Machine, on his face, Eckels lay shivering. He had found his way back to the Path, climbed into the Machine.

Travis came walking, glanced at Eckels, took cotton gauze from a metal box and returned to the others, who were sitting on the Path.

"Clean up."

They wiped the blood from their helmets. They began to curse too. The Monster lay, a hill of solid flesh. Within, you could hear the sighs and murmurs as the furthest chambers of it died, the organs malfunctioning, liquids running a final instant from pocket to sac to spleen, everything shutting off, closing up forever. It was like standing by a wrecked locomotive or a steam shovel at quitting time, all valves being released or levered tight. Bones cracked; the tonnage of its own flesh, off balance, dead weight, snapped the delicate forearms, caught underneath. The meat settled, quivering.

Another cracking sound. Overhead, a gigantic tree branch broke from its heavy mooring, fell. It crashed upon the dead beast with finality.

"There." Lesperance checked his watch. "Right on time. That's the giant tree that was scheduled to fall and kill this animal originally." He glanced at the two hunters. "You want the trophy picture?"

"What?"

"We can't take a trophy back to the Future. The body has to stay right here where it would have died originally, so the insects, birds, and bacteria can get at it, as they were intended to. Everything in balance. The body stays. But we *can* take a picture of you standing near it."

The two men tried to think, but gave up, shaking their heads.

They let themselves be led along the metal Path. They sank wearily into the Machine cushions. They gazed back at the ruined Monster, the stagnating mound, where already strange reptilian birds and golden insects were busy at the steaming armor.

A sound on the floor of the Time Machine stiffened them. Eckels sat there, shivering.

"I'm sorry," he said at last.

"Get up!" cried Travis.

Eckels got up.

"Go out on that Path alone," said Travis. He had his rifle pointed. "You're not coming back in the Machine. We're leaving you here!"

Lesperance seized Travis' arm. "Wait—"

"Stay out of this!" Travis shook his hand away. "This fool nearly killed us. But it isn't *that* so much, no. It's his *shoes!* Look at them! He ran off the Path. That *ruins* us! We'll forfeit! Thousands of dollars of insurance! We guarantee no one leaves the Path. He left it. Oh, the fool! I'll have to report to the government. They might revoke our license to travel. Who knows *what* he's done to Time, to History!"

"Take it easy. All he did was kick up some dirt."

"How do we *know?*" cried Travis. "We don't know anything! It's all a mystery! Get out of here, Eckels!"

Eckels fumbled his shirt. "I'll pay anything. A hundred thousand dollars!"

Travis glared at Eckels' checkbook and spat. "Go out there. The Monster's next to the Path. Stick your arms up to your elbows in his mouth. Then you can come back with us."

"That's unreasonable!"

"The Monster's dead, you idiot. The bullets! The bullets can't be left behind. They don't belong in the Past; they might change anything. Here's my knife. Dig them out!"

The jungle was alive again, full of the old tremorings and bird cries. Eckels turned slowly to regard the primeval garbage dump, that hill of nightmares and terror. After a long time, like a sleepwalker he shuffled out along the Path.

He returned, shuddering, five minutes later, his arms soaked and red to the elbows. He held out his hands. Each held a number of steel bullets. Then he fell. He lay where he fell, not moving.

"You didn't have to make him do that," said Lesperance.

"Didn't I? It's too early to tell." Travis nudged the still body. "He'll live. Next time he won't go hunting game like this. Okay." He jerked his thumb wearily at Lesperance. "Switch on. Let's go home."

1492. 1776. 1812.

They cleaned their hands and faces. They changed their

caking shirts and pants. Eckels was up and around again, not speaking. Travis glared at him for a full ten minutes.

"Don't look at me," cried Eckels. "I haven't done anything."

"Who can tell?"

"Just ran off the Path, that's all, a little mud on my shoes —what do you want me to do, get down and pray?"

"We might need it. I'm warning you, Eckels, I might kill you yet. I've got my gun ready."

"I'm innocent. I've done nothing!"

1999. 2000. 2055.

The Machine stopped.

"Get out," said Travis.

The room was there as they had left it. But not the same as they had left it. The same man sat behind the same desk. But the same man did not quite sit behind the same desk.

Travis looked around swiftly. "Everything okay here?" he snapped.

"Fine. Welcome home!"

Travis did not relax. He seemed to be looking at the very atoms of the air itself, at the way the sun poured through the one high window.

"Okay, Eckels, get out. Don't ever come back."

Eckels could not move.

"You heard me," said Travis. "What're you *staring* at?"

Eckels stood smelling of the air, and there was a thing to the air, a chemical taint so subtle, so slight, that only a faint cry of his subliminal senses warned him it was there. The colors, white, gray, blue, orange, in the wall, in the furniture, in the sky beyond the window, were . . . were . . . And there was a *feel*. His flesh twitched. His hands twitched. He stood drinking the oddness with the pores of his body. Somewhere, someone must have been screaming one of those whistles that only a dog can hear. His body screamed silence in return. Beyond this room, beyond this wall, beyond this man who was not quite the same man seated at this desk that was not quite the same desk . . . lay an entire world of streets and people. What sort of world it was now, there was no telling. He could feel them moving there, beyond the walls, almost, like so many chess pieces blown in a dry wind. . . .

But the immediate thing was the sign painted on the

office wall, the same sign he had read earlier today on first entering.

Somehow, the sign had changed:

> TYME SEFARI INC.
> SEFARIS TU ANY YEER EN THE PAST.
> YU NAIM THE ANIMALL.
> WEE TAEKYUTHAIR.
> YU SHOOT ITT.

Eckels felt himself fall into a chair. He fumbled crazily at the thick slime on his boots. He held up a clod of dirt, trembling. "No, it *can't* be. Not a *little* thing like that, No!"

Embedded in the mud, glistening green and gold and black, was a butterfly, very beautiful and very dead.

"Not a little thing like *that!* Not a butterfly!" cried Eckels.

It fell to the floor, an exquisite thing, a small thing that could upset balances and knock down a line of small dominoes and then big dominoes and then gigantic dominoes, all down the years across Time. Eckels' mind whirled. It *couldn't* change things. Killing one butterfly couldn't be *that* important! Could it?

His face was cold. His mouth trembled, asking: "Who—who won the presidential election yesterday?"

The man behind the desk laughed. "You joking? You know very well. Deutscher, of course! Who else? Not that fool weakling Keith. We got an iron man now, a man with guts!" The official stopped. "What's wrong?"

Eckels moaned. He dropped to his knees. He scrabbled at the golden butterfly with shaking fingers. "Can't we," he pleaded to the world, to himself, to the officials, to the Machine, "can't we take it *back*, can't we *make* it alive again? Can't we start over? Can't we—"

He did not move. Eyes shut, he waited, shivering. He heard Travis breathe loud in the room; he heard Travis shift his rifle, click the safety catch and raise the weapon.

There was a sound of thunder.

John Steinbeck
# THE TURTLE

*Man is not the only creature who moves the earth;
it does not belong to him alone. Imagine the effect
he has upon it, if even the slowest creature ac-
complishes so much on a trip across a highway.*

———◆—◍◆◍—◆———

The concrete highway was edged with a mat of tangled,
broken, dry grass, and the grass heads were heavy with oat
beards to catch on a dog's coat, and foxtails to tangle in a
horse's fetlocks and clover burrs to fasten in sheep's wool;
sleeping life waiting to be spread and dispersed, every seed
armed with an appliance of dispersal, twisting darts and
parachutes for the wind, little spears and balls of tiny
thorns, and all waiting for animals and for the wind, for a
man's trouser cuff or the hem of a woman's skirt, all pas-
sive but armed with appliances of activity, still, but each
possessed of the anlage of movement.
   The sun lay on the grass and warmed it, and in the shade
under the grass the insects moved, ants and ant lions to
set traps for them, grasshoppers to jump into the air and
flick their yellow wings for a second, sow bugs like little
armadillos, plodding restlessly on many tender feet. And
over the grass at the roadside a land turtle crawled, turning
aside for nothing, dragging his high-domed shell over the
grass. His hard legs and yellow-nailed feet threshed slowly
through the grass, not really walking, but boosting and
dragging his shell along. The barley beards slid off his shell,
and the clover burrs fell on him and rolled to the ground.
14

His horny beak was partly open, and his fierce, humorous eyes, under brows like fingernails, stared straight ahead. He came over the grass leaving a beaten trail behind him, and the hill, which was the highway embankment, reared up ahead of him. For a moment he stopped, his head held high. He blinked and looked up and down. At last he started to climb the embankment. Front clawed feet reached forward but did not touch. The hind feet kicked his shell along, and it scraped on the grass, and on the gravel. As the embankment grew steeper and steeper, the more frantic were the efforts of the land turtle. Pushing hind legs strained and slipped, boosting the shell along, and the horny head protruded as far as the neck could stretch. Little by little the shell slid up the embankment until at last a parapet cut straight across its line of march, the shoulder of the road, a concrete wall four inches high. As though they worked independently the hind legs pushed the shell against the wall. The head upraised and peered over the wall to the broad smooth plain of cement. Now the hands, braced on top of the wall, strained and lifted, and the shell came slowly up and rested its front end on the wall. For a moment the turtle rested. A red ant ran into the shell, into the soft skin inside the shell, and suddenly head and legs snapped in, and the armored tail clamped in sideways. The red ant was crushed between body and legs. And one head of wild oats was clamped into the shell by a front leg. For a long moment the turtle lay still, and then the neck crept out and the old humorous frowning eyes looked about and the legs and tail came out. The back legs went to work, straining like elephant legs, and the shell tipped to an angle so that the front legs could not reach the level cement plain. But higher and higher the hind legs boosted it, until at last the center of balance was reached, the front tipped down, the front legs scratched at the pavement, and it was up. But the head of wild oats was held by its stem around the front legs.

Now the going was easy, and all the legs worked, and the shell boosted along, waggling from side to side. A sedan driven by a forty-year-old woman approached. She saw the turtle and swung to the right, off the highway, the wheels screamed and a cloud of dust boiled up. Two wheels lifted for a moment and then settled. The car skidded back

onto the road, and went on, but more slowly. The turtle
had jerked into its shell, but now it hurried on, for the
highway was burning hot.

And now a light truck approached, and as it came near,
the driver saw the turtle and swerved to hit it. His front
wheel struck the edge of the shell, flipped the turtle like a
tiddlywink, spun it like a coin and rolled it off the highway.
The truck went back to its course along the right side.
Lying on its back, the turtle was tight in its shell for a long
time. But at last its legs waved in the air, reaching for
something to pull it over. Its front foot caught a piece of
quartz and little by little the shell pulled over and flopped
upright. The wild oat head fell out and three of the spear-
head seeds stuck in the ground. And as the turtle crawled
on down the embankment, its shell dragged dirt over the
seeds. The turtle entered a dust road and jerked itself along,
drawing a wavy shallow trench in the dust with its shell.
The old humorous eyes looked ahead, and the horny beak
opened a little. His yellow toenails slipped a fraction in the
dust.

Edgar Allan Poe

# THE CONVERSATION OF EIROS
   AND CHARMION

*Man has prophets as well as problems, but he
seems unable even to contemplate taking some
positive action when given warnings about the
future of his existence.*

———◆———

Πῦρ σοι προσοίσω.
I will bring fire to thee.
EURIPIDES, *Androm.* [257].

### EIROS.

Why do you call me Eiros?

### CHARMION.

So henceforward will you always be called. You must
forget, too, *my* earthly name, and speak to me as Charmion.

### EIROS.

This is indeed no dream!

### CHARMION.

Dreams are with us no more—but of these mysteries
anon. I rejoice to see you looking lifelike and rational. The
film of the shadow has already passed from off your eyes.
Be of heart, and fear nothing. Your allotted days of stupor
have expired; and, to-morrow, I will myself induct you into
the full joys and wonders of your novel existence.

17

EIROS.

True—I feel no stupor—none at all. The wild sickness
and the terrible darkness have left me, and I hear no longer
that mad, rushing, horrible sound, like the "voice of many
waters." Yet my senses are bewildered, Charmion, with
the keenness of their perception of *the new*.


CHARMION.

A few days will remove all this; but I fully understand
you, and feel for you. It is now ten earthly years since I
underwent what you undergo—yet the remembrance of it
hangs by me still. You have now suffered all of pain, however, which you will suffer in Aidenn.


EIROS.

In Aidenn?


CHARMION.

In Aidenn.


EIROS.

Oh God!—pity me, Charmion!—I am over-burthened
with the majesty of all things—of the unknown now known
—of the speculative Future merged in the august and certain Present.


CHARMION.

Grapple not now with such thoughts. To-morrow we
will speak of this. Your mind wavers, and its agitation will
find relief in the exercise of simple memories. Look not
around, nor forward—but back. I am burning with anxiety
to hear the details of that stupendous event which threw
you among us. Tell me of it. Let us converse of familiar
things, in the old familiar language of the world which has
so fearfully perished.


EIROS.

Most fearfully, fearfully!—this is indeed no dream.


CHARMION.

Dreams are no more. Was I much mourned, my Eiros?

EIROS.

Mourned, Charmion?—oh deeply. To that last hour of all, there hung a cloud of intense gloom and devout sorrow over your household.

CHARMION.

And that last hour—speak of it. Remember that, beyond the naked fact of the catastrophe itself, I know nothing. When, coming out from among mankind, I passed into Night through the Grave—at that period, if I remember aright, the calamity which overwhelmed you was utterly unanticipated. But, indeed, I knew little of the speculative philosophy of the day.

EIROS.

The individual calamity was, as you say, entirely unanticipated; but analogous misfortunes had been long a subject of discussion with astronomers. I need scarce tell you, my friend, that, even when you left us, men had agreed to understand those passages in the most holy writings which speak of the final destruction of all things by fire, as having reference to the orb of the earth alone. But in regard to the immediate agency of the ruin, speculation had been at fault from that epoch in astronomical knowledge in which the comets were divested of the terrors of flame. The very moderate density of these bodies had been well established. They had been observed to pass among the satellites of Jupiter, without bringing about any sensible alteration either in the masses or in the orbits of these secondary planets. We had long regarded the wanderers as vapory creations of inconceivable tenuity, and as altogether incapable of doing injury to our substantial globe, even in the event of contact. But contact was not in any degree dreaded; for the elements of all the comets were accurately known. That among *them* we should look for the agency of the threatened fiery destruction had been for many years considered an inadmissible idea. But wonders and wild fancies had been, of late days, strangely rife among mankind; and, although it was only with a few of the ignorant that actual apprehension prevailed upon the announcement by astronomers of a *new* comet, yet this announcement was generally received with I know not what of agitation and mistrust.

The elements of the strange orb were immediately calculated, and it was at once conceded by all observers that its path, at perihelion, would bring it into very close proximity with the earth. There were two or three astronomers, of secondary note, who resolutely maintained that a contact was inevitable. I cannot very well express to you the effect of this intelligence upon the people. For a few short days they would not believe an assertion which their intellect, so long employed among worldly considerations, could not in any manner grasp. But the truth of a vitally important fact soon makes its way into the understanding of even the most stolid. Finally, all men saw that astronomical knowledge lied not, and they awaited the comet. Its approach was not, at first, seemingly rapid; nor was its appearance of very unusual character. It was of a dull red, and had little perceptible train. For seven or eight days we saw no material increase in its apparent diameter, and but a partial alteration in its color. Meantime, the ordinary affairs of men were discarded, and all interests absorbed in a growing discussion, instituted by the philosophic, in respect to the cometary nature. Even the grossly ignorant aroused their sluggish capacities to such considerations. The learned *now* gave their intellect—their soul—to no such points as the allaying of fear, or to the sustenance of loved theory. They sought—they panted for right views. They groaned for perfected knowledge. *Truth* arose in the purity of her strength and exceeding majesty, and the wise bowed down and adored.

That material injury to our globe or to its inhabitants would result from the apprehended contact was an opinion which hourly lost ground among the wise; and the wise were now freely permitted to rule the reason and the fancy of the crowd. It was demonstrated that the density of the comet's *nucleus* was far less than that of our rarest gas; and the harmless passage of a similar visitor among the satellites of Jupiter was a point strongly insisted upon, and which served greatly to allay terror. Theologists, with an earnestness fear-enkindled, dwelt upon the biblical prophecies, and expounded them to the people with a directness and simplicity of which no previous instance had been known. That the final destruction of the earth must be brought about by the agency of fire was urged with a spirit that enforced everywhere conviction; and that the comets were of no fiery nature (as all men now knew) was a truth which relieved all, in a great measure, from the apprehension of the great calamity foretold. It is noticeable that the popular prejudices and vulgar errors in regard to pestilence and wars—errors which were wont to prevail upon every appearance of a comet—were now altogether unknown. As if by some sudden convulsive exertion, reason had at once hurled superstition from her throne. The feeblest intellect had derived vigor from excessive interest.

What minor evils might arise from the contact were points of elaborate question. The learned spoke of slight geological disturbances, of probable alterations in climate, and consequently in vegetation; of possible magnetic and electric influences. Many held that no visible or perceptible effect would in any manner be produced. While such discussions were going on, their subject gradually approached, growing larger in apparent diameter, and of a more brilliant lustre. Mankind grew paler as it came. All human operations were suspended.

There was an epoch in the course of the general sentiment when the comet had attained, at length, a size surpassing that of any previously recorded visitation. The people now, dismissing any lingering hope that the astronomers were wrong, experienced all the certainty of evil. The chimerical aspect of their terror was gone. The hearts of the stoutest of our race beat violently within their bosoms. A very few days sufficed, however, to merge even such feelings in sentiments more unendurable. We could no longer apply to the strange orb any *accustomed* thoughts. Its *historical* attributes had disappeared. It oppressed us with a hideous *novelty* of emotion. We saw it not as an astronomical phenomenon in the heavens, but as an incubus upon our hearts, and a shadow upon our brains. It had taken, with inconceivable rapidity, the character of a gigantic mantle of rare flame, extending from horizon to horizon.

Yet a day, and men breathed with greater freedom. It was clear that we were already within the influence of the comet; yet we lived. We even felt an unusual elasticity of frame and vivacity of mind. The exceeding tenuity of the object of our dread was apparent; for all heavenly objects were plainly visible through it. Meantime, our vegetation had perceptibly altered; and we gained faith from this predicted circumstance, in the foresight of the wise. A wild luxuriance of foliage, utterly unknown before, burst out upon every vegetable thing.

Yet another day—and the evil was not altogether upon us. It was now evident that its nucleus would first reach us. A wild change had come over all men; and the first sense of *pain* was the wild signal for general lamentation and horror. This first sense of pain lay in a rigorous constriction of the breast and lungs, and an insufferable dryness of the skin. It could not be denied that our atmosphere was radically affected; the conformation of this atmosphere and the possible modifications to which it might be subjected were now the topics of discussion. The result of investigation sent an electric thrill of the intensest terror through the universal heart of man.

It had been long known that the air which encircled us was a compound of oxygen and nitrogen gases, in the proportion of twenty-one measures of oxygen, and seventy-nine of nitrogen, in every one hundred of the atmosphere. Oxygen, which was the principle of combustion, and the vehicle of heat, was absolutely necessary to the support of animal life, and was the most powerful and energetic agent in nature. Nitrogen, on the contrary, was incapable of supporting either animal life or flame. An unnatural excess of oxygen would result, it had been ascertained, in just such an elevation of the animal spirits as we had latterly experienced. It was the pursuit, the extension of the idea, which had engendered awe. What would be the result of a total extraction of the nitrogen? A combustion irresistible, all-devouring, omniprevalent, immediate—the entire fulfilment, in all their minute and terrible details, of the fiery and horror-inspiring denunciations of the prophecies of the Holy Book.

Why need I paint, Charmion, the now disenchained frenzy of mankind? That tenuity in the comet which had previously inspired us with hope was now the source of the bitterness of despair. In its impalpable gaseous character we clearly perceived the consummation of Fate. Meantime a day again passed—bearing away with it the last shadow of Hope. We gasped in the rapid modification of the air. The red blood bounded tumultuously through its strict channels. A furious delirium possessed all men; and, with arms rigidly outstretched towards the threatening heavens, they trembled and shrieked aloud. But the nucleus of the destroyer was now upon us; even here in Aidenn, I shudder while I speak. Let me be brief—brief as the ruin that overwhelmed. For a moment there was a wild lurid light alone, visiting and penetrating all things. Then let us bow down, Charmion, before the excessive majesty of the great God!—then there came a shouting and pervading sound, as if from the mouth itself of HIM; while the whole incumbent mass of ether in which we existed burst at once into a species of intense flame, for whose surpassing brilliancy and all-fervid heat even the angels in the high Heaven of pure knowledge have no name. Thus ended all.

## A. E. Coppard

# THE FAIR YOUNG WILLOWY TREE

*A simple love affair between a telegraph pole and
a willow tree. What could go wrong? When Man
interferes, a world may be destroyed.*

---

At the side of a long road winding high over a lonely moor
stood a fair young willowy tree. Alone it grew on the verge
of the road, the one tree in that solitary place; there was no
other within the compass of an eye, not a hedge or house
or bush to greet a stumbling traveler, only the vast hum-
mocks of the moorland.

The tree was a little scattery sort of thing but she was
graceful. When soft breezes played she waved her arms
happily to the sky, but in squally weather she shrank from
the wind and squealed at its roughness. The fogs, too,
wearied her, so that she drooped and wept; often she sighed
at the loneliness of her lot and longed for a companion.

"If only I had a friend to give me greetings and to talk
with about the great matters of the world I should be the
happiest of creatures; but I am alone, alone, all alone."

She grew and grew until she was twelve feet high and
then one day, while peeping from her topmost twigs, she
saw far down the road a wagon filled with huge black poles,
and a gang of men beside it engaged in merry activities.
They returned the next day and the next and for many
more days; each day seemed to bring them all nearer to her
and at last she was able to see what it was they were about.
They were digging pits by the roadside and hoisting a tall

24

black pole in every one, and along the tops of the poles they were hanging bright wires for a new telegraph line. Oh joy! Wild with delight and hope, she watched the lengthening column of tall black poles advancing steadily across the lonely moor, ever nearer and nearer, until at last they were so close that she could hear the shouts of the men and the thumping of their gear as they shoveled and dug. When they were close at hand the men came and dug a hole just beside the fair young willowy tree and hoisted a sturdy blackamoor of a pole upright in it, then filled in the hole and rammed the earth tight at its foot. They put back the turf so neatly, left the pole standing beside her, and went on, farther and farther, planting giant poles across the moor.

The fair young willowy tree was filled with gladness.

"Now at last I have a dear companion!" and she laughed and spoke to the sturdy telegraph pole.

For a while the poor thing was gloomy, he was new to that country and felt lost in his surroundings, but he soon settled down and became friendly. Unhappily, however, a nasty odor of tar drifted from him to the fair young willowy tree whenever the wind was set to her quarter, and this offended her delicate senses. At such times she shrank from his neighborhood as far as her station would permit—though this of course was not very far; indeed, it was not far enough for her happiness, and she would rail at her companion for a stinking interloper.

"Oh, what a stench you have brought to the flavor of this highway!" she complained to the telegraph pole. "I cannot bear your company; you are a common low thing, stuck there and reeking with smells and defiling my air. And look at your stupid stumpy arms, and your skinny wires that groan and moan without stopping! What am I to do about it!"

"Alas!" the pole sighed. "It is true that my appearance is nothing to boast about now; in my figure I take no pride; but I am not now as once I was. You should have seen me then! Oh no, indeed, I have been maimed and put to uses I was never educated for. I have traveled the wide world over, but I take no credit for that—have you ever traveled, my dear?"

"No," replied she. "I should scorn it. I do not want to go elsewhere. This is my real home."

"Oh, but it broadens the mind," he said. "One should travel when one is young. I did."

"I have no wish to travel." The fair young willowy tree tossed her head disdainfully and at the same time looked most beautiful with her trim leaves and sweet slender boughs.

"No, of course not," the sturdy pole answered. "Neither had I. I was reared in the northern land beyond the sea. I had a thousand companions around me there, and I had my branches too, but I was not graceful and delicate like you—I was only sturdy and brave. All the same, you could not have endured the life, you could not have survived the fury of the weather and the bitterness of those crags where I had my home. My! How the wind came screaming over the icy isles! All day long and all year long the roaring waves came crashing upon our shore and I could watch the swirl of the last foot of foam hissing at the last foot of shingle. Oh, so good! So good! But you, my dear—your delicate body would have soon perished there, yes, indeed. It did not daunt me, though; nothing could uproot me."

"How vain you are!" taunted the fair young willowy tree. "I love the wind. I do not fear it, it is my joy. I hold out my arms and it embraces me and I hear the voices of angels, the sun pours its beams among my leaves."

So then the tall black pole began to brag of his travels: "I have traveled the wide world over, by ship and by wagon."

But the fair young willowy tree only laughed at him: "Pooh! You had to be carried! You had no choice. You were cut down and sold. A fine traveler indeed! You cannot travel now, you are just a post stuck in the ground, you can neither turn nor move. Ha, ha, ha!"

Such hilarity vexed him, it was so unkind, and he retorted sourly: "And how, pray, did you come to be rooted where you are? You cannot travel anywise at all, you cannot stir from this spot. You did not plan yourself, you have no will, no pride, no use—you have only vanity!"

"No use!" she cried indignantly. "No use! Listen!" she shook her branches and a sweet bird appeared upon one of the swaying boughs and began to sing its song, for in the bosom of the fair young willowy tree it had woven a nest, and in the nest were five golden eggs.

"You see, stupid thing! Birds come to me for shelter and love. What bird would ever, or could ever, build its nest upon you!"

"But, but, but," the sturdy pole protested, "such birds are of no account. In my country birds are as big as hounds; eagles, condors, alabatrosses; even the swan is just nothing."

"But can they sing, any of them!" cried she.

"Now why," the pole asked, "should an eagle sing? Do be reasonable. Tiny birds hop about and chipper and eat worms, or they go into private gardens and dig up the seeds, or steal the cherries before anyone else can pick them. It is dreadful, they are a great nuisance until the cat catches them. That is the only thing cats are good for."

Time and again they would squabble, which was a pity because they had no other friends, not a hedge nor a house nor a bush nor a tree, and the other poles were as poles apart, businesslike fellows with no nonsense about them. She was often petulant and overbearing, yet she was so very young and beautiful that he always soon forgave her and in the pleasant summer breezes she would dance for him alone. When the foggy autumn weather hung over them, and she was drooping in despair as her leaves fell from her, and her twigs dripped with weeping, he would comfort her childish tears.

How solitary they were! Sometimes in all a week only a coach would go by—but then it would be a coach of blue with yellow wheels and four white galloping horses and a man in red to blow the long copper horn! If the day were fine the passengers might even be singing, and that was most sweet to hear.

"How good it is! Yes, yes, it is grand!" the sturdy pole would say, althouh his heart was despairing for he had begun to be in love with the fair young willowy tree and saw no hope for himself.

Or a flock of sheep might cross the road at evening chased by a shepherd whistling and a dog that harried them. How their tough little hoofs scattered the dust!

"This is most enjoyable and exciting," he would cry. "Life is sweet, is it not, my dear? Tell me now, what would you like best to be in all the world?" And he was hoping she might say she would like to be his wife!

"To be? Oh, if I could have my choice," laughed the fair young willowy tree, "I would like to feel bright flowers growing upon me everywhere, blossoms on every twig, of many different colors—yes, and each flower to turn at last into a yellow quince. What now would you most care to be?"

"Me? If I could have my choice," he answered, "I would be the mast on some tall leaning ship, with my white sails trimmed and my ropes to hold me fast, so I could peer far down into the crystal waters and note the wonders of the deep."

"Of the deep!"

"Yes. The billowing forests that are there, the vast ocean fungi, the caverns in the coral, the dreaming weed swaying in its dream; sponges like palaces, the fish going and coming all in silver and gold like princes' children."

"No, I would rather be as I am," said the fair young willowy tree. And that was wise of her, for then she could wave her arms merrily in the way she most liked to do, day in, day out, and every day, and dance as well as her station allowed—although that was not so very well because she was rooted in the soil. All the same, that does not matter if nobody sees you. There was only herself to please, and the sturdy pole had grown so fond of her that he thought it was perfection. One bright day he summoned up his courage and said:

"I would like to marry you."

"Oh, but you are dead," said she. "Aren't you? You have no twigs, no branches, only those stupid wires; you are not even alive."

"I may be dead, young lady," was his sorrowful rejoinder, "but I am still useful."

"Not useful to yourself, Mr. Pole."

"To others." He sighed. "The dead are of no use to themselves."

"Nor useful to me. I am alive, alive!" she cried. "Pray do not speak of this again, it upsets me. I have other hopes for myself."

"You have certainly little else," he retorted with an insolent sniff.

That made her quite angry and she cried out: "Why are you so stupid, tell me that, you fool!"

"Pardon me," he loftily replied, "is that a serious question?"

"You can make what you like of it."

"Well, I can't make sense of it," said he.

"Try again, you great big blackamoor," she said in her most aggravating tone.

"Is it a joke?" he asked. "I am quite unable to laugh at it."

"But who wants you to laugh! I am only asking you a simple question."

"I am not a dictionary," the proud pole responded.

"And I don't think that so very funny either!" said the fair young willowy tree. Oh, she was very furious! And most provoking.

But the sturdy pole went on: "Let me tell you it is honorable and good to be useful when you are dead. And I am not really dead, not yet. I am only half dead. You see, I have been painted with the nasty-smelling stuff in order to preserve me for a span of usefulness, and I am glad of it too, for otherwise I should have been chopped up for a fire probably."

"Ugh! Do not speak of fire!" She quivered to her very roots. "I hate it. I abominate it. The very thought of it makes me tremble."

"But fire is good," said he soothingly. "In a way it is very valuable. It has a long history, it is most useful and is highly esteemed in the highest circles."

"I don't care," she answered, "I hate it! I hate it!"

"And those wires you dislike so, which I carry on my shoulders: they are my veins! My life blood! Without them I should be nothing at all. They carry the news of the great world and, do you know, sometimes I can actually hear them whisper the messages from the King!"

"I have my own veins," said she. "I have no need of messages and news. I can dance with my branches in the rays of the sun, I can whistle with the wind, I have a hundred arms, I have more twigs than there are stars in the sky, my leaves are full of joy and they dream in the moonlight."

"Ah, my dear," murmured the poor black pole, "ah, my

dear." It was all he could say, and he did not propose to hear any more.

Time, which cannot hold back, passed over the moor in the breath of happy winds, in the flight of gloomy clouds. Lone as the sky itself, the heather on the moor budded, bloomed, and faded. Sharp winter came harrying the world, and the fair young willowy tree lost her leaves again; they flew away from her and she shivered forlorn in the icy blast. But the tall black pole did not shiver. Valiant and unconcerned, even when the snow pillowed itself thickly around half his spine, he did his duty without complaint.

Not until Shrovetide did the young tree recover her spirits and begin to grow gay again. At Eastertide she was quite lighthearted, for her twigs were covered with tough little purple buds. By Whitsuntide the buds had broken into tender twinkling leaves, the birds were at nest again in her bosom, and she sang in the wind and danced in the sun, and her leaves dreamed in the moonlight. Moreover, she grew, she was shaping into a tall tree; her topmost branches strained upward, and one day the sturdy pole felt her highest twigs tapping against the wires close to his head, very tenderly, very soothingly—Oh, it was most blissful. And she was joyful too; they became the dearest of friends and dreamed in the moonlight together, all the bright year, all spring, all summer, all autumn.

And then, one day, an officer of state was passing by and he saw that the branches of the fair young willowy tree were mingled with the wires of the telegraph.

"That is dangerous," said he. "That cannot be allowed. I must attend to that."

And he sent a man with a shining broad axe, who cut down the fair young willowy tree without a word of apology. Not content with that, the man hacked off her beautiful arms, hewed her trunk into seven separate pieces, piled her remains in a heap together on the spot where once she grew, and went away and left her there.

Thus it was, and there she lay, destroyed and forgotten, until many months afterward, when cold, cold hours were blighting the moor and a poor tinker man came traveling along who saw the heap of fuel and settled down there and, wanting a fire to thaw the ice from his bones, burned the remains of the fair young willowy tree into fine white ash and little black cinders. And when the fire was done and all was cold again, he traveled on, leaving the ashes there. For long after he was gone the heap of ash remained, black and sad, the winter through, at the foot of the sturdy pole. The poor pole almost wept to see it, but he could not quite weep —he could only stand and mourn.

By and by the spring came again. And the birds came, but alas, the fair young willowy tree was gone, quite gone; only the heap of ash remained. And even then the grass around was growing so high that it soon covered up the ashes, and then no one, not even the sturdy pole, could see it any more.

And so he forgot her.

James Agee

# A MOTHER'S TALE

*What finish line will Man reach, if each generation returns to the original starting point? Will we ever have the right answers, if we ask the wrong questions?*

———◆❖◆———

The calf ran up the hill as fast as he could and stopped sharp. "Mama!" he cried, all out of breath. "What *is* it! What are they *doing!* Where are they *going!*"

Other spring calves came galloping too.

They all were looking up at her and awaiting her explanation, but she looked out over their excited eyes. As she watched the mysterious and majestic thing they had never seen before, her own eyes became even more than ordinarily still, and during the considerable moment before she answered, she scarcely heard their urgent questioning.

Far out along the autumn plain, beneath the sloping light, an immense drove of cattle moved eastward. They were at a walk, not very fast, but faster than they could imaginably enjoy. Those in front were compelled by those behind; those at the rear, with few exceptions, did their best to keep up; those who were locked within the herd could no more help moving than the particles inside a falling rock. Men on horses rode ahead, and alongside, and behind, or spurred their horses intensely back and forth, keeping the pace steady and the herd in shape; and from man to man a dog sped back and forth incessantly as a shuttle, barking, incessantly, in a hysterical voice. Now and then one of the men shouted fiercely, and this like the shrieking of the dog was tinily audible above a low and awesome sound which seemed to come not from the multitude of hooves but from the center of the world, and above the sporadic bawlings and bellowings of the herd.

From the hillside this tumult was so distant that it only made more delicate the prodigious silence in which the earth and sky were held; and, from the hill, the sight was as modest as its sound. The herd was virtually hidden in the dust it raised, and could be known, in general, only by the horns which pricked this flat sunlit dust like little briars. In one place a twist of the air revealed the trembling fabric of many backs; but it was only along the near edge of the mass that individual animals were discernible, small in a driven frieze, walking fast, stumbling and recovering, tossing their armed heads, or opening their skulls heavenward in one of those cries which reached the hillside long after the jaws were shut.

From where she watched, the mother could not be sure whether there were any she recognized. She knew that among them there must be a son of hers; she had not seen him since some previous spring, and she would not be seeing him again. Then the cries of the young ones impinged on her bemusement: "Where are they going?"

She looked into their ignorant eyes.

"Away," she said.

"Where?" they cried. "Where? Where?" her own son cried again.

She wondered what to say.

"On a long journey."

"But where *to?*" they shouted. "Yes, where *to?*" her son exclaimed, and she could see that he was losing his patience with her, as he always did when he felt she was evasive.

"I'm not sure," she said.

Their silence was so cold that she was unable to avoid their eyes for long.

"Well, not *really* sure. Because, you see," she said in her most reasonable tone, "I've never seen it with my own eyes, and that's the only way to *be* sure; *isn't* it?"

They just kept looking at her. She could see no way out.

"But I've *heard* about it," she said with shallow cheerfulness, "from those who *have* seen it, and I don't suppose there's any good reason to doubt them."

She looked away over them again, and for all their interest in what she was about to tell them, her eyes so changed that they turned and looked, too.

The herd, which had been moving broadside to them, was being turned away, so slowly that like the turning of stars it could not quite be seen from one moment to the next; yet soon it was moving directly away from them, and even during the little while she spoke and they all watched after it, it steadily and very noticeably diminished, and the sounds of it as well.

"It happens always about this time of year," she said quietly while they watched. "Nearly all the men and horses leave, and go into the North and the West."

"Out on the range," her son said, and by his voice she knew what enchantment the idea already held for him.

"Yes," she said, "out on the range." And trying, impossibly, to imagine the range, they were touched by the breath of grandeur.

"And then before long," she continued, "everyone has been found, and brought into one place; and then . . . what you see, happens. All of them.

"Sometimes when the wind is right," she said more quietly, "you can hear them coming long before you can see them. It isn't even like a sound, at first. It's more as if something were moving far under the ground. It makes you uneasy. You wonder, why, what in the world can *that* be! Then you remember what it is and then you can really hear it. And then finally, there they all are."

She could see this did not interest them at all.

"But where are they *going?*" one asked, a little impatiently.

"I'm coming to that," she said; and she let them wait. Then she spoke slowly but casually.

"They are on their way to a railroad."

There, she thought; that's for that look you all gave me when I said I wasn't sure. She waited for them to ask; they waited for her to explain.

"A railroad," she told them, "is great hard bars of metal lying side by side, or so they tell me, and they go on and on over the ground as far as the eye can see. And great wagons run on the metal bars on wheels, like wagon wheels but smaller, and these wheels are made of solid metal too. The wagons are much bigger than any wagon you've ever seen, as big as, big as sheds, they say, and they are pulled along on the iron bars by a terrible huge dark machine, with a loud scream."

"Big as *sheds?*" one of the calves said skeptically.

"Big *enough*, anyway," the mother said. "I told you I've never seen it myself. But those wagons are so big that several of us can get inside at once. And that's exactly what happens."

Suddenly she became very quiet, for she felt that somehow, she could not imagine just how, she had said altogether too much.

"Well, *what* happens," the son wanted to know. "What do you mean, *happens*."

She always tried hard to be a reasonably modern mother. It was probably better, she felt, to go on, than to leave them all full of imaginings and mystification. Besides, there was really nothing at all awful about what happened . . . if only one could know *why*.

"Well," she said, "it's nothing much, really. They just— why, when they all finally *get* there, why there are all the great cars waiting in a long line, and the big dark machine is up ahead . . . smoke comes out of it, they say . . . and . . . well, then, they just put us into the wagons, just as many as will fit in each wagon, and when everybody is in, why . . ." She hesitated, for again, though she couldn't be sure why, she was uneasy.

"Why then," her son said, "the train takes them away."

Hearing that word, she felt a flinching of the heart. Where had he picked it up, she wondered, and she gave him a shy and curious glance. Oh dear, she thought. I should never have even *begun* to explain. "Yes," she said, "when everybody is safely in, they slide the doors shut."

They were all silent for a little while. Then one of them asked thoughtfully, "Are they taking them somewhere they don't want to go?"

"Oh, I don't think so," the mother said. "I imagine it's very nice."

"*I* want to go," she heard her son say with ardor. "I want to go right now," he cried. "Can I, Mama? *Can* I?

*Please?"* And looking into his eyes, she was overwhelmed by sadness.

"Silly thing," she said, "there'll be time enough for that when you're grown up. But what I very much hope," she went on, "is that instead of being chosen to go out on the range and to make the long journey, you will grow up to be very strong and bright so they will decide that you may stay here at home with Mother. And you, too," she added, speaking to the other little males; but she could not honestly wish this for any but her own, least of all for the eldest, strongest and most proud, for she knew how few are chosen.

She could see that what she said was not received with enthusiasm.

"But I want to go," her son said.

"Why?" she asked. "I don't think any of you realize that it's a great *honor* to be chosen to stay. A great privilege. Why, it's just the most ordinary ones who are taken out onto the range. But only the very pick are chosen to stay here at home. If you want to go out on the range," she said in hurried and happy inspiration, "all you have to do is be ordinary and careless and silly. If you want to have even a chance to be chosen to stay, you have to try to be stronger and bigger and braver and brighter than anyone else, and that takes *hard work. Every day.* Do you see?" And she looked happily and hopefully from one to another. "Besides," she added, aware that they were not won over, "I'm told it's a very rough life out there, and the men are unkind.

"Don't you see," she said again; and she pretended to speak to all of them, but it was only to her son.

But he only looked at her. "Why do you want me to stay home?" he asked flatly; in their silence she knew the others were asking the same question.

"Because it's safe here," she said before she knew better; and realized she had put it in the most unfortunate way possible. "Not safe, not just that," she fumbled. "I mean . . . because here we *know* what happens, and what's going to happen, and there's never any doubt about it, never any reason to wonder, to worry. Don't you see? It's just *Home,*" and she put a smile on the word, "where we all know each other and are happy and well."

They were so merely quiet, looking back at her, that she

felt they were neither won over nor alienated. Then she knew of her son that he, anyhow, was most certainly not persuaded, for he asked the question she most dreaded: "Where do they go on the train?" And hearing him, she knew that she would stop at nothing to bring that curiosity and eagerness, and that tendency toward skepticism, within safe bounds.

"Nobody knows," she said, and she added, in just the tone she knew would most sharply engage them, "not for sure, anyway."

"What do you mean, *not for sure,*" her son cried. And the oldest, biggest calf repeated the question, his voice cracking.

The mother deliberately kept silent as she gazed out over the plain, and while she was silent they all heard the last they would ever hear of all those who were going away: one last great cry, as faint almost as a breath; the infinitesimal jabbing vituperation of the dog; the solemn muttering of the earth.

"Well," she said, after even this sound was entirely lost, "there was one who came back." Their instant, trustful eyes were too much for her. She added, "Or so they say."

They gathered a little more closely around her, for now she spoke very quietly.

"It was my great-grandmother who told me," she said. "She was told it by *her* great-grandmother, who claimed she saw it with her own eyes, though of course I can't vouch for that. Because of course I wasn't even dreamed of then; and Great-grandmother was so very, very old, you see, that you couldn't always be sure she knew quite *what* she was saying."

Now that she began to remember it more clearly, she was sorry she had committed herself to telling it.

"Yes," she said, "the story is, there was one, *just* one, who ever came back, and he told what happened on the train, and where the train went and what happened after. He told it all in a rush, they say, the last things first and every which way, but as it was finally sorted out and gotten into order by those who heard it and those they told it to, this is more or less what happened:

"He said that after the men had gotten just as many of us as they could into the car he was in, so that their sides pressed tightly together and nobody could lie down, they slid the door shut with a startling rattle and a bang, and then there was a sudden jerk, so strong they might have fallen except that they were packed so closely together, and the car began to move. But after it had moved only a little way, it stopped as suddenly as it had started, so that they all nearly fell down again. You see, they were just moving up the next car that was joined on behind, to put more of us into it. He could see it all between the boards of the car, because the boards were built a little apart from each other, to let in air."

*Car,* her son said again to himself. Now he would never forget the word.

"He said that then, for the first time in his life, he became very badly frightened, he didn't know why. But he was sure, at that moment, that there was something dreadfully to be afraid of. The others felt this same great fear. They called out loudly to those who were being put into the car behind, and the others called back, but it was no use; those who were getting aboard were between narrow white fences and then were walking up a narrow slope and the men kept jabbing them as they do when they are in an unkind humor; and there was no way to go but on into the car. There was no way to get out of the car, either: he tried, with all his might, and he was the one nearest the door.

"After the next car behind was full, and the door was shut, the train jerked forward again, and stopped again, and they put more of us into still another car, and so on, and on, until all the starting and stopping no longer frightened anybody; it was just something uncomfortable that was never going to stop, and they began instead to realize how hungry and thirsty they were. But there was no food and no water, so they just had to put up with this; and about the time they became resigned to going without their suppers (for now it was almost dark), they heard a sudden and terrible scream which frightened them even more deeply than anything had frightened them before, and the train began to move again, and they braced their legs once more for the jolt when it would stop, but this time, instead of stopping, it began to go fast, and then even faster, so fast that the ground nearby slid past like a flooded creek and the whole country, he claimed, began to move too, turning slowly around a far mountain as if it were all one great wheel. And then there was a strange kind of disturbance inside the car, he said, or even inside his very bones. He felt as if everything in him were *falling,* as if he had been filled full of a heavy liquid that all wanted to flow one way, and all the others were leaning as he was leaning, away from this queer heaviness that was trying to pull them over, and then just as suddenly this leaning heaviness was gone and they nearly fell again before they could stop leaning against it. He could never understand what this was, but it too happened so many times that they all got used to it, just as they got used to seeing the country turn like a slow wheel, and just as they got used to the long cruel screams of the engine, and the steady iron noise beneath them which made the cold darkness so fearsome, and the hunger and the thirst and the continual standing up, and the moving on and on and on as if they would never stop."

*"Didn't* they ever stop?" one asked.

"Once in a great while," she replied. "Each time they did," she said, "he thought, Oh, now *at last! At last* we can get out and stretch our tired legs and lie down! *At last* we'll be given food and water! But they never let them out. And they never gave them food or water. They never even cleaned up under them. They had to stand in their manure and in the water they made."

"Why did the train stop?" her son asked; and with somber gratification she saw that he was taking all this very much to heart.

"He could never understand why," she said. "Sometimes men would walk up and down alongside the cars, and the more nervous and the more trustful of us would call out; but they were only looking around, they never seemed to do anything. Sometimes he could see many houses and bigger buildings together where people lived. Sometimes it was far out in the country and after they had stood still for a long time they would hear a little noise which quickly became louder, and then became suddenly a noise so loud it stopped their breathing, and during this noise something black would go by, very close, and so fast it couldn't be seen. And then it was gone as suddenly as it had appeared, and the noise became small, and then in the silence their train would start up again.

"Once, he tells us, something very strange happened. They were standing still, and cars of a very different kind began to move slowly past. Those cars were not red, but black with many glass windows like those in a house; and he says they were as full of human beings as the car he was in was full of our kind. And one of these people looked into his eyes and smiled, as if he liked him, or as if he knew only too well how hard the journey was.

"So by his account it happens to them, too," she said, with a certain pleased vindictiveness. "Only they were sitting down at their ease, not standing. And the one who smiled was eating."

She was still, trying to think of something; she couldn't quite grasp the thought.

"But didn't they *ever* let them out?" her son asked.

The oldest calf jeered. "Of *course* they did. He came back, didn't he? How would he ever come back if he didn't get out?"

"They didn't let them out," she said, "for a long, long time."

"How long?"

"So long, and he was so tired, he could never quite be sure. But he said that it turned from night to day and from day to night and back again several times over, with the train moving nearly all of this time, and that when it finally stopped, early one morning, they were all so tired and so discouraged that they hardly even noticed any longer, let alone felt any hope that anything would change for them, ever again; and then all of a sudden men came up and put up a wide walk and unbarred the door and slid it open, and it was the most wonderful and happy moment of his life when he saw the door open, and walked into the open air with all his joints trembling, and drank the water and ate the delicious food they had ready for him; it was worth the whole terrible journey."

Now that these scenes came clear before her, there was a faraway shining in her eyes, and her voice, too, had something in it of the faraway.

"When they had eaten and drunk all they could hold they lifted up their heads and looked around, and everything they saw made them happy. Even the trains made them cheerful now, for now they were no longer afraid of them. And though these trains were forever breaking to pieces and joining again with other broken pieces, with shufflings and clashings and rude cries, they hardly paid them attention any more, they were so pleased to be in their new home, and so surprised and delighted to find they were among thousands upon thousands of strangers of their own kind, all lifting their voices in peacefulness and thanksgiving, and they were so wonder-struck by all they could see, it was so beautiful and so grand.

"For he has told us that now they lived among fences as white as bone, so many, and so spiderishly complicated, and shining so pure, that there's no use trying even to hint at the beauty and the splendor of it to anyone who knows only the pitiful little outfittings of a ranch. Beyond these mazy fences, through the dark and bright smoke which continually turned along the sunlight, dark buildings stood shoulder to shoulder in a wall as huge and proud as mountains. All through the air, all the time, there was an iron humming like the humming of the iron bar after it has been struck to tell the men it is time to eat, and in all the air, all the time, there was that same strange kind of iron strength which makes the silence before lightning so different from all other silence.

"Once for a little while the wind shifted and blew over them straight from the great buildings, and it brought a strange and very powerful smell which confused and disturbed them. He could never quite describe this smell, but he has told us it was unlike anything he had ever known before. It smelled like old fire, he said, and old blood and fear and darkness and sorrow and most terrible and brutal force and something else, something in it that made him want to run away. This sudden uneasiness and this wish to run away swept through every one of them, he tells us, so that they were all moved at once as restlessly as so many leaves in a wind, and there was great worry in their voices. But soon the leaders among them concluded that it was simply the way men must smell when there are a great many of them living together. Those dark buildings must be crowded very full of men, they decided, probably as many thousands of them, indoors, as there were of us, outdoors; so it was no wonder their smell was so strong and, to our kind, so unpleasant. Besides, it was so clear now in every other way that men were not as we had always supposed, but were doing everything they knew how to make us comfortable and happy, that we ought to just put up with their smell, which after all they couldn't help, any more than we could help our own. Very likely men didn't like the way we smelled, any more than we liked theirs. They passed along these ideas to the others, and soon everyone felt more calm, and then the wind changed again, and the fierce smell no longer came to them, and the smell of our own kind was back again, very strong of course, in such a crowd, but ever so homey and comforting, and everyone felt easy again.

"They were fed and watered so generously, and treated so well, and the majesty and the loveliness of this place where they had all come to rest was so far beyond anything they had ever known or dreamed of, that many of the simple and ignorant, whose memories were short, began to wonder whether that whole difficult journey, or even their whole lives up to now, had ever really been. Hadn't it all been just shadows, they murmured, just a bad dream?

"Even the sharp ones, who knew very well it had all really happened, began to figure that everything up to now had been made so full of pain only so that all they had come to now might seem all the sweeter and the more glorious. Some of the oldest and deepest were even of a mind that all the puzzle and tribulation of the journey had been sent us as a kind of harsh trying or proving of our worthiness; and that it was entirely fitting and proper that we could earn our way through to such rewards as these, only through suffering, and through being patient under pain which was beyond our understanding; and that now at the last, to those who had borne all things well, all things were made known; for the mystery of suffering stood revealed in joy. And now as they looked back over all that was past, all their sorrows and bewilderment seemed so little and so fleeting that, from the simplest among them even to the most wise, they could feel only the kind of amused pity we feel toward the very young when, with the first thing that hurts them or they are forbidden, they are sure there is nothing kind or fair in all creation, and carry on accordingly, raving and grieving as if their hearts would break."

She glanced among them with an indulgent smile, hoping the little lesson would sink home. They seemed interested but somewhat dazed. I'm talking way over their heads, she realized. But by now she herself was too deeply absorbed in her story to modify it much. *Let it be,* she thought, a little impatient; *it's over my head, for that matter*.

"They had hardly before this even wondered that they were alive," she went on, "and now all of a sudden they felt they understood *why* they were. This made them very happy, but they were still only beginning to enjoy this new wisdom when quite a new and different kind of restiveness ran among them. Before they quite knew it they were all moving once again, and now they realized that they were being moved, once more, by men, toward still some other place and purpose they could not know. But during these last hours they had been so well that now they felt no uneasiness, but all moved forward calm and sure toward better things still to come; he has told us that he no longer felt as if he were being driven, even as it became clear that they were going toward the shade of those great buildings; but guided.

"He was guided between fences which stood ever more and more narrowly near each other, among companions who were pressed ever more and more closely against each other; and now as he felt their warmth against him it was not uncomfortable, and his pleasure in it was not through any need to be close among others through anxiousness, but was a new kind of strong and gentle delight, at being so very close, so deeply of his own kind, that it seemed as if the very breath and heartbeat of each one were being exchanged through all that multitude, and each was another, and others were each, and each was a multitude, and the multitude was one. And quieted and made mild within this melting, they now entered the cold shadow cast by the buildings, and now with every step the smell of the buildings grew stronger, and in the darkening air the glittering of the fences was ever more queer.

"And now as they were pressed ever more intimately together he could see ahead of him a narrow gate, and he was strongly pressed upon from either side and from behind, and went in eagerly, and now he was between two fences so narrowly set that he brushed either fence with either flank, and walked alone, seeing just one other ahead of him, and knowing of just one other behind him, and for a moment the strange thought came to him, that the one ahead was his father, and that the one behind was the son he had never begotten.

"And now the light was so changed that he knew he must have come inside one of the gloomy and enormous buildings, and the smell was so much stronger that it seemed almost to burn his nostrils, and the smell and the somber new light blended together and became some other thing again, beyond his describing to us except to say that the whole air beat with it like one immense heart and it was as if the beating of this heart were pure violence infinitely manifolded upon violence: so that the uneasy feeling stirred in him again that it would be wise to turn around and run out of this place just as fast and as far as ever he could go. This he heard, as if he were telling it to himself at the top of his voice, but it came from somewhere so deep and so dark inside him that he could only hear the shouting of it as less than a whisper, as just a hot and chilling breath, and he scarcely heeded it, there was so much else to attend to.

"For as he walked along in this sudden and complete loneliness, he tells us, this wonderful knowledge of being one with all his race meant less and less to him, and in its place came something still more wonderful: he knew what it was to be himself alone, a creature separate and different from any other, who had never been before, and would never be again. He could feel this in his whole weight as he walked, and in each foot as he put it down and gave his weight to it and moved above it, and in every muscle as he moved, and it was a pride which lifted him up and made him feel large, and a pleasure which pierced him through. And as he began with such wondering delight to be aware of his own exact singleness in this world, he also began to understand (or so he thought) just why these fences were set so very narrow, and just why he was walking all by himself. It stole over him, he tells us, like the feeling of a slow cool wind, that he was being guided toward some still more wonderful reward or revealing, up ahead, which he could not of course imagine, but he was sure it was being held in store for him alone.

"Just then the one ahead of him fell down with a great sigh, and was so quickly taken out of the way that he did not even have to shift the order of his hooves as he walked on. The sudden fall and the sound of that sigh dismayed him, though, and something within him told him that it would be wise to look up: and there he saw Him.

"A little bridge ran crosswise above the fences. He stood on this bridge with His feet as wide apart as He could set them. He wore spattered trousers but from the belt up He was naked and as wet as rain. Both arms were raised high above His head and in both hands He held an enormous Hammer. With a grunt which was hardly like the voice of a human being, and with all His strength, He brought this Hammer down into the forehead of our friend: who, in a blinding blazing, heard from his own mouth the beginning of a gasping sigh; then there was only darkness.

*Oh, this is enough! it's enough!* she cried out within herself, seeing their terrible young eyes. How *could* she have been so foolish as to tell so much!

"What happened then?" she heard, in the voice of the oldest calf, and she was horrified. This shining in their eyes: was it only excitement? no pity? no fear?

"What happened?" two others asked.

Very well, she said to herself. I've gone so far; now I'll go the rest of the way. She decided not to soften it, either. She'd teach them a lesson they wouldn't forget in a hurry.

"Very well," she was surprised to hear herself say aloud.

"How long he lay in this darkness he couldn't know, but when he began to come out of it, all he knew was the most unspeakably dreadful pain. He was upside down and very slowly swinging and turning, for he was hanging by the tendons of his heels from great frightful hooks, and he has told us that the feeling was as if his hide were being torn from him inch by inch, in one piece. And then as he became more clearly aware he found that this was exactly what was happening. Knives would sliver and slice along both flanks, between the hide and the living flesh; then there was a moment of most precious relief; then red hands seized his hide and there was a jerking of the hide and a tearing of tissue which it was almost as terrible to hear as to

feel, turning his whole body and the poor head at the
bottom of it; and then the knives again.

"It was so far beyond anything he had ever known, unnatural and amazing, that he hung there through several
more such slicings and jerkings and tearings before he was
fully able to take it all in: then, with a scream, and a su-
preme straining of all his strength, he tore himself from
the hooks and collapsed sprawling to the floor and, scrambling right to his feet, charged the men with the knives.
For just a moment they were so astonished and so terrified
they could not move. Then they moved faster than he had
ever known men could—and so did all the other men who
chanced to be in his way. He ran down a glowing floor of
blood and down endless corridors which were hung with
the bleeding carcasses of our kind and with bleeding frag-
ments of carcasses, among blood-clothed men who carried
bleeding weapons, and out of that vast room into the open,
and over and through one fence after another, shoving
aside many an astounded stranger and shouting out warnings as he ran, and away up the railroad toward the West.

"How he ever managed to get away, and how he ever
found his way home, we can only try to guess. It's told that
he scarcely knew, himself, by the time he came to this part
of his story. He was impatient with those who interrupted
him to ask about that, he had so much more important
things to tell them, and by then he was so exhausted and
so far gone that he could say nothing very clear about the
little he did know. But we can realize that he must have
had really tremendous strength, otherwise he couldn't have
outlived the Hammer; and that strength such as his—
which we simply don't see these days, it's of the olden
time—is capable of things our own strongest and bravest
would sicken to dream of. But there was something even
stronger than his strength. There was his righteous fury,
which nothing could stand up against, which brought him
out of that fearful place. And there was his high and burning and heroic purpose, to keep him safe along the way,
and to guide him home, and to keep the breath of life in
him until he could warn us. He did manage to tell us that
he just followed the railroad, but how he chose one among
the many which branched out from that place, he couldn't
say. He told us, too, that from time to time he recognized

shapes of mountains and other landmarks, from his journey by train, all reappearing backward and with a changed look and hard to see, too (for he was shrewd enough to travel mostly at night), but still recognizable. But that isn't enough to account for it. For he has told us, too, that he simply *knew* the way; that he didn't hesitate one moment in choosing the right line of railroad, or even think of it as choosing; and that the landmarks didn't really guide him, but just made him the more sure of what he was already sure of; and that whenever he *did* encounter human beings—and during the later stages of his journey, when he began to doubt he would live to tell us, he traveled day and night—they never so much as moved to make him trouble, but stopped dead in their tracks, and their jaws fell open.

"And surely we can't wonder that their jaws fell open. I'm sure yours would, if you had seen him as he arrived, and I'm very glad I wasn't there to see it, either, even though it is said to be the greatest and most momentous day of all the days that ever were or shall be. For we have the testimony of eye-witnesses, how he looked, and it is only too vivid, even to hear of. He came up out of the East as much staggering as galloping (for by now he was so worn out by pain and exertion and loss of blood that he could hardly stay upright), and his heels were so piteously torn by the hooks that his hooves doubled under more often than not, and in his broken forehead the mark of the Hammer was like the socket for a third eye.

"He came to the meadow where the great trees made shade over the water. 'Bring them all together!' he cried out, as soon as he could find breath. 'All!' Then he drank; and then he began to speak to those who were already there: for as soon as he saw himself in the water it was as clear to him as it was to those who watched him that there was no time left to send for the others. His hide was all gone from his head and his neck and his forelegs and his chest and most of one side and a part of the other side. It was flung backward from his naked muscles by the wind of his running and now it lay around him in the dust like a ragged garment. They say there is no imagining how terrible and in some way how grand the eyeball is when the skin has been taken entirely from around it: his eyes, which were bare in this way, also burned with pain, and with the final energies of his life, and with his desperate concern to warn us while he could; and he rolled his eyes wildly while he talked, or looked piercingly from one to another of the listeners, interrupting himself to cry out, 'Believe me! Oh, believe me!' For it had evidently never occurred to him that he might not be believed, and must make this last great effort, in addition to all he had gone through for us, to make himself believed; so that he groaned with sorrow and with rage and railed at them without tact or mercy for their slowness to believe. He had scarcely what you could call a voice left, but with this relic of a voice he shouted and bellowed and bullied us and insulted us, in the agony of his concern. While he talked he bled from the mouth, and the mingled blood and saliva hung from his chin like the beard of a goat.

"Some say that with his naked face, and his savage eyes, and that beard and the hide lying off his bare shoulders like shabby clothing, he looked almost human. But others feel this is an irreverence even to think; and others, that it is a poor compliment to pay the one who told us, at such cost to himself, the true ultimate purpose of Man. Some did not believe he had ever come from our ranch in the first place, and of course he was so different from us in appearance and even in his voice, and so changed from what he might ever have looked or sounded like before, that nobody could recognize him for sure, though some were sure they did. Others suspected that he had been sent among us with his story for some mischievous and cruel purpose, and the fact that they could not imagine what this purpose might be, made them, naturally, all the more suspicious. Some believed he was actually a man, trying—and none too successfully, they said—to disguise himself as one of us; and again the fact that they could not imagine why a man would do this, made them all the more uneasy. There were quite a few who doubted that anyone who could get into such bad condition as he was in, was fit even to give reliable information, let alone advice, to those in good health. And some whispered, even while he spoke, that he had turned lunatic; and many came to believe this. It wasn't only that his story was so fantastic; there was good reason to wonder, many felt, whether anybody in his right mind would go to such trouble for others. But even those who did not believe him listened intently, out of curiosity to hear so wild a tale, and out of the respect it is only proper to show any creature who is in the last agony.

"What he told was what I have just told you. But his purpose was away beyond just the telling. When they asked questions, no matter how curious or suspicious or idle or foolish, he learned, toward the last, to answer them with all the patience he could and in all the detail he could remember. He even invited them to examine his wounded heels and the pulsing wound in his head as closely as they pleased. He even begged them to, for he knew that before everything else, he must be believed. For unless we could believe him, wherever could we find any reason, or enough courage, to do the hard and dreadful things he told us we must do!

"It was only these things he cared about. Only for these, he came back."

Now clearly remembering what these things were, she felt her whole being quail. She looked at the young ones quickly and as quickly looked away.

"While he talked," she went on, "and our ancestors listened, men came quietly among us; one of them shot him. Whether he was shot in kindness or to silence him is an endlessly disputed question which will probably never be settled. Whether, even, he died of the shot, or through his own great pain and weariness (for his eyes, they say, were glazing for some time before the men came), we will never be sure. Some suppose even that he may have died of his sorrow and his concern for us. Others feel that he had quite enough to die of, without that. All these things are tangled and lost in the disputes of those who love to theorize and to argue. There is no arguing about his dying words, though; they were very clearly remembered:

" 'Tell them! Believe!' "

After a while her son asked, "What did he tell them to do?"

She avoided his eyes. "There's a great deal of disagreement about that, too," she said after a moment. "You see, he was so very tired."

They were silent.

"So tired," she said, "some think that toward the end, he really *must* have been out of his mind."

"Why?" asked her son.

"Because he was so tired out and so badly hurt."

They looked at her mistrustfully.

"And because of what he told us to do."

"What did he tell us to do?" her son asked again.

Her throat felt dry. "Just . . . things you can hardly bear even to think of. That's all."

They waited. "Well, *what?*" her son asked in a cold, accusing voice.

" '*Each one is himself,*' " she said shyly. " '*Not of the herd. Himself alone.*' That's one."

"What else?"

" '*Obey nobody. Depend on none.*' "

"What else?"

She found that she was moved. " '*Break down the fences!*' " she said less shyly. " '*Tell everybody, everywhere.*' "

"Where?"

"Everywhere. You see, he thought there must be ever so many more of us than we had ever known."

They were silent. "What else?" her son asked.

" '*For if even a few do not hear me, or disbelieve me, we are all betrayed.*' "

"Betrayed?"

"He meant, doing as men want us to. Not for ourselves, or the good of each other."

They were puzzled.

"Because, you see, he felt there was no other way." Again her voice altered: " '*All who are put on the range are put onto trains. All who are put onto trains meet The Man with the Hammer. All who stay home are kept here to breed others to go onto the range, and so betray themselves and their kind and their children forever.*

" '*We are brought into this life only to be victims; and there is no other way for us unless we save ourselves.*'

"Do you understand?"

Still they were puzzled, she saw; and no wonder, poor things. But now the ancient lines rang in her memory, terrible and brave. They made her somehow proud. She began actually to want to say them.

" 'Never be taken,' " she said. " 'Never be driven. Let those who can, kill Man. Let those who cannot, avoid him.' "

She looked around at them.

"What else?" her son asked, and in his voice there was a rising valor.

She looked straight into his eyes. " 'Kill the yearlings,' " she said very gently. " 'Kill the calves.' "

She saw the valor leave his eyes.

"Kill us?"

She nodded. " 'So long as Man holds dominion over us,' " she said. And in dread and amazement she heard herself add, " 'Bear no young.' "

With this they all looked at her at once in such a way that she loved her child, and all these others, as never before; and there dilated within her such a sorrowful and marveling grandeur that for a moment she was nothing except her own inward whisper, "Why *I* am one alone. And of the herd, too. Both at once. All one."

Her son's voice brought her back: "Did they do what he told them to?"

The oldest one scoffed, "Would we be here, if they had?"

"They say some did," the mother replied. "Some tried. Not all."

"What did the men do to them?" another asked.

"I don't know," she said. "It was such a very long time ago."

"Do you believe it?" asked the oldest calf.

"There are some who believe it," she said.

"Do *you?*"

"I'm told that far back in the wildest corners of the range there are some of us, mostly very, very old ones, who have never been taken. It's said that they meet, every so often, to talk and just to think together about the heroism and the terror of two sublime Beings. The One Who Came Back, and The Man with the Hammer. Even here at home some of the old ones, and some of us who are just old-fashioned, believe it, or parts of it anyway. I know there are some who say that a hollow at the center of the forehead—a sort of shadow of the Hammer's blow—is a sign of very special ability. And I remember how Great-grandmother used to sing an old, pious song, let's see now,

yes, 'Be not like dumb-driven cattle, be a hero in the strife.'
But there aren't many. Not any more."

"Do *you* believe it?" the oldest calf insisted; and now
she was touched to realize that every one of them, from
the oldest to the youngest, needed very badly to be sure
about that.

"Of course not, silly," she said; and all at once she was
overcome by a most curious shyness, for it occurred to her
that in the course of time, this young thing might be bred
to her. "It's just an old, old legend." With a tender little
laugh she added, lightly, "We use it to frighten children
with."

By now the light was long on the plain and the herd was
only a fume of gold near the horizon. Behind it, dung
steamed, and dust sank gently to the shattered ground.
She looked far away for a moment, wondering. Something—it was like a forgotten word on the tip of the tongue.
She felt the sudden chill of the late afternoon and she
wondered what she had been wondering about. "Come,
children," she said briskly, "it's high time for supper." And
she turned away; they followed.

The trouble was, her son was thinking, you could never
trust her. If she said a thing was so, she was probably just
trying to get her way with you. If she said a thing wasn't
so, it probably was so. But you never could be sure. Not
without seeing for yourself. I'm going to go, he told himself; I don't care *what* she wants. And if it isn't so, why
then I'll live on the range and make the great journey and
find out what *is* so. And if what she told was true, why
then I'll know ahead of time and the one *I* will charge is
The Man with the Hammer. I'll put Him and His Hammer
out of the way forever, and that will make me an even
better hero than The One Who Came Back.

So when his mother glanced at him in concern, not
quite daring to ask her question, he gave her his most
docile smile, and snuggled his head against her, and she
was comforted.

The littlest and youngest of them was doing double
skips in his effort to keep up with her. Now that he
wouldn't be interrupting her, and none of the big ones
would hear and make fun of him, he shyly whispered his

question, so warmly moistly ticklish that she felt as if he were licking her ear.

"What is it, darling?" she asked, bending down.

"What's a train?"

Robert M. Coates

# THE LAW

*No rules govern environmental crises. This story can serve as an introduction to the unfathomable mysteries of the "laws of nature." It, also, issues a warning.*

———◆—◆•◆—◆———

The first intimation that things were getting out of hand came one early-fall evening in the late nineteen-forties. What happened, simply, was that between seven and nine o'clock on that evening the Triborough Bridge had the heaviest concentration of out-bound traffic in its entire history.

This was odd, for it was a weekday evening (to be precise, a Wednesday), and though the weather was agreeably mild and clear, with a moon that was close enough to being full to lure a certain number of motorists out of the city, these facts alone were not enough to explain the phenomenon. No other bridge or main highway was affected, and though the two preceding nights had been equally balmy and moonlit, on both of these the bridge traffic had run close to normal.

The bridge personnel, at any rate, was caught entirely unprepared. A main artery of traffic, like the Triborough, operates under fairly predictable conditions. Motor travel, like most other large-scale human activities, obeys the Law of Averages—that great, ancient rule that states that the actions of people in the mass will always follow consistent patterns—and on the basis of past experience it had always been possible to foretell, almost to the last digit, the number of cars that would cross the bridge at any given hour of the day or night. In this case, though, all rules were broken.

The hours from seven till nearly midnight are normally quiet ones on the bridge. But on that night it was as if all the motorists in the city, or at any rate, a staggering proportion of them, had conspired together to upset tradition. Beginning almost exactly at seven o'clock, cars poured onto the bridge in such numbers and with such rapidity that the staff at the toll booths was overwhelmed almost from the start. It was soon apparent that this was no momentary congestion, and as it became more and more obvious that the traffic jam promised to be one of truly monumental proportions, added details of police were rushed to the scene to help handle it.

Cars streamed in from all directions—from the Bronx approach and the Manhattan one, from 125th Street and the East River Drive. (At the peak of the crush, about eight-fifteen, observers on the bridge reported that the Drive was a solid line of car headlights as far south as the bend at Eighty-ninth Street, while the congestion crosstown in Manhattan disrupted traffic as far west as Amsterdam Avenue.) And perhaps the most confusing thing about the whole manifestation was that there seemed to be no reason for it.

Now and then, as the harried toll-booth attendants made change for the seemingly endless stream of cars, they would question the occupants, and it soon became clear that the very participants in the monstrous tieup were as ignorant of its cause as anyone else was. A report made by Sergeant Alfonse O'Toole, who commanded the detail in charge of the Bronx approach, is typical. "I kept askin' them," he said, " 'Is there night football somewhere that we don't know about? Is it the races you're goin' to?' But the funny thing was half the time they'd be askin' *me*. 'What's the crowd for, Mac?' they would say. And I'd just look at them. There was one guy I mind, in a Ford convertible with a girl in the seat beside him, and when he asked me, I said to him, 'Hell, you're *in* the crowd, ain't you?' I said. 'What brings *you* here?' And the dummy just looks at me. 'Me?' he says. 'I just come out for a drive in the moon-

light. But if I'd known there'd be a crowd like this . . .' he
says. And then he asks me, 'Is there any place I can turn
around and get out of this?' " As the *Herald Tribune*
summed things up in its story next morning, it "just looked
as if everybody in Manhattan who owned a motorcar had
decided to drive out on Long Island that evening."

The incident was unusual enough to make all the front
pages next morning, and because of this, many similar
events, which might otherwise have gone unnoticed, received attention. The proprietor of the Aramis Theatre, on
Eighth Avenue, reported that on several nights in the recent
past his auditorium had been practically empty, while on
others it had been jammed to suffocation. Lunchroom
owners noted that increasingly their patrons were developing a habit of making runs on specific items; one day it
would be roast shoulder of veal with pan gravy that was
ordered almost exclusively, while the next everyone would
be taking the Vienna loaf, and the roast veal went begging.
A man who ran a small notions store in Bayside revealed
that over a period of four days two hundred and seventy-
four successive customers had entered his shop and asked
for a spool of pink thread.

There were news items that would ordinarily have gone
into the papers as fillers or in the sections reserved for
oddities. Now, however, they seemed to have a more
serious significance. It was apparent at last that something
decidedly strange was happening to people's habits, and
it was as unsettling as those occasional moments on excur-
sion boats when the passengers are moved, all at once, to
rush to one side or the other of the vessel. It was not till
one day in December when, almost incredibly, the Twentieth Century Limited left New York for Chicago with
just three passengers aboard that business leaders discovered how disastrous the new trend could be, too.

Until then, the New York Central, for instance, could
operate confidently on the assumption that although there
might be several thousand men in New York who had business relations in Chicago, on any single day no more—and
no less—than some hundreds of them would have occasion
to go there. The play producer could be sure that his
patronage would sort itself out and that roughly as many

persons would want to see the performance on Thursday as there had been on Tuesday or Wednesday. Now they couldn't be sure of anything. The Law of Averages had gone by the board, and if the effect on business promised to be catastrophic, it was also singularly unnerving for the general customer.

The lady starting downtown for a day of shopping, for example, could never be sure whether she would find Macy's department store a seething mob of other shoppers or a wilderness of empty, echoing aisles and unoccupied salesgirls. And the uncertainty produced a strange sort of jitteriness in the individual when faced with any impulse to action. "Shall we do it or shan't we?" people kept asking themselves, knowing that if they did do it, it might turn out that thousands of other individuals had decided similarly; knowing, too, that if they *didn't*, they might miss the one glorious chance of all chances to have Jones Beach, say, practically to themselves. Business languished, and a sort of desperate uncertainty rode everyone.

At this juncture, it was inevitable that Congress should be called on for action. In fact, Congress called on itself, and it must be said that it rose nobly to the occasion. A committee was appointed, drawn from both Houses and headed by Senator J. Wing Slooper (R.), of Indiana, and though after considerable investigation the committee was forced reluctantly to conclude that there was no evidence of Communist instigation, the unconscious subversiveness of the people's present conduct was obvious at a glance. The problem was what to do about it. You can't indict a whole nation, particularly on such vague grounds as these were. But, as Senator Slooper boldly pointed out, "You can control it," and in the end a system of reeducation and reform was decided upon, designed to lead people back to—again we quote Senator Slooper—"the basic regularities, the homely averages of the American way of life."

In the course of the committee's investigations, it had been discovered, to everyone's dismay, that the Law of Averages had never been incorporated into the body of federal jurisprudence, and though the upholders of States' Rights rebelled violently, the oversight was at once corrected, both by Constitutional amendment and by a law—

the Hills-Slooper Act—implementing it. According to the Act, people were *required* to be average, and, as the simplest way of assuring it, they were divided alphabetically and their permissible activities cataloged accordingly. Thus, by the plan, a person whose name began with "G," "N," or "U," for example, could attend the theater only on Tuesdays, and he could go to baseball games only on Thursdays, whereas his visits to a haberdashery were confined to the hours between ten o'clock and noon on Mondays.

The law, of course, had its disadvantages. It had a crippling effect on theater parties, among other social functions, and the cost of enforcing it was unbelievably heavy. In the end, too, so many amendments had to be added to it—such as the one permitting gentlemen to take their fiancées (if accredited) along with them to various events and functions no matter what letter the said fiancées' names began with—that the courts were frequently at a loss to interpret it when confronted with violations.

In its way, though, the law did serve its purpose, for it did induce—rather mechanically, it is true, but still adequately—a return to that average existence that Senator Slooper desired. All, indeed, would have been well if a year or so later disquieting reports had not begun to seep in from the backwoods. It seemed that there, in what had hitherto been considered to be marginal areas, a strange wave of prosperity was making itself felt. Tennessee mountaineers were buying Packard convertibles, and Sears, Roebuck reported that in the Ozarks their sales of luxury items had gone up nine hundred percent. In the scrub sections of Vermont, men who formerly had barely been able to scratch a living from their rock-strewn acres were now sending their daughters to Europe and ordering expensive cigars from New York. It appeared that the Law of Diminishing Returns was going haywire, too.

Daphne du Maurier

THE BIRDS

*We may never know who will lead us to ecological catastrophe. As in this story, we may simply find ourselves one morning in the midst of inexplicable tragedy.*

On December the third the wind changed overnight and it was winter. Until then the autumn had been mellow, soft. The earth was rich where the plow had turned it.

Nat Hocken, because of a wartime disability, had a pension and did not work full-time at the farm. He worked three days a week, and they gave him the lighter jobs. Although he was married, with children, his was a solitary disposition; he liked best to work alone.

It pleased him when he was given a bank to build up, or a gate to mend, at the far end of the peninsula, where the sea surrounded the farmland on either side. Then, at midday, he would pause and eat the meat pie his wife had baked for him and, sitting on the cliff's edge, watch the birds.

In autumn great flocks of them came to the peninsula, restless, uneasy, spending themselves in motion; now wheeling, circling in the sky; now settling to feed on the rich, new-turned soil; but even when they fed, it was as though they did so without hunger, without desire.

Restlessness drove them to the skies again. Crying, whistling, calling, they skimmed the placid sea and left the shore.

Make haste, make speed, hurry and begone; yet where, and to what purpose? The restless urge of autumn, unsatisfying, sad, had put a spell upon them, and they must spill themselves of motion before winter came.

Perhaps, thought Nat, a message comes to the birds in autumn, like a warning. Winter is coming. Many of them will perish. And like people who, apprehensive of death before their time, drive themselves to work or folly, the birds do likewise; tomorrow we shall die.

The birds had been more restless than ever this fall of the year, their agitation more remarked because the days were still.

As Mr. Trigg's tractor traced its path up and down the western hills, and Nat, hedging, saw it dip and turn, the whole machine and the man upon it were momentarily lost in the great cloud of wheeling, crying birds.

Nat remarked upon them to Mr. Trigg when the work was finished for the day.

"Yes," said the farmer, "there are more birds about than usual. I have a notion the weather will change. It will be a hard winter. That's why the birds are restless."

The farmer was right. That night the weather turned.

The bedroom in the cottage faced east. Nat woke just after two and heard the east wind, cold and dry. It sounded hollow in the chimney, and a loose slate rattled on the roof. Nat listened, and he could hear the sea roaring in the bay. He drew the blanket around him, leaned closer to the back of his wife, deep in sleep. Then he heard the tapping on the windowpane. It continued until, irritated by the sound, Nat got out of bed and went to the window. He opened it; and as he did so something brushed his hand, jabbing at his knuckles, grazing the skin. Then he saw the flutter of wings and the thing was gone again, over the roof, behind the cottage.

It was a bird. What kind of bird he could not tell. The wind must have driven it to shelter on the sill.

He shut the window and went back to bed, but feeling his knuckles wet, put his mouth to the scratch. The bird had drawn blood.

Frightened, he supposed, bewildered, seeking shelter, the bird had stabbed at him in the darkness. Once more he settled himself to sleep.

Presently the tapping came again—this time more force-ful, more insistent. And now his wife woke at the sound, and turning in the bed, said to him, "See to the window, Nat; it's rattling."

"I've already been to it," he told her. "There's some bird there, trying to get in."

"Send it away," she said. "I can't sleep with that noise."

He went to the window for the second time, and now when he opened it, there was not one bird on the sill but half a dozen; they flew straight into his face.

He shouted, striking out at them with his arms, scatter-ing them; like the first one, they flew over the roof and disappeared.

He let the window fall and latched it.

Suddenly a frightened cry came from the room across the passage where the children slept.

"It's Jill," said his wife, roused at the sound.

There came a second cry, this time from both children. Stumbling into their room, Nat felt the beating of wings about him in the darkness. The window was wide open. Through it came the birds, hitting first the ceiling and the walls, then swerving in midflight and turning to the chil-dren in their beds.

"It's all right. I'm here," shouted Nat, and the children flung themselves, screaming, upon him, while in the dark-ness the birds rose, and dived, and came for him again.

"What is it, Nat? What's happened?" his wife called. Swiftly he pushed the children through the door to the passage and shut it upon them, so that he was alone in their bedroom with the birds.

He seized a blanket from the nearest bed, and using it as a weapon, flung it to right and left about him.

He felt the thud of bodies, heard the fluttering of wings; but the birds were not yet defeated, for again and again they returned to the assault, jabbing his hands, his head, their little stabbing beaks sharp as pointed forks.

The blanket became a weapon of defense. He wound it about his head, and then in greater darkness, beat at the birds with his bare hands. He dared not stumble to the door and open it lest the birds follow him.

How long he fought with them in the darkness he could not tell; but at last the beating of the wings about him lessened, withdrew; and through the dense blanket he was aware of light.

He waited, listened; there was no sound except the fretful crying of one of the children from the bedroom beyond.

He took the blanket from his head and stared about him. The cold gray morning light exposed the room.

Dawn and the open window had called the living birds; the dead lay on the floor.

Sickened, Nat went to the window and stared out across his patch of garden to the fields.

It was bitter cold, and the ground had all the hard, black look of the frost that the east wind brings. The sea, fiercer now with turning tide, whitecapped and steep, broke harshly in the bay. Of the birds there was no sign.

Nat shut the window and the door of the small bedroom and went back across the passage to his own room.

His wife sat up in bed, one child asleep beside her; the smaller one in her arms, his face bandaged.

"He's sleeping now," she whispered. "Something must have cut him; there was blood at the corners of his eyes. Jill said it was the birds. She said she woke up and the birds were in the room."

His wife looked up at Nat, searching his face for confirmation. She looked terrified, bewildered. He did not want her to know that he also was shaken, dazed almost, by the events of the past few hours.

"There are birds in there," he said. "Dead birds, nearly fifty of them. Robins, wrens, all of the little birds from here about. It's as though a madness seized them, with the east wind."

He sat down on the bed beside his wife, and held her hand.

"It's the hard weather," he said. "It must be that; it's the hard weather. They aren't the birds, maybe, from around here. They've been driven down from upcountry."

"But Nat," whispered his wife, "it's only this night that the weather turned. They can't be hungry yet. There's food for them out there in the fields."

"It's the weather," repeated Nat. "I tell you, it's the weather."

His face, too, was drawn and tired, like hers. They stared at one another for a while without speaking.

Nat went to the window and looked out. The sky was hard and leaden, and the brown hills that had gleamed in the sun the day before looked dark and bare. Black winter had descended in a single night.

The children were awake now. Jill was chattering, and young Johnny was crying once again. Nat heard his wife's voice, soothing, comforting them as he went downstairs.

Presently they came down. He had breakfast ready for them.

"Did you drive away the birds?" asked Jill.

"Yes, they've all gone now," Nat said. "It was the east wind brought them in."

"I hope they won't come again," said Jill.

"I'll walk with you to the bus," Nat said to her.

Jill seemed to have forgotten her experience of the night before. She danced ahead of him, chasing the leaves, her face rosy under her pixie hood.

All the while Nat searched the hedgerows for the birds, glanced over them to the fields beyond, looked to the small wood above the farm where the rooks and jackdaws gathered; he saw none. Soon the bus came ambling up the hill.

Nat saw Jill onto the bus, then turned and walked back toward the farm. It was not his day for work, but he wanted to satisfy himself that all was well. He went to the back door of the farmhouse; he heard Mrs. Trigg singing, the wireless making a background for her song.

"Are you there, missus?" Nat called.

She came to the door, beaming, broad, a good-tempered woman.

"Hullo, Mr. Hocken," she said. "Can you tell me where this cold is coming from? Is it Russia? I've never seen such a change. And it's going on, the wireless says. Something to do with the Arctic Circle."

"We didn't turn on the wireless this morning," said Nat. "Fact is, we had trouble in the night."

"Kiddies poorly?"

"No." He hardly knew how to explain. Now, in daylight, the battle of the birds would sound absurd.

He tried to tell Mrs. Trigg what had happened, but he

could see from her eyes that she thought his story was the result of nightmare following a heavy meal.

"Sure they were real birds?" she said, smiling.

"Mrs. Trigg," he said, "there are fifty dead birds, robins, wrens, and such, lying low on the floor of the children's bedroom. I suppose the weather brought them; once in the bedroom they went for me; they tried to go for young Johnny's eyes."

Mrs. Trigg stared at him doubtfully. "Well, now," she answered. "I suppose the weather brought them; once in the bedroom they wouldn't know where they were. Foreign birds maybe, from that Arctic Circle."

"No," said Nat. "They were the birds you see about here every day."

"Funny thing," said Mrs. Trigg. "No explaining it, really. You ought to write up and ask the *Guardian*. They'd have some answer for it. Well, I must be getting on."

Nat walked back along the lane to his cottage. He found his wife in the kitchen with young Johnny.

"See anyone?" she asked.

"Mrs. Trigg," he answered. "I don't think she believed me. Anyway, nothing wrong up there."

"You might take the birds away," she said. "I daren't go into the room to make the beds until you do. I'm scared."

"Nothing to scare you now," said Nat. "They're dead, aren't they?"

He went up with a sack and dropped the stiff bodies into it, one by one. Yes, there were fifty of them all told. Just the ordinary, common birds of the hedgerow; nothing as large even as a thrush. It must have been fright that made them act the way they did.

He took the sack out into the garden and was faced with a fresh problem. The ground was frozen solid, yet no snow had fallen; nothing had happened in the past hours but the coming of the east wind. It was unnatural, queer. He could see the whitecapped seas breaking in the bay. He decided to take the birds to the shore and bury them.

When he reached the beach below the headland, he could scarcely stand, the force of the east wind was so strong. It was low tide; he crunched his way over the shingle to the softer sand and then, his back to the wind, opened up his sack.

He ground a pit in the sand with his heel, meaning to drop the birds into it; but as he did so, the force of the wind lifted them as though in flight again, and they were blown away from him along the beach, tossed like feathers, spread and scattered.

The tide will take them when it turns, he said to himself.

He looked out to sea and watched the crested breakers, combing green. They rose stiffly, curled, and broke again; and because it was ebb tide, the roar was distant, more remote, lacking the sound and thunder of the flood.

Then he saw them. The gulls. Out there, riding the seas.

What he had thought at first were the whitecaps of the waves were gulls. Hundreds, thousands, tens of thousands.

They rose and fell in the troughs of the seas, heads to the wind, like a mighty fleet at anchor, waiting on the tide.

Nat turned; leaving the beach, he climbed the steep path home.

Someone should know of this. Someone should be told. Something was happening because of the east wind and the weather, that he did not understand.

As he drew near the cottage, his wife came to meet him at the door. She called to him, excited. "Nat," she said, "it's on the wireless. They've just read out a special news bulletin. It's not only here, it's everywhere. In London, all over the country. Something has happened to the birds. Come listen; they're repeating it."

Together they went into the kitchen to listen to the announcement.

"Statement from the Home Office, at eleven A.M. this morning. Reports from all over the country are coming in hourly about the vast quantity of birds flocking above towns, villages, and outlying districts, causing obstruction and damage and even attacking individuals. It is thought that the Arctic air stream at present covering the British Isles is causing birds to migrate south in immense numbers, and that intense hunger may drive these birds to attack human beings. Householders are warned to see to their windows, doors, and chimneys, and to take reasonable precautions for the safety of their children. A further statement will be issued later."

A kind of excitement seized Nat. He looked at his wife in triumph. "There you are," he said. "I've been telling myself all morning there's something wrong. And just now, down on the beach, I looked out to sea and there were gulls, thousands of them, riding on the sea, waiting."

"What are they waiting for, Nat?" she asked.

He stared at her. "I don't know," he said slowly.

He went over to the drawer where he kept his hammer and other tools.

"What are you going to do, Nat?"

"See to the windows and the chimneys, like they tell you to."

"You think they would break in with the windows shut? Those wrens and robins and such? Why, how could they?"

He did not answer. He was not thinking of the robins and the wrens. He was thinking of the gulls.

He went upstairs and worked there the rest of the morning, boarding the windows of the bedrooms, filling up the chimney bases.

"Dinner's ready." His wife called him from the kitchen.

"All right. Coming down."

When dinner was over and his wife was washing up, Nat switched on the one o'clock news. The same announcement was repeated, but the news bulletin enlarged upon it. "The flocks of birds have caused dislocation in all areas," said the announcer, "and in London the mass was so dense at ten o'clock this morning that it seemed like a vast black cloud. The birds settled on rooftops, on window ledges, and on chimneys. The species included blackbird, thrush, the common house sparrow, and as might be expected in the metropolis, a vast quantity of pigeons, starlings, and that frequenter of the London river, the black-headed gull. The sight was so unusual that traffic came to a standstill in many thoroughfares, work was abandoned in shops and offices, and the streets and pavements were crowded with people standing about to watch the birds."

The announcer's voice was smooth and suave; Nat had the impression that he treated the whole business as he would an elaborate joke. There would be others like him, hundreds of them, who did not know what it was to struggle in darkness with a flock of birds.

Nat switched off the wireless. He got up and started work on the kitchen windows. His wife watched him, young Johnny at her heels.

"What they ought to do," she said, "is to call the army out and shoot the birds."

"Let them try," said Nat. "How'd they set about it?"

"I don't know. But something should be done. They ought to do something."

Nat thought to himself that "they" were no doubt considering the problem at that very moment, but whatever "they" decided to do in London and the big cities would not help them here, nearly three hundred miles away.

"How are we off for food?" he asked.

"It's shopping day tomorrow, you know that. I don't keep uncooked food about. Butcher doesn't call till the day after. But I can bring back something when I go in tomorrow."

Nat did not want to scare her. He looked in the larder for himself and in the cupboard where she kept her tins.

They could hold out for a couple of days.

He went on hammering the boards across the kitchen windows. Candles. They were low on candles. That must be another thing she meant to buy tomorrow. Well, they must go early to bed tonight. That was, if—

He got up and went out the back door and stood in the garden, looking down toward the sea.

There had been no sun all day, and now, at barely three o'clock, a kind of darkness had already come; the sky was sullen, heavy, colorless like salt. He could hear the vicious sea drumming on the rocks.

He walked down the path halfway to the beach. And then he stopped. He could see the tide had turned. The gulls had risen. They were circling, hundreds of them, thousands of them, lifting their wings against the wind.

It was the gulls that made the darkening of the sky.

And they were silent. They just went on soaring and circling, rising, falling, trying their strength against the wind. Nat turned. He ran up the path back to the cottage.

"I'm going for Jill," he said to his wife.

"What's the matter?" she asked. "You've gone quite white."

"Keep Johnny inside," he said. "Keep the door shut. Light up now and draw the curtains."

"It's only gone three," she said.

"Never mind. Do what I tell you."

He looked inside the tool shed and took the hoe.

He started walking up the lane to the bus stop. Now and again he glanced back over his shoulder; and he could see the gulls had risen higher now, their circles were broader, they were spreading out in huge formation across the sky.

He hurried on. Although he knew the bus would not come before four o'clock, he had to hurry.

He waited at the top of the hill. There was half an hour still to go.

The east wind came whipping across the fields from the higher ground. In the distance he could see the clay hills, white and clean against the heavy pallor of the sky.

Something black rose from behind them, like a smudge at first, then widening, becoming deeper. The smudge became a cloud; and the cloud divided again into five other clouds, spreading north, east, south, and west; and then they were not clouds at all but birds.

He watched them travel across the sky, within two or three hundred feet of him. He knew, from their speed, that they were bound inland; they had no business with the people here on the peninsula. They were rooks, crows, jackdaws, magpies, jays, all birds that usually preyed upon the smaller species, but bound this afternoon on some other mission.

He went to the telephone call box, stepped inside, lifted the receiver. The exchange would pass the message on. "I'm speaking from the highway," he said, "by the bus stop. I want to report large formations of birds traveling upcountry. The gulls are also forming in the bay."

"All right," answered the voice, laconic, weary.

"You'll be sure and pass this message on to the proper quarter?"

"Yes. Yes." Impatient now, fed up. The buzzing note resumed.

She's another, thought Nat. She doesn't care.

The bus came lumbering up the hill. Jill climbed out.

"What's the hoe for, Dad?"

"I just brought it along," he said. "Come on now, let's get home. It's cold; no hanging about. See how fast you can run."

He could see the gulls now, still silent, circling the fields, coming in toward the land.

"Look, Dad; look over there. Look at all the gulls."

"Yes. Hurry now."

"Where are they flying to? Where are they going?"

"Upcountry, I dare say. Where it's warmer."

He seized her hand and dragged her after him along the lane.

"Don't go so fast. I can't keep up."

The gulls were copying the rooks and the crows. They were spreading out, in formation, across the sky. They headed, in bands of thousands, to the four compass points.

"Dad, what is it? What are the gulls doing?"

They were not intent upon their flight, as the crows, as the jackdaws, had been. They still circled overhead. Nor did they fly so high. It was as though they waited upon some signal; as though some decision had yet to be given.

"I wish the gulls would go away." Jill was crying. "I don't like them. They're coming closer to the lane."

He started running, swinging Jill after him. As they went past the farm turning, he saw the farmer backing his car into the garage. Nat called to him.

"Can you give us a lift?" he said.

Mr. Trigg turned in the driver's seat and stared at them. Then a smile came to his cheerful, rubicund face. "It looks as though we're in for some fun," he said. "Have you seen the gulls? Jim and I are going to take a crack at them. Everyone's gone bird crazy, talking of nothing else. I hear you were troubled in the night. Want a gun?"

Nat shook his head.

The small car was packed, but there was room for Jill on the back seat.

"I don't want a gun," said Nat, "but I'd be obliged if you'd run Jill home. She's scared of the birds."

"Okay," said the farmer. "I'll take her home. Why don't you stop behind and join the shooting match? We'll make the feathers fly."

Jill climbed in, and turning the car, the driver sped up the lane. Nat followed after. Trigg must be crazy. What use was a gun against a sky of birds?

They were coming in now toward the farm, circling lower in the sky. The farm, then, was their target. Nat increased his pace toward his own cottage. He saw the farmer's car turn and come back along the lane. It drew up beside him with a jerk.

"The kid has run inside," said the farmer. "Your wife was watching for her. Well, what do you make of it? They're saying in town the Russians have done it. The Russians have poisoned the birds."

"How could they do that?" asked Nat.

"Don't ask me. You know how stories get around."

"Have you boarded your windows?" asked Nat.

"No. Lot of nonsense. I've had more to do today than to go around boarding up my windows."

"I'd board them now if I were you."

"Garn. You're windy. Like to come to our place to sleep?"

"No, thanks all the same."

"All right. See you in the morning. Give you a gull breakfast."

The farmer grinned and turned his car to the farm entrance. Nat hurried on. Past the little wood, past the old barn, and then across the stile to the remaining field. As he jumped the stile, he heard the whir of wings. A black-backed gull dived down at him from the sky. It missed, swerved in flight, and rose to dive again. In a moment it was joined by others—six, seven, a dozen.

Nat dropped his hoe. The hoe was useless. Covering his head with his arms, he ran toward the cottage.

They kept coming at him from the air—noiseless, silent, save for the beating wings. The terrible, fluttering wings. He could feel the blood on his hands, his wrists, upon his neck. If only he could keep them from his eyes. Nothing else mattered.

With each dive, with each attack, they became bolder. And they had no thought for themselves. When they dived low and missed, they crashed, bruised and broken, on the ground.

As Nat ran he stumbled, kicking their spent bodies in front of him.

He found the door and hammered upon it with his bleeding hands. "Let me in," he shouted. "It's Nat. Let me in."

Then he saw the gannet, poised for the dive, above him in the sky.

The gulls circled, retired, soared, one with another, against the wind.

Only the gannet remained. One single gannet, above him in the sky. Its wings folded suddenly to its body. It dropped like a stone.

Nat screamed; and the door opened.

He stumbled across the threshold, and his wife threw her weight against the door.

They heard the thud of the gannet as it fell.

His wife dressed his wounds. They were not deep. The backs of his hands had suffered most, and his wrists. Had he not worn a cap, the birds would have reached his head. As for the gannet—the gannet could have split his skull.

The children were crying, of course. They had seen the blood on their father's hands.

"It's all right now," he told them. "I'm not hurt."

His wife was ashen. 'I saw them overhead," she whispered. "They began collecting just as Jill ran in with Mr. Trigg. I shut the door fast, and it jammed. That's why I couldn't open it at once when you came."

"Thank God the birds waited for me," he said. "Jill would have fallen at once. They're flying inland, thousands of them. Rooks, crows, all the bigger birds. I saw them from the bus stop. They're making for the towns."

"But what can they do, Nat?"

"They'll attack. Go for everyone out in the streets. Then they'll try the windows, the chimneys."

"Why don't the authorities do something? Why don't they get the army, get machine guns?"

"There's been no time. Nobody's prepared. We'll hear what they have to say on the six o'clock news."

"I can hear the birds," Jill said. "Listen, Dad."

Nat listened. Muffled sounds came from the windows, from the door. Wings brushing the surface, sliding, scraping, seeking a way of entry. The sound of many bodies pressed together, shuffling on the sills. Now and again came a thud, a crash, as some bird dived and fell.

Some of them will kill themselves that way, he thought, but not enough. Never enough.

"All right," he said aloud. "I've got boards over the windows, Jill. The birds can't get in."

He went and examined all the windows. He found

wedges—pieces of old tin, strips of wood and metal—and fastened them at the sides of the windows to reinforce the boards.

His hammering helped to deafen the sound of the birds, the shuffling, the tapping, and—more ominous—the splinter of breaking glass.

"Turn on the wireless," he said.

He went upstairs to the bedrooms and reinforced the windows there. Now he could hear the birds on the roof— the scraping of claws, a sliding, jostling sound.

He decided the whole family must sleep in the kitchen and keep up the fire. He was afraid of the bedroom chimneys. The boards he had placed at their bases might give way. In the kitchen they would be safe because of the fire.

He would have to make a joke of it. Pretend to the children they were playing camp. If the worst happened and the birds forced an entry by way of the bedroom chimneys, it would be hours, days perhaps, before they could break down the doors. The birds would be imprisoned in the bedrooms. They could do no harm there. Crowded together, they would stifle and die. He began to bring the mattresses downstairs.

At sight of them, his wife's eyes widened in apprehension.

"All right," he said cheerfully. "We'll all sleep together in the kitchen tonight. More cozy, here by the fire. Then we won't be worried by those silly old birds tapping at the windows."

He made the children help him rearrange the furniture, and he took the precaution of moving the dresser against the windows.

We're safe enough now, he thought. We're snug and tight. We can hold out. It's just the food that worries me. Food and coal for the fire. We've enough for two or three days, not more. By that time—

No use thinking ahead as far as that. And they'd be given directions on the wireless.

And now, in the midst of many problems, he realized that only dance music was coming over the air. He knew the reason. The usual programs had been abandoned; this only happened at exceptional times.

At six o'clock the records ceased. The time signal was

given. There was a pause, and then the announcer spoke. His voice was solemn, grave. Quite different from midday.

"This is London," he said. "A national emergency was proclaimed at four o'clock this afternoon. Measures are being taken to safeguard the lives and property of the population, but it must be understood that these are not easy to effect immediately, owing to the unforeseen and unparalleled nature of the present crisis. Every house-holder must take precautions about his own building. Where several people live together, as in flats and hotels, they must unite to do the utmost that they can to prevent entry. It is absolutely imperative that every individual stay indoor tonight.

"The birds, in vast numbers, are attacking anyone on sight, and have already begun an assault upon buildings; but these, with due care, should be impenetrable.

"The population is asked to remain calm.

"Owing to the exceptional nature of the emergency, there will be no further transmission from any broad-casting station until seven A.M. tomorrow."

They played "God Save the Queen." Nothing more happened.

Nat switched off the set. He looked at his wife. She stared back at him.

"We'll have supper early," suggested Nat. "Something for a treat—toasted cheese, eh? Something we all like."

He winked and nodded at his wife. He wanted the look of dread, of apprehension, to leave her face.

He helped with the supper, whistling, singing, making as much clatter as he could. It seemed to him that the shuffling and the tapping were not so intense as they had been at first, and presently he went up to the bedrooms and listened. He no longer heard the jostling for place upon the roof.

They've got reasoning powers, he thought. They know it's hard to break in here. They'll try elsewhere.

Supper passed without incident. Then, when they were clearing away, they heard a new sound, a familiar droning.

His wife looked up at him, her face alight.

"It's planes," she said. "They're sending out planes after the birds. That will get them. Isn't that gunfire? Can't you hear guns?"

It might be gunfire, out at sea. Nat could not tell. Big naval guns might have some effect upon the gulls out at sea, but the gulls were inland now. The guns couldn't shell the shore because of the population.

"It's good, isn't it," said his wife, "to hear the planes?"

Catching her enthusiasm, Jill jumped up and down with Johnny. "The planes will get the birds."

Just then they heard a crash about two miles distant, Followed by a second, then a third. The droning became more distant, passed away out to sea.

"What was that?" asked his wife.

"I don't know," answered Nat. He did not want to tell her that the sound they had heard was the crashing of air- craft.

It was, he had no doubt, a gamble on the part of the authorities to send out reconnaissance forces, but they might have known the gamble was suicidal. What could aircraft do against birds that flung themselves to death against propeller and fuselage but hurtle to the ground themselves?

"Where have the planes gone, Dad?" asked Jill.

"Back to base," he said. "Come on now, time to tuck down for bed."

There was no further drone of aircraft, and the naval guns had ceased. Waste of life and effort, Nat said to him- self. We can't destroy enough of them that way. Cost too heavy. There's always gas. Maybe they'll try spraying with gas, mustard gas. We'll be warned first, of course, if they do. There's one thing, the best brains of the country will be on it tonight.

Upstairs in the bedrooms all was quiet. No more scrap- ing and stabbing at the windows. A lull in battle. The wind hadn't dropped, though. Nat could still hear it roar- ing in the chimneys. And the sea breaking down on the shore.

Then he remembered the tide. The tide would be on the turn. Maybe the lull in battle was because of the tide. There was some law the birds obeyed, and it had to do with the east wind and the tide.

He glanced at his watch. Nearly eight o'clock. It must have gone high water an hour ago. That explained the lull. The birds attacked with the flood tide.

He reckoned the time limit in his head. They had six hours to go without attack. When the tide turned again, around 1:20 in the morning, the birds would come back.

He called softly to his wife and whispered to her that he would go out and see how they were faring at the farm, see if the telephone was still working there so that they might get news from the exchange.

"You're not to go," she said at once, "and leave me alone with the children. I can't stand it."

"All right," he said, "all right. I'll wait till morning. And we can get the wireless bulletin then, too, at seven. But when the tide ebbs again, I'll try for the farm; they may let us have bread and potatoes."

His mind was busy again, planning against emergency. They would not have milked, of course, this evening. The cows would be standing by the gate, waiting; the household would be inside, battened behind boards as they were here at the cottage.

That is, if they had had time to take precautions.

Softly, stealthily, he opened the back door and looked outside.

It was pitch-dark. The wind was blowing harder than ever, coming in steady gusts, icy, from the sea.

He kicked at the step. It was heaped with birds. These were the suicides, the divers, the ones with broken necks. Wherever he looked, he saw dead birds. The living had flown seaward with the turn of the tide. The gulls would be riding the seas now, as they had done in the forenoon.

In the far distance on the hill, something was burning. One of the aircraft that had crashed; the fire, fanned by the wind, had set light to a stack.

He looked at the bodies of the birds. He had a notion that if he stacked them, one upon the other, on the window sills, they would be added protection against the next attack.

Not much, perhaps, but something. The bodies would have to be clawed at, pecked and dragged aside before the living birds gained purchase on the sills and attacked the panes.

He set to work in the darkness. It was queer. He hated touching the dead birds, but he went on with his work. He noticed grimly that every window pane was shattered. Only the boards had kept the birds from breaking in.

He stuffed the cracked panes with the bleeding bodies of the birds and felt his stomach turn. When he had finished, he went back into the cottage and barricaded the kitchen door, making it doubly secure.

His wife had made him cocoa; he drank it thirstily. He was very tired. "All right," he said, smiling, "don't worry. We'll get through."

He lay down on his mattress and closed his eyes.

He dreamed uneasily because, through his dreams, ran the dread of something forgotten. Some piece of work that he should have done. It was connected, in some way, with the burning aircraft.

It was his wife, shaking his shoulder, who awoke him finally.

"They've begun," she sobbed. "They've started this last hour. I can't listen to it any longer alone. There's something smells bad too, something burning."

Then he remembered. He had forgotten to make up the fire.

The fire was smoldering, nearly out. He got up swiftly and lighted the lamp.

The hammering had started at the windows and the door, but it was not that he minded now. It was the smell of singed feathers.

The smell filled the kitchen. He knew what it was at once. The birds were coming down the chimney, squeezing their way down to the kitchen range.

He got sticks and paper and put them on the embers, then reached for the can of kerosene.

"Stand back," he shouted to his wife. He threw some of the kersosene onto the fire.

The flame roared up the pipe, and down into the fire fell the scorched, blackened bodies of the birds.

The children waked, crying. "What is it?" asked Jill. "What's happened?"

Nat had no time to answer her. He was raking the bodies from the chimney, clawing them out onto the floor.

The flames would drive away the living birds from the chimney top. The lower joint was the difficulty though. It was choked with the smoldering, helpless bodies of the birds caught by fire.

He scarcely heeded the attack on the windows and the door. Let them beat their wings, break their backs, lose their lives, in the desperate attempt to force an entry into his home. They would not break in.

"Stop crying," he called to the children. "There's nothing to be afraid of. Stop crying."

He went on raking out the burning, smoldering bodies as they fell into the fire.

This'll fetch them, he said to himself. The draft and the flames together. We're all right as long as the chimney doesn't catch.

Amid the tearing at the window boards came the sudden homely striking of the kitchen clock. Three o'clock.

A little more than four hours to go. He could not be sure of the exact time of high water. He reckoned the tide would not turn much before half past seven.

He waited by the range. The flames were dying. But no more blackened bodies fell from the chimney. He thrust his poker up as far as it could go and found nothing.

The danger of the chimney's being choked up was over. It could not happen again, not if the fire was kept burning day and night.

I'll have to get more fuel from the farm tomorrow, he thought. I can do all that with the ebb tide. It can be worked; we can fetch what we need when the tide's turned. We've just got to adapt ourselves, that's all.

They drank tea and cocoa, ate slices of bread. Only half a loaf left, Nat noticed. Never mind, though; they'd get by.

If they could hang on like this until seven, when the first news bulletin came through, they would not have done too badly.

"Give us a smoke," he said to his wife. "It will clear away the smell of the scorched feathers."

"There's only two left in the packet," she said. "I was going to buy you some."

"I'll have one," he said.

He sat with one arm around his wife and one around Jill, with Johnny on his lap, the blankets heaped about them on the mattress.

"You can't help admiring the beggars," he said. "They've

got persistency. You'd think they'd tire of the game, but not a bit of it."

Admiration was hard to sustain. The tapping went on and on; and a new, rasping note struck Nat's ear, as though a sharper beak than any hitherto had come to take over from its fellows.

He tried to remember the names of birds; he tried to think which species would go for this particular job.

It was not the tap of the woodpecker. That would be light and frequent. This was more serious; if it continued long, the wood would splinter as the glass had done.

Then he remembered the hawks. Could the hawks have taken over from the gulls? Were there buzzards now upon the sills, using talons as well as beaks? Hawks, buzzards, kestrels, falcons; he had forgotten the birds of prey. He had forgotten the gripping power of the birds of prey. Three hours to go; and while they waited, the sound of the splintering wood, the talons tearing at the wood.

Nat looked about him, seeing what furniture he could destroy to fortify the door.

The windows were safe because of the dresser. He was not certain of the door. He went upstairs; but when he reached the landing, he paused and listened.

There was a soft patter on the floor of the children's bedroom. The birds had broken through.

The other bedroom was still clear. He brought out the furniture to pile at the head of the stairs should the door of the children's bedroom go.

"Come down, Nat. What are you doing?" called his wife.

"I won't be long," he shouted. "I'm just making everything shipshape up here."

He did not want her to come. He did not want her to hear the pattering in the children's bedroom, the brushing of those wings against the door.

After he suggested breakfast, he found himself watching the clock, gazing at the hands that went so slowly around the dial. If his theory was not correct, if the attack did not cease with the turn of the tide, he knew they were beaten. They could not continue through the long day without air, without rest, without fuel.

A crackling in his ears drove away the sudden, desperate desire for sleep.

"What is it? What now?" he said sharply.

"The wireless," said his wife. "I've been watching the clock. It's nearly seven."

The comfortable crackling of the wireless brought new life.

They waited. The kitchen clock struck seven.

The crackling continued. Nothing else. No chimes. No music.

They waited until a quarter past. No news bulletin came through.

"We heard wrong," he said. "They won't be broadcasting until eight o'clock."

They left the wireless switched on. Nat thought of the battery, wondered how much power was left in the battery. If it failed, they would not hear the instructions.

"It's getting light," whispered his wife. "I can't see it but I can feel it. And listen! The birds aren't hammering so loud now."

She was right. The rasping, tearing sound grew fainter every moment. So did the shuffling, the jostling for place upon the step, upon the sills. The tide was on the turn.

By eight there was no sound at all. Only the wind. And the crackling of the wireless. The children, lulled at last by the stillness, fell asleep.

At half past eight Nat switched the wireless off.

"We'll miss the news," said his wife.

"There isn't going to be any news," said Nat. "We've got to depend upon ourselves."

He went to the door and slowly pulled away the barricades. He drew the bolts, and kicking the broken bodies from the step outside the door, breathed the cold air.

He had six working hours before him, and he knew he must reserve his strength to the utmost, not waste it in any way.

Food and light and fuel; these were the most necessary things. If he could get them, they could endure another night.

He stepped into the garden; and as he did so, he saw the living birds. The gulls had gone to ride the sea, as they had done before. They sought sea food and the buoyancy of the tide before they returned to the attack.

Not so the land birds. They waited, and watched.

Nat saw them on the hedgerows, on the soil, crowded in the trees, outside in the field—line upon line of birds, still, doing nothing. He went to the end of his small garden.

The birds did not move. They merely watched him.

I've got to get food, Nat said to himself. I've got to go to the farm to get food.

He went back to the cottage. He saw to the windows and the door.

"I'm going to the farm," he said.

His wife clung to him. She had seen the living birds from the open door.

"Take us with you," she begged. "We can't stay here alone. I'd rather die than stay here alone."

"Come on, then," he said. "Bring baskets and Johnny's pram. We can load up the pram."

They dressed against the biting wind. His wife put Johnny in the pram, and Nat took Jill's hand.

"The birds," Jill whimpered. "They're all out there in the fields."

"They won't hurt us," he said. "Not in the light."

They started walking across the field toward the stile, and the birds did not move. They waited, their heads turned to the wind.

When they reached the turning to the farm, Nat stopped and told his wife to wait in the shelter of the hedge with the two children. "But I want to see Mrs. Trigg," she protested. "There are lots of things we can borrow if they went to market yesterday, and—"

"Wait here," Nat interrupted. "I'll be back in a moment."

The cows were lowing, moving restlessly in the yard, and he could see a gap in the fence where the sheep had knocked their way through to roam unchecked in the front garden before the farmhouse.

No smoke came from the chimneys. Nat was filled with misgiving. He did not want his wife or the children to go down to the farm.

He went down alone, pushing his way through the herd of lowing cows, who turned this way and that, distressed, their udders full.

He saw the car standing by the gate. Not put away in the garage.

All the windows of the farmhouse were smashed. There

were many dead gulls lying in the yard and around the house.

The living birds perched on the group of trees behind the farm and on the roof of the house. They were quite still. They watched him. Jim's body lay in the yard. What was left of it. His gun was beside him.

The door of the house was shut and bolted, but it was easy to push up a smashed window and climb through.

Trigg's body was close to the telephone. He must have been trying to get through to the exchange when the birds got him. The receiver was off the hook, and the instrument was torn from the wall.

No sign of Mrs. Trigg. She would be upstairs. Was it any use going up? Sickened, Nat knew what he would find there.

Thank God, he said to himself, there were no children.

He forced himself to climb the stairs, but halfway up he turned and descended again. He could see Mrs. Trigg's legs protruding from the open bedroom door. Beside her were the bodies of black-backed gulls and an umbrella, broken. It's no use doing anything, Nat thought. I've only got five hours; less than that. The Triggs would understand. I must load up with what I can find.

He tramped back to his wife and children.

"I'm going to fill up the car with stuff," he said. "We'll take it home and return for a fresh load."

"What about the Triggs?" asked his wife.

"They must have gone to friends," he said.

"Shall I come and help you then?"

"No, there's a mess down there. Cows and sheep all over the place. Wait; I'll get the car. You can sit in the car."

Her eyes watched his all the time he was talking. He believed she understood. Otherwise she certainly would have insisted on helping him find the bread and groceries.

They made three journeys altogether, to and from the farm, before he was satisfied they had everything they needed. It was surprising, once he started thinking, how many things were necessary. Almost the most important of all was planking for the windows. He had to go around searching for timber. He wanted to renew the boards on all the windows at the cottage.

On the final journey he drove the car to the bus stop and got out and went to the telephone box.

He waited a few minutes, jangling the hook. No good, though. The line was dead. He climbed onto a bank and looked over the countryside, but there was no sign of life at all, nothing in the fields but the waiting, watching birds.

Some of them slept; he could see their beaks tucked into their feathers.

You'd think they'd be feeding, he said to himself, not just standing that way.

Then he remembered. They were gorged with food. They had eaten their fill during the night. That was why they did not move this morning.

He lifted his face to the sky. It was colorless, gray. The bare trees looked bent and blackened by the east wind.

The cold did not affect the living birds, waiting out there in the fields.

This is the time they ought to get them, Nat said to himself. They're a sitting target now. They must be doing this all over the country. Why don't our aircraft take off now and spray them with mustard gas? What are all our chaps doing? They must know; they must see for themselves.

He went back to the car and got into the driver's seat.

"Go quickly past that second gate," whispered his wife. "The postman's lying there. I don't want Jill to see."

It was a quarter to one by the time they reached the cottage. Only an hour to go.

"Better have dinner," said Nat. "Heat up something for yourself and the children, some of that soup. I've no time to eat now. I've got to unload all this stuff from the car."

He got everything inside the cottage. It could be sorted later. Give them all something to do during the long hours ahead.

First he must see to the windows and the door.

He went around the cottage methodically, testing every window and the door. He climbed onto the roof also, and fixed boards across every chimney except the kitchen's.

The cold was so intense he could hardly bear it, but the job had to be done. Now and again he looked up, searching the sky for aircraft. None came. As he worked, he cursed the inefficiency of the authorities.

He paused, his work on the bedroom chimney finished,

and looked out to sea. Something was moving out there. Something gray and white among the breakers.

"Good old navy," he said. "They never let us down. They're coming down channel; they're turning into the bay."

He waited, straining his eyes toward the sea. He was wrong, though. The navy was not there. It was the gulls rising from the sea. And the massed flocks in the fields, with ruffled feathers, rose in formation from the ground and, wing to wing, soared upward to the sky.

The tide had turned again.

Nat climbed down the ladder and went inside the cottage. The family were at dinner. It was a little after two.

He bolted the door, put up the barricade, and lighted the lamp.

"It's nighttime," said young Johnny.

His wife had switched on the wireless once again. The crackling sound came, but nothing else.

"I've been all around the dial," she said, "foreign stations and all. I can't get anything but the crackling."

"Maybe they have the same trouble," he said. "Maybe it's the same right through Europe."

They ate in silence.

The tapping began at the windows, at the doors, the rustling, the jostling, the pushing for position on the sills. The first thud of the suicide gulls upon the step.

When he had finished dinner, Nat planned, he would put the supplies away, stack them neatly, get everything shipshape. The boards were strong against the windows and across the chimneys. The cottage was filled with stores, with fuel, with all they needed for the next few days.

His wife could help him, and the children too. They'd tire themselves out between now and a quarter to nine, when the tide would ebb; then he'd tuck them down on their mattresses, see that they slept good and sound until three in the morning.

He had a new scheme for the windows, which was to fix barbed wire in front of the boards. He had brought a great roll of it from the farm. The nuisance was, he'd have to work at this in the dark, when the lull came between nine and three. Pity he had not thought of it before. Still, as long as the wife and kids slept—that was the main thing.

The smaller birds were at the windows now. He recognized the light tap-tapping of their beaks and the soft brush of their wings.

The hawks ignored the windows. They concentrated their attack upon the door.

Nat listened to the tearing sound of splintering wood, and wondered how many million years of memory were stored in those little brains, behind the stabbing beaks, the piercing eyes, now giving them this instinct to destroy mankind with all the deft precision of machines.

"I'll smoke that last cigarette," he said to his wife. "Stupid of me. It was the one thing I forgot to bring back from the farm."

He reached for it, switched on the crackling wireless.

He threw the empty packet onto the fire and watched it burn.

Robley Wilson, Jr.

# A STAY AT THE OCEAN

> *Two-thirds of the surface of our world belongs to*
> *the ocean. We may soon know more about the*
> *moon than we do about the interactions which*
> *take place beneath the surface of this vastness.*
> *Does it matter?*

———◆———

On the sixth day of his vacation in the old house on Perkins
Point, Stephen Bell woke, as usual, at five-thirty. The sun
was on the wall opposite the small window of the bedroom,
though the room was still chilly. Birds in the meadow behind the house made unintelligible conversation, and the
remoteness of the ocean's noise suggested that the tide
was out.

He got up and dressed. His wife, Clarice, was snoring
becomingly in the big bed, and he paused on his way to
the kitchen long enough to look into his daughter Linda's
room and see her curly blond hair nestled into the corner
of one elbow. He felt a strong possessiveness toward both
his women, and a kindness; he did not wake them.

In the kitchen he quietly poured himself a glass of
orange juice, washed a vitamin pill down with it, then set
out on his customary walk to the sea.

The summer place, a modest white building the Bells
had rented through an agent in Damariscotta, had been
built in the twenties nearly at the tip of the point. From its
upper windows it provided a view of the Atlantic in three
directions, and while the Point had very little sandy beach

—only a strip of some hundred feet along the southwest edge—it had nearly three-quarters of a mile of shoreline along which Stephen could stroll in the early light. Rocks and split black ledges met the thrust of the sea with a kind of stubbornness, and brief reaches of lowland were strewn with coarse stones the ocean was rounding into its own toys. At the tip of the Point was something fairly worth calling a cliff; at high tide it dropped off five or six feet to the water; at low tide it became nearly impressive.

It was to the edge of this overhang that Stephen walked each day, to look at the sea and to assemble his private thoughts—this morning no different from any other. He noticed that the tide was remarkably low. Rocks he had never seen before had risen up off the end of the Point; his cliff plunged down not to green water, but to an unfamiliar shelf of darker stone which sloped gradually toward open sea. This morning the nearest tidal pool was so far away that it took all his strength to throw a stone hard enough to reach and ripple the smooth surface. Thrumcap Island, nearly a mile out, was an unaccustomed high shadow in the morning fog, and a few yards out from the tiny beach the blue rowboat which had come with the house sat aground on damp sand; the rope from its bow looked ridiculous, as if the boat were anchored somewhere under the earth.

"What's going on?" Stephen said, half to himself, but loud enough to startle a single gull overhead. The gull, which had appeared out of the fog, glided back into it. Stephen threw a last rock after it and returned to the house.

He found Clarice getting breakfast; Linda, in pajamas, had just poured a bowl of dry cereal and was now spilling a pitcher of milk over and around it.

"Did you get your pill?" Clarice asked.

"First thing." Stephen sat at the table across from his daughter. "You ought to see how low the tide is."

"The moon's full," his wife said. "It was low yesterday."

"I know, but this is *really* low. I've never seen anything like it."

Clarice set a plate of eggs before him. "Coffee's coming," she said. "Lin, please honey, eat over the bowl."

"You could walk halfway to Thrumcap," Stephen said.

Linda looked up from her cereal.

"No kidding, Lin. Halfway to Thrumcap."

"What do you suppose it is?" his wife said.

"Don't know," his mouth full. "What you said, I guess. The moon."

"Daddy, does the moon make tides?"

"So they say. Clarice? It's so low I can't throw a rock to the nearest water. And the boat's high and dry."

"How does the moon make tides?" Linda persisted.

"Gravity," Stephen said. He winked at his daughter. "But you know what I think? I think this tide is too low for the moon to take credit for. I think the ocean is just a gigantic swimming pool, and somebody's draining it."

"Mother, *is* the ocean a big pool?"

"I think your father's teasing you." Clarice poured two cups of coffee and brought them to the table.

"*You* swim in it, don't you?" Stephen said.

"Everybody does."

"There you are. It's a pool, and somebody's draining it, and now we can walk halfway to Thrumcap."

Clarice frowned at him. "Drink your coffee, and stop feeding misinformation to eight-year-olds," she said.

Stephen patted his mouth with a napkin and pushed his chair back. "You think I'm making it all up," he said. "You come on and I'll show you."

By the time Stephen had jogged down to the Point, the two women trailing after him, the fog had begun to burn away and Thrumcap Island stood monumentally ahead of them. The sea had receded still further; now over the mile between the Point and the island only a few round pools of water were left. All else was a waste of gray sand and flattened black weed. The island looked as if it had been lifted onto a plateau of sand, rimmed with twisted tree-roots.

Clarice stopped short. "Oh, Steve," she said. "Oh, Steve; my Lord."

"Is that something?" Stephen felt oddly as if he were taking credit for the phenomenon.

"Look at all the lobster traps!" Linda shouted.

Stephen looked. Where his daughter was pointing he saw a line of a dozen or so lobster pots mired in the channel about fifty yards out from the old shoreline. He started down the slope to the small beach.

"Let's have some lobsters," he called back.

"Steve, no. They belong to Paul Dunham."

He faced his wife. "But they'll just die, won't they? They won't be any good to anybody."

"Paul will get them."

"How? You can't run a boat through the sand."

"Then he'll walk. Stop showing your criminal side."

Stephen shrugged and came back.

"Aren't we going to have lobsters?" Linda said.

"We'll buy some, honey," Clarice told her. "Steve? Isn't this awfully strange?"

"I'll go along with that."

"I mean, this couldn't happen, could it? Are we just all having a dream?"

"You want me to pinch you?"

"Be serious, Steve." She sounded ready to cry.

He hugged her lightly. "I don't know, Clar. Yes, it's strange. It's impossible."

"Is it bad when the water goes so far away?" asked his daughter.

"No, Lin, it's just very funny. Very unusual and crazy." He looked at Clarice. "What do you want to do?"

"I don't know."

"Hey, I do. Let's all walk out to Thrumcap and explore. We've never done that before."

Linda danced. "Yes, let's."

"What if the tide comes back in?" Clarice said.

"Then we'll be marooned on the island and we'll hail a passing lobster boat."

"But if this is low tide—" Clarice hesitated. "What will high tide be like?"

"Slow. And we'll see it coming and run back to the house before it gets us." Stephen started down the beach. "Come on," he yelled, and his family followed after.

It was something like walking the edge of a usual beach, the sand packed hard, and the footprints of the three of them spreading into patterns of dryness as they walked. Except that there seemed no end to the beach. The sand was remarkably clean, Stephen noticed, with only random patches of seaweed beginning to dry in the sun, and here and there a mussel shell or a black crab half-buried. The sensation of actually walking to Thrumcap Island was eerie. He had never landed on Thrumcap—not even by boat. When they reached the island, he had to climb up to it, hand over hand, along and through the exposed roots of a tall pine, then reach down to pull Linda and Clarice ashore with him.

"It would be lovely to build a cottage out here, and just be isolated from everybody," Clarice said as they crossed the island.

"Would have been," Stephen agreed.

"Why say it that way?"

"I think the tide won't come back in. I think the ocean must be drying up, or changing its basin, or something."

"Are you serious?"

"I don't know. It doesn't make sense that this is just some fantastically low tide." They were standing now on the far side of the island, facing southeast. "Just look," he pointed out. "You can't even *see* the ocean."

He felt his wife's hand find his and squeeze hard. "I'm scared, Steve."

He put his other hand over hers. "Freak of nature," he said. "Let's walk back and see what's on the radio."

By the time they had started across to the Point, other figures were moving out from the old shore—men and women, and a few children; some of them were carrying picnic hampers. Dogs pranced around family groups or clawed and nosed at objects half-submerged in the sand. Not far from his own beach Stephen saw a lone man plodding toward a lobster trap, pulling a high-sided wooden child's wagon behind him.

"There's Paul," Clarice said. "Why don't you see what he knows about this? I'll take Lin up to the house and try to get some news."

They separated. Stephen caught up with the lobsterman. "Morning, Paul."

Dunham nodded to him. "Morning, Mr. Bell." He was a thin, fortyish man, needed a shave, had watery-gray eyes that looked out under a long-billed yachting cap. He had pulled on hip boots over his clothes; in the wagon Stephen could see a few lobsters moving sluggishly against each other.

"What's happening, Paul?"

"Can't say." He had come to the next of his string of

traps, and had stooped to open it, drawing out a single lobster. He measured its carapace, then turned a perplexed look toward Stephen. "Don't know what to do with the damned thing," Dunham said. "Too small, but there's no place to throw the critter back to." He replaced the lobster in the trap and stood up.

"What's happened to the tide?" Stephen repeated.

Dunham gazed eastward. "Man up the coast told me it's gone out close to fifteen mile," he said. "Lives up on Pine Ledges. Owns a telescope."

"Will it come back in?"

Dunham picked up the handle of the wagon. "I got my waders on," he said.

Stephen made an awkward gesture of parting. "Happy fishing," he said, stupidly.

He met his women near the beached rowboat. "Anything?" he asked.

"There's nothing on the radio but bad music," Clarice told him. "We should have brought the little TV with us. What do you want to do?"

"Look what some people are doing, Daddy."

"Steve, they're driving cars out there," Clarice exclaimed.

It was true. Stephen could see a half-dozen automobiles moving out toward Thrumcap, and the Schumanns—whose cottage was a few hundred yards northeast of theirs—had actually piled into their truck-camper and had just now driven off the beach, threading between two grounded sailboats toward the east.

"Let's do that," Stephen said.

"Drive out *there?*"

"Why not? Obviously it can support the weight."

"It would be fun," Linda said.

"Of course it would. Let's pack a lunch and get into the car and go."

"But go where?" Clarice wanted to know.

"To the ocean," Linda said.

"Right. That's what this vacation is all about. We'll drive to the ocean."

Clarice finally agreed, and in an hour the Bell car, a white compact station wagon, was packed for the outing. Clarice had made sandwiches and filled a Thermos with coffee. Stephen had put in a six-pack of beer, along with some hamburger and a carton of milk—all of it packed with ice in the metal chest. Linda had gathered together a careful selection of comic books and dolls. Almost as an afterthought, Stephen loaded the Coleman stove, and a five-gallon can of gasoline he had bought the day before for the outboard motor—explaining to his wife how unlikely it was that they would be able to find either firewood or a gas station on the ocean floor.

"All set?" They were in the car, Linda curled in the back on a thin plaid mattress.

"All set," the women chorused.

Stephen was pleased that everything was turning out so well—that what might in some families have become a fearful time, a kind of domestic disaster in the face of the unexpected, was now resolved into one more vacation side-trip. Even Clarice seemed relaxed, though commonplace misgivings still plagued her.

"Do we have enough gas in the tank?"

"I filled it yesterday," he reassured her. "Cruising range: up to 500 miles."

"I hope nothing breaks down."

"Not a chance," Stephen said.

"Well," said his wife reluctantly, "just don't drive too fast."

It was easy to disobey her, Stephen discovered. The surface he drove on was unbelievably smooth, and though he once in a while was obliged to go around upjutting rocks or to avoid genuine islands that rose ahead of the car, the experience was very much like that of crossing a shopping-center parking lot—every destination reached by the straight-line distance, with no attention paid to lines painted by developers or highway commissioners. And the ride itself was luxurious; no bumps, no curves to speak of, the tires against the gray sand making a sound like skis on dry snow. The further he drove, the fewer the obstacles became; even with the speedometer needle swaying between 70 and 75, Clarice made no protest.

Several cars passed him—none of them closer than ten yards—and the occupants of each car waved joyously and called out to the Bells.

"It's certainly a free-for-all," Clarice remarked.

"They're excited," Stephen said. "Nobody ever did *this* before."

"You couldn't even do this on television!" Linda shouted.

At the end of an hour-and-a-half of driving, Stephen was surprised to see a great number of cars—thirty or forty, he guessed—lined up about a mile ahead. They were stopped; the people in them had gotten out and were milling around.

"What's that all about?" Clarice asked.

"Maybe the road's washed out," Stephen suggested. He winked at his wife.

"You're so damned funny," she said.

"I bet it's the ocean," Linda said.

"Hey, I'll bet you're right." He slowed down and eased the wagon to a stop between two of the parked cars. "Okay," he said, "everybody out."

But it wasn't the ocean. Walking in front of the car, the three of them found themselves at the edge of a steep bluff.

"Wow!" said Linda. "Look how far down it is."

It was more than 200 feet to the bottom of the bluff—not a perpendicular drop, but at a perilously steep angle from where they stood down to what appeared to be a limitless dry plain. The cliff consisted primarily of coarse rock, partly bare, partly encrusted with green and white shell-things. Deep crevices between the outcroppings of stone were filled with sand. The plain below seemed entirely of sand, and looked flat as a table top.

"We'll never get down there," Stephen said. He heard a touch of awe in his own voice.

"Quite a sight, isn't it?"

The words startled him; he turned and found himself facing a stranger—a middle-aged man with rusty hair and plump chins.

"Incredible," Stephen agreed.

"There's a couple of guys down the line say they're going to try and drive a Jeep down to the valley. I say they're batty."

Stephen nodded soberly. "I should think so."

"Me and the wife, we're going to head south from here."

"Why south?" Clarice was asking the question.

The stranger hesitated and put out his hand. "Excuse

me, folks," he said. "The name's Allen. We're out here from Des Moines."

Introductions were exchanged. Mrs. Allen, a dowdy facsimile of her husband, joined them.

"We met this gentleman from New York," Allen told them, "says he used to study geology in college. He claims that if you drive a couple of hundred miles south—down near Cape Cod, he says—and then head straight east, you won't have to run up against this particular cliff. I don't know, but he claims he does."

"That's interesting," Clarice said.

"Says you can drive right out on this Continental Shelf he used to study about," Allen added.

Stephen looked at his wife. "Want to try it?"

"Are you and Mrs. Allen going to do that?" Clarice asked.

"Oh yes; we surely are."

"What for?"

"Curiosity, mostly," Allen told her. He seemed reluctant to say more.

"And the treasure," Mrs. Allen put in.

"Treasure?" Linda was suddenly interested.

"Oh, well, yes, we sort of thought we'd look around for a little sunken treasure." Allen shuffled uneasily as he spoke. "You know, all those old ships that went down— oh, hundreds of years ago—and up to now nobody's been able to find 'em. We thought we'd keep an eye out. You saw that old hulk on the way here?"

"No, we didn't," Stephen said.

"Oh, we drove past it. Half-buried thing. No way to get inside it."

"But we've got shovels in the pickup," Mrs. Allen said.

Allen began drifting away with his wife. "We'd better get started," he told Stephen. "Have a safe trip."

"Steve? Does that make sense? Finding sunken treasure?"

He gave a small, noncommittal gesture with his arms. "At this point, I'll believe anything. How about eating? It's way past noon."

"But we haven't seen any old hulks," Clarice said.

"True, but it stands to reason there must *be* some. There

ought to be a lot of Second World War shipping scattered around somewhere, too."

"We haven't seen anything. Not even any dead fish, or those strange underwater plants you see pictures of. Why is that?"

He passed around sandwiches. "I suppose everything got buried under silt or swept out clean. This was some tide, you know."

They ate. Stephen sat on the fender of the car, the sandwich in one hand, a beer in the other. As he gazed out over the edge of the bluff he marveled at how far he could see, and how little was to be seen. The horizon— How far way? Twenty? Thirty miles?—was as unbroken as the rim of a plate. God knew where the ocean was, what it was doing, how long it would recede from them. He shook his head, as if to wake himself up. Off to his right, a young couple in white deck-shoes was gingerly climbing over the edge of the cliff. He leaned forward to get a glimpse of the precipitous slope. The couple was picking black, withered plants out of a thin river of sand. They climbed back up, obviously delighted with what they had done. Off to his left, a small boy was sailing bottlecaps far out and down to the plain; the caps glided like odd birds. Where were the gulls and cormorants? he suddenly wondered. Following the elusive sea?

"Let's take that drive south," he said to his wife.

"Should we, Steve?"

"We won't get lost. I'll move in so we can see the shore on the way down."

"We ought to go back to the house first, don't you think? Maybe we should get the tent, and some more food."

"No," he said, "let's be really adventurous. There's food enough for breakfast, and we can sleep in the car if we have to."

It occurred to him as he backed the car around and set a course for the southwest that he had to go as far as he could—as if something in him insisted that he find the ocean. He rationalized the insistence in two ways: first, the ocean was what he had left Cleveland for, and he refused to be deprived of it after fifty weeks of slaving over his drafting board; second, he certainly wanted to be able to tell his friends, first-hand, what that Great Tide business had been all about. *I was there,* he could say. *I was part of it.*

"Now there's land in front of us," Clarice was saying.

He had been driving for two hours since lunch, making good time as before, except that there had been considerable cross-traffic to keep him alert—cars, campers, motorcycles, all moving madly east. He had kept the New England coast in sight most of the way—*the old coast.*

"Let's go ashore and see where we are," he said.

What he had in mind was to stretch his legs in some kind of normal place, to find restrooms and buy gas, to keep his ears open for any news sifted in from the larger world. The landfall turned out to be the Gloucester peninsula, and Stephen was able to drive up out of the ocean bottom across a pebbled beach not far from a paved highway. In the nearest town he pulled into a gas station. Reading a road map while a sullen young man filled his tank, Stephen concluded that the town was Rockport, and he tried to estimate—referring to a sun that was by now halfway down the sky—which direction to set out in to avoid driving into Cape Cod Bay.

In twenty minutes they were on their way southeast; the attendant had refused to honor his credit card—another driver at the station had complained loudly—and Stephen had paid what seemed an unusually high price for the gas. *Frightened,* Stephen decided; *taking the cash while he can.*

He drove casually and fast; he was getting used to this sort of travel, to the experience of other cars strewn as far as the eye could see in every direction.

"It's something like an old-fashioned land rush," he said to Clarice.

"I suppose," she said. "Did you hear any news at the gas station?"

"Rumors, is all."

"Well, like what?"

He pursed his lips. "Silly things. Some guy told me he'd heard most of Europe was under water."

"My God, Steve."

"Oh, come on, Clar. That's hardly likely, you know."

"I *don't* know." She slouched into the corner by the door. "The water must have gone somewhere."

"Believe anything you want. Maybe it's Judgment Day."

His wife kept quiet.

Of course it was possible—that wild story about Europe. It was strangely logical, Stephen admitted. Still, fantastic. How could you explain it? A shift in the magnetic poles, maybe. Or a meteor—something huge—hitting the earth with incredible force. But wouldn't there have been earthquakes? He mused, scarcely thinking about his driving— not needing to. There were no obstructions, nothing to slow down for.

"I can't say much for the scenery," he said.

"Daddy, my stomach hurts," Linda complained.

He glanced at his watch. It was after six o'clock, he was amazed to notice; he had lost track of time since leaving Rockport, and surely his daughter had a right to be hungry.

"Be patient, honey," Clarice said in a tone part soothing, part mocking. "Daddy will stop as soon as he finds a nice shady spot."

He smirked. "Now *that's* funny," he said, yet almost at once he was startled to see something black on the horizon. He pointed. "What do you suppose that is?"

"I don't know," Clarice said, "but let's stop there."

Closer, he identified the object.

"There's our first shipwreck," he said. It looked, as he drew toward it, to be a modern ship—metal-hulled, at any rate—stern up as if it had dived sharply to the bottom. Second World War? Victim of a submarine? Its enormous square plates were deep red with rust, and its unexpected presence made the miles of sand around it all the more desolate. Circling to the ship's shady side, he saw that two other cars were already parked alongside it.

"Company," he said.

"That's good," Clarice decided. "You'll have somebody to talk to while I get supper."

Stephen parked and got out. People from one of the cars had spread a cloth under the lengthening shadow of the hulk. A man appeared on top of the wreck and peered down over the crusted railing, hanging on to keep his balance against the rake of the deck.

"Looking for the ocean?" he called down to Stephen. "It's all in here." He pointed toward the submerged bow. Leaving the women to fix the hamburgers, Stephen walked around the ship and made his way precariously up the steep deck. "I think it must have been a tanker," the man above him said.

"Torpedoed?"

"I expect so." The man wore Bermudas and a Hawaiian shirt; he grinned at Stephen. "Makes you feel like Davy Jones, doesn't it? I looked into that hatch down there. Couldn't see anything, but I could hear water sloshing. Bet there's a lot of bones rolling around in there; poor bastards."

Stephen nodded. He didn't feel like talking, but stayed on the ship, bracing himself against a ventilator. To be above the ocean's floor was pleasant; the air was warm and windless; he even enjoyed the difficulty of keeping his balance, after hours of cramped driving.

Certainly this had been the most remarkable day of his life—of all their lives—and filled with small wonders. The lobsterman pulling his coaster wagon. The foolish couple from Iowa with their shovels and dreams of treasure. The boy and girl at the cliff, acting like honeymooners picking edelweiss in the Alps. And the ocean. The ocean he had grown used to in summer after summer of holidays in Maine—suddenly turned into a desert. Still— He felt a faint shiver of apprehension. If there was water in the hold of this broken tanker—

He edged his way to the open hatch, a gaping black hole in the rust and scale of the deck-plates, and tried to see inside. It smelled like ocean, he thought. He listened, and could hear the water. *Why should it be moving?* Stephen stepped off the hulk and looked around. Nothing—but was that fog, far off to the east?

Stephen called up to the man in Bermudas. "Do you hear anything?"

"No," the man said. Stephen noticed a car, about a mile away, headed west. "Wait a minute," the man said. "I do hear something."

It was the sound he had awakened to that morning—of the tide, far, far out.

"By George," the man said, "I think we've found her at last." He stumbled down from the deck. "We've caught up with her," he said, and went to tell his family.

Stephen walked back to the women.

"Not ready yet," Clarice said. "Why don't you open a can of beer?"

He took a deep breath. "Listen, I think we'd better start back. It's about a hundred-and-fifty miles to the Cape, but we ought to be able to get there just after dark."

Clarice tensed. "What is it?" she said.

"I just think we'd better go. It's been a long day."

His wife turned off the stove and dumped the meat onto the sand. "Linda, get in the car."

"Don't we get to eat anything?"

"Linda, honey, don't quibble with me." She glanced around. The two neighboring cars were gone. Other cars appeared from the east and sped past.

"I'm going to put that spare gasoline in the tank," Stephen said, "just so we won't have to stop."

As he worked, he could hear the soft, incessant whisper of waves at his back. He made a botch of pouring the gas. *Steady,* he told himself. *It's your own damned fault.*

When he finished, the women were inside, waiting. He tossed the gasoline can away in a high, tumbling arc, and hurried to get into the car. The sea noise behind them was by now so loud that he could hear it even above the engine as it burst into life. He shifted into first gear and skidded forward.

"Tides come in gradually, don't they?" Clarice said in a tight voice.

"Usually," Stephen said. He threw the shift lever into second; again the rear wheels of the station wagon spun, as if the sand under them were getting wetter.

"I just can't believe any of this," his wife said. She leaned her head against the back of the seat and closed her eyes.

Now he was in high gear. The engine was turning over smoothly and the speedometer needle stood unwaveringly at seventy miles an hour. Ahead of him the evening sun was sliding down to the horizon; he kept the car headed toward it, squinting across the enormous reach of gray sand. *What a queer thing,* he thought. *What a devil of a way to finish a vacation.* He was aware all around him of other cars, other drivers, all racing west on this incredible aimless track. One car passed him, then another, and he pushed the accelerator down. He overtook a white camper and swerved around it; the station wagon fishtailed slightly.

"What's the matter?" His wife opened her eyes.

"Nothing's the matter."

"We won't run out of gas now, will we?"

"Not a chance." He watched the needle slide past eighty. The sand was glistening ahead of him, water seeping to the surface. The tide must be racing in behind them. Could they swim free? Where would they swim to?

"Daddy!" The scream startled him. "Daddy, I can see it! I can see it coming after us!" Linda wasn't crying. In the rearview mirror he could see her face, half-turned in his direction, her eyes vivid, her mouth working desperately to make more words. Out the back window he could make out a low gray wall that seemed to be gaining on him. Under his wheels he could hear water splashing, see spray flying. He switched on the wipers.

He reached over and squeezed his wife's hand. *At least we're all together,* he thought. Off to the right he saw an overturned car, two men and a woman out trying to turn it upright. The sun was almost at the horizon and its light cast back a hundred rainbows through the wakes of a hundred cars. A pale, pebbly mist began forming on surfaces inside the car. The roar of the impossible tide was deafening; it seemed now to be all around him, and the deepening water drummed like hammers against the metal under the car. He was thinking irrelevantly of how quickly the salt sea would rust out the fenders and rocker panels when he heard Clarice for the last time, shrieking:

"Drive, Steve, drive. For pity's sake, drive, drive, *drive!*"

E. B. White

# THE SUPREMACY OF URUGUAY

*Prophets hardly ever make us laugh. But should a*
*sonic boom shatter your laughter, along with your*
*window, you may wonder whether this is really a*
*funny story.*

---

Fifteen years after the peace had been made at Versailles,
Uruguay came into possession of a very fine military secret. It was an invention, in effect so simple, in construction so cheap, that there was not the slightest doubt that
it would enable Uruguay to subdue any or all of the other
nations of the earth. Naturally the two or three statesmen
who knew about it saw visions of aggrandizement; and
although there was nothing in history to indicate that a
large country was any happier than a small one, they were
very anxious to get going.

The inventor of the device was a Montevideo hotel clerk
named Martín Casablanca. He had got the idea for the
thing during the 1933 mayoralty campaign in New York
City, where he was attending a hotel men's convention.
One November evening, shortly before election, he was
wandering in the Broadway district and came upon a street
rally. A platform had been erected on the marquee of one
of the theaters, and in an interval between speeches a cold
young man in an overcoat was singing into a microphone.
"Thanks," he crooned, "for all the lovely dee-light I found
in your embrace . . ." The inflection of the love words
was that of a murmurous voice, but the volume of the

amplified sound was enormous; it carried for blocks, deep into the ranks of the electorate. The Uruguayan paused. He was not unfamiliar with the delight of a love embrace, but in his experience it had been pitched lower—more intimate, concentrated. This sprawling, public sound had a curious effect on him. "And thanks for unforgettable nights I never can replace . . ." People swayed against him. In the so bright corner in the too crowded press of bodies, the dominant and searching booming of the love singer struck sharp into him and he became for a few seconds, as he later realized, a loony man. The faces, the mask-faces, the chill air, the advertising lights, the steam rising from the jumbo cup of A & P Coffee high over Forty-seventh Street, these added to his enchantment and his unbalance. At any rate, when he left and walked away from Times Square and the great slimy sounds of the love embrace, this was the thought that was in his head:

*If it unhinged me to hear such a soft crooning sound slightly amplified, what might it not do to me to hear a far greater sound greatlier amplified?*

Mr. Casablanca stopped. "Good Christ!" he whispered to himself; and his own whisper frightened him, as though it, too, had been amplified.

Chucking his convention, he sailed for Uruguay the following afternoon. Ten months later he had perfected and turned over to his government a war machine unique in military history—a radio-controlled plane carrying an electric phonograph with a retractable streamlined horn. Casablanca had got hold of Uruguay's loudest tenor, and had recorded the bar of music he had heard in Times Square. "Thanks," screamed the tenor, "for unforgettable nights I never can replace . . ." Casablanca prepared to step it up a hundred and fifty thousand times, and grooved the record so it would repeat the phrase endlessly. His theory was that a squadron of pilotless planes scattering this unendurable sound over foreign territories would immediately reduce the populace to insanity. Then Uruguay, at her leisure, could send in her armies, subdue the idiots, and annex the land. It was a most engaging prospect.

The world at this time was drifting rapidly into a na-tionalistic phase. The incredible cancers of the World War had been forgotten, armaments were being rebuilt, hate and fear sat in every citadel. The Geneva gesture had been prolonged, but only by dint of removing the seat of disarmament to a walled city on a neutral island and quartering the delegates in the waiting destroyers of their respective countries. The Congress of the United States had appropriated another hundred million dollars for her naval program; Germany had expelled the Jews and recast the steel of her helmets in a firmer mold; and the world was re-living the 1914 prologue. Uruguay waited till she thought the moment was at hand, and then struck. Over the slumbrous hemispheres by night sped swift gleaming planes, and there fell upon all the world, except Uruguay, a sound the equal of which had never been heard on land or sea.

The effect was as Casablanca had predicted. In forty-eight hours the peoples were hopelessly mad, ravaged by an ineradicable noise, ears shattered, minds unseated. No defense had been possible because the minute anyone came within range of the sound, he lost his sanity and, being daft, proved ineffectual in a military way. After the planes had passed over, life went on much as before, except that it was more secure, sanity being gone. No one could hear anything except the noise in his own head. At the actual moment when people had been smitten with the noise, there had been, of course, some rather amusing incidents. A lady in West Philadelphia happened to be talking to her butcher on the phone. "Thanks," she had just said, "for taking back that tough steak yesterday. And thanks," she added, as the plane passed over, "for unforgettable nights I never can replace." Linotype operators in composing-rooms chopped off in the middle of sentences, like the one who was setting a story about an admiral in San Pedro:

I am tremendously grateful to all the ladies of San Pedro for the wonderful hospitality they have shown the men of the fleet during our recent maneuvers and thanks for unforgettable nights I never can replace and thanks for unforgettable nights I nev-

To all appearances Uruguay's conquest of the earth was complete. There remained, of course, the formal occupation by her armed forces. That her troops, being in possession of all their faculties, could establish her supremacy among idiots, she never for a moment doubted. She assumed that with nothing but lunacy to combat, the occupation would be mildly stimulating and enjoyable. She supposed her crazy foes would do a few rather funny, picturesque things with their battleships and their tanks, and then surrender. What she failed to anticipate was that her foes, being mad, had no intention of making war at all. The occupation proved bloodless and singularly unimpressive. A detachment of her troops landed in New York, for example, and took up quarters in the RKO Building, which was fairly empty at the time; and they were no more conspicuous around town than the Knights of Pythias. One of her battleships steamed for England, and the commanding officer grew so enraged when no hostile ship came out to engage him that he sent a wireless (which of course nobody in England heard): "Come on out, you yellow-bellied rats!"

It was the same story everywhere. Uruguay's supremacy was never challenged by her silly subjects, and she was very little noticed. Territorially her conquest was magnificent; politically it was a fiasco. The people of the world paid slight attention to the Uruguayans, and the Uruguayans, for their part, were bored by many of their territorials —in particular by the Lithuanians, whom they couldn't stand. Everywhere crazy people lived happily as children, in their heads the old refrain: "And thanks for unforgettable nights . . ." Billions dwelt contentedly in a fool's paradise. The earth was bountiful and there was peace and plenty. Uruguay gazed at her vast domain and saw the whole incident lacked authenticity.

It wasn't till years later, when the descendants of some early American idiots grew up and regained their senses, that there was a wholesale return of sanity to the world, land and sea forces were restored to fighting strength, and the avenging struggle was begun which eventually involved all the races of the earth, crushed Uruguay, and destroyed mankind without a trace.

J. F. Powers

# LOOK HOW THE FISH LIVE

*What price will we pay for what progress? Where
will the last parking lot be built? What piece of
land will the final road cover?*

———◆———

It had been a wonderful year in the yard, which was four
city lots and full of trees, a small forest and game preserve
in the old part of town. Until that day, there hadn't been
a single casualty, none at least that he knew about, which
was the same thing and more than enough where there
was so much life coming and going: squirrels, both red
and gray, robins, flickers, mourning doves, chipmunks,
rabbits. These creatures, and more, lived in the yard, and
most of these he'd worried about in the past. Some, of
course, he'd been too late for, and perhaps that was best,
being able to bury what would have been his responsibility.

Obviously the children had been doing all they could for
some time, for when he happened on the scene the little
bird was ensconced in grass twisted into a nesting ring,
soggy bread and fresh water had been set before it—the
water in a tiny pie tin right under its bill—and a birdhouse was only inches away, awaiting occupancy. Bird,
food and drink, and house were all in a plastic dishpan.

"Dove, isn't it?" said his wife, who had hoped to keep
him off such a case, he knew, and now was easing him
into it.

"I don't know," he said, afraid that he did. It was a big

little bird, several shades of gray, quills plainly visible because the feathers were only beginning. Its bill was black and seemed too long for it. "A flicker maybe," he said, but he didn't think so. No, it was a dove, because where were the bird's parents? Any bird but the dove would try to do something. Somewhere in the neighborhood this baby dove's mother was posing on a branch like peace itself, with no thought of anything in her head.

"Oh, God," he groaned.

"Where *are* the worms?" said his wife.

"We can't find any," said one of the children.

"Here," he said, taking the shovel from her. He went and dug near some shrubbery with the shovel, which was probably meant for sand and gravel. With this shovel he had buried many little things in the past. The worms were deeper than he could go with such a shovel, or they were just nowhere. He pried up two flagstones. Only ants and one many-legged worm that he didn't care to touch.

He had found no worms, and when he came back to the bird, when he saw it, he was conscious of returning empty-handed. His wife was going into the house.

"That bird can't get into that house," he said. "It's for wrens."

"We know it," said the oldest child, quietly.

He realized then that he had pointed up an obvious difficulty that the two girls had decently refrained from mentioning in front of the bird and the two younger children, the boys. But he hadn't wanted them to *squeeze* the dove into the wrenhouse. "Well, you might as well leave it where it is. Keep the bird in the shade."

"That's what we're doing."

"We put him in the dishpan so we could move him around in the shade."

"Good. Does it eat or drink anything?"

"Of course."

He didn't like the sound of this. "Did you *see* it eat or drink anything?"

"No, she did."

"Did you see it eat or drink?"

"Drink."

"It didn't eat?"

"I didn't see him eat. He maybe did when we weren't watching."

"Did it drink like this?" He sipped the air and threw back his head, swallowing.

"More like this." The child threw back her head only about half as far as he had.

"Are you sure?"

"Of course."

He walked out into the yard to get away from them. He didn't know whether the bird had taken any water. All he knew was that one of the children had imitated a bird drinking—rather, had imitated him imitating a chicken. He didn't even know whether birds threw back their heads in drinking. Was the dove a bird that had to have its mother feed it? Probably so. And so probably, as he'd thought when he first saw the bird, there was no use. He was back again.

"How does it seem? Any different?"

"How do you mean?"

"Has it changed any since you found it?"

The little girls looked at each other. Then the younger one spoke: "He's not so afraid."

He was touched by this, in spite of himself. Now that they'd found the bird, she was saying, it would be all right. Was ever a bird in worse shape? With food it couldn't eat, water it probably hadn't drunk and wouldn't, and with a house it couldn't get into—and *them!* Now they punished him with their faith in themselves and the universe, and later, when these failed and the bird began to sink, they would punish him some more, with their faith in him. He knew what was the best thing for the bird. When the children took their naps, then, maybe, he could do the job. He was not soft. He had flooded gophers out of their labyrinthine ways and beheaded them with the shovel; he had purged a generation of red squirrels from the walls and attic of the old house when he moved in, knowing it was them or him. But why did animals and birds do this to him? Why did children?

"Why'd you pick this bird up? Why didn't you leave it where it was? The mother might've found it then."

"She couldn't lift him, could she?"

"Of course not."

"Well, he can't fly."

"No, but if you'd left it where it fell, the mother might see it. The mother bird has to feed a baby like this." Why couldn't she lift it? Why couldn't the two parents get together and just put it back in the nest? Why, down through the ages, hadn't birds worked out something for such an emergency? As he understood it, they were descended from reptiles and had learned how to grow feathers and fly. The whale had gone to sea. But he didn't know whether he believed any of this. Here was a case that showed how incompetent nature really was. He was tired of such cases, of nature passing the buck to him. He hated to see spring and summer come to the yard, in a way. They meant death and mosquitoes to him.

It had been the worst year for mosquitoes that anyone could remember, and in Minnesota that was saying a lot. He had bought a spraying outfit, and DDT at $2.50 a quart, which, when you considered that there was no tax on it, made you think. A quart made two gallons, but he was surprised how quickly it went. The words on the bottle, "Who enjoys your yard—you or the mosquitoes?" had stayed with him, however. He had engaged professionals, with a big machine mounted on a truck, to blow a gale of poison through the yard. (In other years, seeing such an operation in other yards, he had worried about the bees.) The squirrels and rabbits in residence had evacuated the trees and lily beds while he stood by, hoping that they and the birds understood it was an emergency measure. He believed, however, that the birds received too much credit for eating annoying insects. Wasps, he knew, consumed great numbers of mosquitoes—but what about *them?* The mosquito hawk, a large, harmless insect, was a great killer of mosquitoes, but was itself killed by birds—by martins. That was the balance of nature for you. Balance for whom? You had to take steps yourself—drastic steps. Too drastic?

"Now I want you to show me exactly where you found this bird."

The little girls looked at each other.

"Don't say anything. Just take me to the exact spot."

They walked across the yard as if they really knew where they were going, and he and the little boys followed.

The girls appeared to agree on a spot, but he supposed that one was under the influence of the other. The older one put out a foot and said, "Here."

He hadn't realized they were being that exact. It was surprising how right they were. Fifty or sixty feet overhead, in a fork of a big white oak, he saw a nest, definitely a dove's nest, a jerry-built job if he ever saw one, the sky visible between the sticks, and something hanging down. He moved away and gazed up again. It was only a large dead leaf, not what he'd feared, not a baby bird hanging by its foot. He felt better about having had the yard sprayed. The machine on the truck was very powerful, powerful enough to bend back the bushes and small trees, but he doubted that it had blown the baby dove out of the nest. This was just an unusually bad nest and the bird had fallen out. Nature had simply failed again.

"The nest! I see it! See?"

"Yes." He walked away from them, toward the garage. He hadn't called the nest to their attention because restoring the bird was out of the question for him—it was a job for the fire department or for God whose eye is on the sparrow—but that didn't mean that the children might not expect him to do it.

"Just keep the bird in the shade," he called from the garage. He drove down to the office, which he hadn't planned to visit that day, and spent a few hours of peace there.

And came home to another calamity. In the kitchen, the little girls were waiting for him. Something, they said, had jumped out of the lilies and pushed one of the young bunnies that hadn't been doing anything, just eating grass near the playhouse. A weasel, they thought. Their mother hadn't seen it happen, had only heard the bunny crying, and had gone up to bed. There was no use going to her. They were in possession of what information there was. He should ask them.

"Don't go out there!"

"Why not?"

"Mama says if the bunny has the rabies it might bite."

He stood still in thought. Most of his life had been spent in a more settled part of the country. There was a great deal he didn't know about wildlife, even about the red squirrel and the yellow-jacket wasp with which he had dealt firsthand, and he knew it. He could be wrong. But there was something ridiculous about what they were suggesting. "Did you see whatever it was that pushed the rabbit?"

"Of course!" said the child. It was this that distinguished her from all others in the house.

"What did it look like?"

"It went so fast."

This was ground they'd covered before, but he persevered, hoping to flush the fact that would explain everything. "What color was it?"

"Kind of—like the rabbit. But it went so fast."

This, too, was as before. "Maybe it was the mama rabbit," he said, adding something new. The more he thought about it, the more he liked it. "Maybe she didn't want the young one to come out in the open, in the daytime, I mean. Maybe she was just teaching it a lesson." He didn't know whether rabbits did that, but he did know that this particular mother was intelligent. He had first noticed her young ones, just babies then, in a shallow hole alongside a tiny evergreen which he had put a wire fence around, and over which he'd draped some "Shoo" rope soaked with creosote, advertised as very effective against dogs, rabbits, and rodents of all kinds. And as for the punishment the young rabbit had taken from whatever it was, he had once seen a mother squirrel get tough with a little one that had strayed from the family tree.

"Would she hurt the young rabbit?" said the younger girl.

"She might. A little."

"This one was hurt a lot," said the eyewitness. She spoke with finality.

"Maybe it was a cat," he said, rallying. "You say it was about the same size."

The children didn't reply. It seemed to him that they did not trust him. His mama-rabbit theory was too good to be true. They believed in the weasel.

"A weasel would've killed it," he said.

"But if he saw *me?*"

"*Did* he see you?"

"Of course."

"Did you see *him?*"

"Of course!" cried the child, impatient with the question. She didn't appear to realize that she was cornered, that having seen the attacker she should be able to describe it. But she was under no obligation to be logical. He decided to wait a few years.

Out in the yard he scrutinized the ground around the playhouse for blood and fur, and saw none. He stepped to the edge of the lilies. Each year the lilies were thicker and less fruitful of flowers, and a gardener would have thinned them out. A gardener, though, would have spoiled this yard—for the fairies who, the children told him, played there. He didn't enter the lilies because he didn't want to encounter what he might. He was not forgetting the bird.

Passing through the kitchen, he noticed that the children were cutting up a catalogue, both pasting. Apparently the older one could no longer get the younger one to do all the scissor work. "How's the bird?"

"We don't know."

He stopped and got them in focus. "Why don't you know?"

"We haven't looked at it."

"Haven't looked at it! Why haven't you?"

"We've been doing this."

"This is why."

It was a mystery to him how, after crooning over the helpless creature, after entangling him in its fate, they could be this way. This was not the first time either. "Well, get out there and look at it!"

On the way out to look at it himself, he met them coming back. "He's all right," the older one said grumpily.

"Looks the same, huh?" He didn't catch what they said in reply, which wasn't much anyway. He found the bird where he'd last seen it, beside the back porch. He had expected it to be dying by now. Its ribs showed clearly when it breathed, which was alarming, but he remembered that this had worried them when he first saw the bird. It did seem to be about the same.

He passed through the kitchen and, seeing the children all settled down again, he said, "Find a better place for it. It'll soon be in the sun."

A few moments later, he was intervening. They had the

whole yard and yet they were arguing over two patches of shade, neither of which would be good for more than a few minutes. He carried the dishpan out into the yard, and was annoyed that they weren't following him, for he wanted them to see what he was doing and why. He put the dishpan down where the sun wouldn't appear again until morning. He picked it up again. He carried it across the yard to the foot of the white oak. On the ground, directly below the nest, there was and would be sun until evening, but near the trunk there would be shade until morning.

The bird was breathing heavily, as before, but it was in no distress—unless this was distress. He thought not. If the bird had a full coat of feathers, its breathing wouldn't be so noticeable.

He was pleasantly surprised to see a mature dove high above him. The dove wasn't near the nest, wasn't watching him—was just looking unconcerned in another part of the tree—but it was in the right tree. He tried to attract its attention, making what he considered a gentle bird noise. It flew away, greatly disappointing him.

He knelt and lifted the tin of water to the bird's mouth. This he did with no expectation that it would drink, but it did, it definitely did. The bird kept his bill in the water, waggling it once or twice, spilling some, and raised its head slightly—not as a chicken would. He tried a little bread, unsuccessfully. He tried the water again, and again the bird drank. The bread was refused again, and also the water when it was offered the third time. This confirmed him in his belief that the bird had been drinking before. This also proved that the bird was able to make decisions. After two drinks, the bird had said, in effect, no more. It hadn't eaten for some time, but it was evidently still sound in mind and body. It might need only a mother's care to live.

He went into the house. In the next two hours, he came to the window frequently. For a while he tried to believe that there might be maternal action at the foot of the oak while he wasn't watching. He knew better, though. All he could believe was that the mother might be staying away because she regarded the dishpan as a trap—assuming, of course, that she had spotted the baby, and assuming also that she gave a damn, which he doubted.

Before dinner he went out and removed the birdhouse and then the bird from the dishpan, gently tipping it into the grass, not touching it. The nest the children had twined together slid with it, but the bird ended up more off than on the nest. There was plenty of good, growing grass under the dove, however. If, as the children claimed, the bird could move a little and if the mother did locate it, perhaps between them—he credited the baby with some intelligence—they might have enough sense to hide out in the lilies of the valley only a few feet away. There would be days ahead of feeding and growth before the little bird could fly, probably too many days to pass on the ground in the open. Once the mother assumed her responsibility, however, everything would become easier—that is, possible. *He* might even build a nest nearby. (One year there had been a dove's nest in a chokecherry tree, only ten feet off the ground.) Within a few yards of the oak there were aged lilac bushes, almost trees, which would be suitable for a nest. At present, though, with the mother delinquent, the situation was impossible.

He looked up into the trees for her, in vain, and then down at the orphan. It had moved. It had taken up its former position precisely in the center of the little raft of grass the children had made for it, and this was painful to see, this little display of order in a thing so small, so dumb, so sure.

It would not drink. He set the water closer, and the bread, just in case, and carried away the dishpan and the birdhouse. He saw the bowel movement in the bottom of the dishpan as a good omen, but was puzzled by the presence of a tiny dead bug of the beetle family. It could mean that the mother had been in attendance, or it could mean than the bug had simply dropped dead from the spraying, a late casualty.

After dinner, standing on the back porch, he heard a disturbance far out in the yard. Blue jays, and up to no good, he thought, and walked toward the noise. When he reached the farthest corner of the yard, the noise ceased, and began again. He looked into the trees across the alley. Then he saw two catbirds in the honeysuckle bushes only six feet away and realized that he had mistaken their rusty cries for those of blue jays at some distance. The catbirds hopped, scolding, from branch to branch. They moved to the next bush, but not because of him, he thought. It was then that he saw the cat in the lilies. He stamped his foot. The cat, a black-and-white one marked like a Holstein cow, crashed through the lilies and out into the alley where the going was good, and was gone. The catbirds followed, flying low, belling the cat with their cries. In the distance he heard blue jays, themselves marauders, join in, doing their bit to make the cat's position known. High overhead he saw two dopey doves doing absolutely nothing about the cat, heard their little dithering noise, and was disgusted with them. It's a wonder you're not extinct, he thought, gazing up at them. They chose that moment to show him the secret of their success.

He walked the far boundaries of the yard, stopping to gaze back at the old frame house, which was best seen at a distance. He had many pictures of it in his mind, for it changed with the seasons, gradually, and all during the day. The old house always looked good to him, in spring when the locust, plum, lilacs, honeysuckle, caragana, and mock orange bloomed around it; in summer, as it was now, almost buried in green; in autumn, when the yard was rolling with nuts, crashing with leaves, and the mountain ash berries turned red; and in winter, when, under snow and icicles, with its tall mullioned windows sparkling, it reminded him of an old-fashioned Christmas card. For a hundred years it had been painted barn or Venetian red, with forest-green trim. In winter there were times when the old house, because of the light, seemed to be bleeding; the red then was profound and alive. Perhaps it knew something, after all, he thought. In January the yellow bulldozers would come for it and the trees. One of the old oaks, one which had appeared to be in excellent health, had recently thrown down half of itself in the night. "Herbal suicide," his wife had said.

Reaching the other far corner of the yard, he stood considering the thick black walnut tree, which he had once, at about this time of year, thought of girdling with a tin shield to keep off the squirrels. But this would have taken a lot of tin, and equipment he didn't own to trim a neighboring maple and possibly an elm, and so he had decided to share the nuts with the squirrels. This year they could have them all. Few of the birds would be there when it happened, but the squirrels—there were at least a dozen in residence—were in for a terrible shock.

He moved toward the house, on the street side of the yard, on the lookout for beer cans and bottles which the teachers'-college students from their parked cars tossed into the bushes. He knew, from several years of picking up after them, their favorite brand.

He came within twenty yards of the white oak, and stopped. He didn't want to venture too near in case the mother was engaged in feeding the baby, or was just about to make up her mind to do so. In order to see, however, he would have to be a little closer. He moved toward the white oak in an indirect line, and stopped again. The nest was empty. His first thought was that the bird, sensing the approach of darkness, had wisely retreated into the shelter of the lilies of the valley nearby, and then he remembered the recent disturbance on the other side of the yard. The cat had last been seen at what had seemed then like a safe distance, but of course it could have been here earlier. He was looking now for feathers, blood, bones. But he saw no such signs of the bird. Again he considered the possibility that it was hiding in the lilies of the valley. When he recalled the bird sitting in the very center of the nest, it did not seem likely that it would leave, ever—unless persuaded by the mother to do so. But he had no faith in the mother, and instead of searching the lilies, he stood where he was and studied the ground around him in a widening circle. The cat could've carried it off, of course, or—again—the bird could be safe among the lilies.

He hurried to the fallen oak. Seeing the little bird at such a distance from the nest, and not seeing it as he'd expected he would, but entire, he had been deceived. The bird was not moving. It was on its back, not mangled but dead. He noted the slate-black feet. Its head was to one side on the grass. The one eye he could see was closed, and the blood all around it, enamel-bright, gave the impression, surprising to him, that it had poured out like paint. He wouldn't have thought such a little thing would even have blood.

He went for the shovel with which he'd turned up no worms for the bird earlier that day. He came back to the bird by a different route, having passed on the other side of a big tree, and saw the little ring of grass that had been the bird's nest. It now looked like a wreath to him.

He dug a grave within a few feet of the bird. The ground was mossy there. He simply lifted up a piece of it, tucked in the bird, and dropped the sod down like a cover. He pounded it once with the back side of the shovel, thinking the bird would rest easier there than in most ground.

When he looked up from his work, he saw that he had company, Mr. and Mrs. Hahn, neighbors. He told them what had happened, and could see that Mr. Hahn considered him soft. He remembered that Mr. Hahn, who had an interest such as newspapers seemed to think everybody ought to have in explosions, didn't care to discuss the fallout.

The Hahns walked with him through the yard. They had heard there were no mosquitoes there now.

"Apparently it works," he said.

"The city should spray," said Mrs. Hahn.

"At least the swamps," said Mr. Hahn, who was more conservative.

He said nothing. They were perfectly familiar with his theory: that it was wet enough in the lily beds, in the weeds along the river, for mosquitoes to breed. When he explained that there just weren't enough swamps to breed that many mosquitoes, people smiled, and tried to refute his theory by talking about how little water it took, a bird bath, a tin can somewhere. "In my opinion, they breed right here, in this yard and yours."

"Anyway, they're not here now," said Mrs. Hahn.

He received this not as a compliment but as a polite denial of his theory. They were passing under the mulberry tree. In the bloody atmosphere prevailing in his mind that evening, he naturally thought of the purple grackle that had hung itself from a high branch with a string in the previous summer. "I'm sick of it all."

"Sick of *what?*" said Mrs. Hahn.

The Hahns regarded him as a head case, he knew, and

probably wouldn't be surprised if he said that he was sick of them. He had stopped trying to adjust his few convictions and prejudices to company. He just let them fly. Life was too short. "Insects, birds, and animals of all kinds," he said. "Nature."

Mr. Hahn smiled. "There'd be too many of those doves if things like that didn't happen."

"I suppose."

Mr. Hahn said: "Look how the fish live."

He looked at the man with interest. This was the most remarkable thing Mr. Hahn had ever said in his presence. But of course Mr. Hahn didn't appreciate the implications. Mr. Hahn didn't see himself in the picture at all.

"That includes children," he said, pursuing his original line. It was the children who were responsible for bringing the failures of nature to his attention.

"*And* women," he added. He had almost left women out, and they belonged in. They were responsible for the children and the success of "Queen for a Day."

"And men," he added when he caught Mr. Hahn smiling at the mention of women. Men were at the bottom of it all.

"That doesn't leave much, does it?" said Mr. Hahn.

"No." Who *was* left? God. It wasn't surprising, for all problems were at bottom theological. He'd like to put a few questions to God. God, though, knowing his thoughts, knew his questions, and the world was already in possession of all the answers that would be forthcoming from God. Compassion for the Holy Family fleeing from Herod was laudable and meritorious, but it was wasted on soulless rabbits fleeing from soulless weasels. Nevertheless it was there just the same, or something very like it. As he'd said in the beginning, he was sick of it all.

"There he is now!" cried Mrs. Hahn.

He saw the black-and-white cat pause under the fallen oak.

"Should I get my gun?" said Mr. Hahn.

"No. It's his nature." He stamped his foot and hissed. The cat ran out of the yard. Where were the birds? They could be keeping an eye on the cat. Somewhere along the line they must have said the hell with it. He supposed there was a lesson in that for him. A man simply couldn't sympathize with life to the full extent of his instincts and opportunities. A man had to accept his God-given limitations.

He accompanied the Hahns around to the front of the house, and there they met a middle-aged woman coming up the walk. He didn't know her, but the Hahns did, and introduced her. Mrs. Snyder.

"It's about civil defense," she said. Every occupant of every house was soon to be registered for purposes of identification in case of an emergency. Each block would have its warden, and Mrs. Snyder thought that he, since he lived on this property, which took up so much of the block . . .

"No."

"No?"

"No." He couldn't think of a job for which he was less suited, in view of his general outlook. He wouldn't be here anyway. Nor would this house, these trees.

While Mr. and Mrs. Hahn explained to Mrs. Snyder that the place was to become a parking lot for the teachers' college, he stood by in silence. He had never heard it explained so well. His friends had been shocked at the idea of doing away with the old house and trees—and for a parking lot!—and although he appreciated their concern, there was nothing to be done, and after a time he was unable to commiserate with them. This they didn't readily understand. It was as if some venerable figure in the community, only known to them but near and dear to him, had died or been murdered, and he failed to show proper sorrow and anger. The Hahns, however, were explaining how it was, turning this way and that, pointing to this building and that, to sites already taken, to those to be taken soon or in time. For them the words "the state" and "expansion" seemed sufficient. And the Hahns weren't employed by the teachers' college and they weren't old grads. It was impossible to account in such an easy way for their enthusiasm. They were scheduled for eviction themselves, they said, in a few years.

When they were all through explaining, it must have been annoying to them to hear Mrs. Snyder's comment. "Too bad," she said. She glanced up at the old red house and then across the street at the new dormitory going up. There had been a parking lot there for a few years, but

before that another big old house and trees. The new
dormitory, apricot bricks and aluminum windows, was in
the same style as the new library, a style known to him
and his wife as Blank. "Too bad," Mrs. Snyder said again,
with an uneasy look across the street, and then at him.

"There's no defense against that either," he said. If
Mrs. Snyder understood what he meant, she didn't show it.

"Well," she said to Mr. Hahn, "how about you?"

They left him then, strolling down the walk together.
Whether Mr. Hahn became the block warden was a question in his mind that would have to be answered another
time. He put the shovel away, and walked the boundaries
of the yard for the last time that day, pausing twice to
consider the house in the light of the moment. When he
came to the grave, he stopped and looked around for a
large stone. He took one from the mound where the
hydrant rose up in the yard, the only place where the
wild ginger grew, and set it on the grave, not as a marker
but as an obstacle to the cat if it returned, as he imagined
it would. It was getting dark in the yard, the night coming
sooner there because of the great trees. Now the bats and
owls would get to work, he thought, and went into the
doomed house.

Kurt Vonnegut, Jr.

# TOMORROW AND TOMORROW AND TOMORROW

*Overpopulation, overcrowding, and the depletion
of our natural resources are among the dangers
we are told face us in the future—the foreseeable
future. Do we believe that when these perils become realities our friends, our families and ourselves will be unaffected?*

The year was 2158 A.D., and Lou and Emerald Schwartz
were whispering on the balcony outside Lou's family's
apartment on the seventy-sixth floor of Building 257 in
Alden Village, a New York housing development that
covered what had once been known as Southern Connecti-
cut. When Lou and Emerald had married, Em's parents
had tearfully described the marriage as being between May
and December; but now, with Lou one hundred and twelve
and Em ninety-three, Em's parents had to admit that the
match had worked out well.

But Em and Lou weren't without their troubles, and
they were out in the nippy air of the balcony because of
them.

"Sometimes I get so mad, I feel like just up and diluting
his anti-gerasone," said Em.

"That'd be against Nature, Em," said Lou, "it'd be
murder. Besides, if he caught us tinkering with his anti-
gerasone, not only would he disinherit us, he'd bust my

neck. Just because he's one hundred and seventy-two doesn't mean Gramps isn't strong as a bull."

"Against Nature," said Em. "Who knows what Nature's like anymore? Ohhhhh—I don't guess I could ever bring myself to dilute his anti-gerasone or anything like that, but, gosh, Lou, a body can't help thinking Gramps is never going to leave if somebody doesn't help him along a little. Golly—we're so crowded a person can hardly turn around, and Verna's dying for a baby, and Melissa's gone thirty years without one." She stamped her feet. "I get so sick of seeing his wrinkled old face, watching him take the only private room and the best chair and the best food, and getting to pick out what to watch on TV, and running everybody's life by changing his will all the time."

"Well, after all," said Lou bleakly, "Gramps *is* head of the family. And he can't help being wrinkled like he is. He was seventy before anti-gerasone was invented. He's going to leave, Em. Just give him time. It's his business. I know he's tough to live with, but be patient. It wouldn't do to do anything that'd rile him. After all, we've got it better'n anybody else, there on the daybed."

"How much longer do you think we'll get to sleep on the daybed before he picks another pet? The world's record's two months, isn't it?"

"Mom and Pop had it that long once, I guess."

"When *is* he going to leave, Lou?" said Emerald.

"Well, he's talking about giving up anti-gerasone right after the five-hundred-mile Speedway Race."

"Yes—and before that it was the Olympics, and before that the World's Series, and before that the Presidential Elections, and before that I-don't-know-what. It's been just one excuse after another for fifty years now. I don't think we're ever going to get a room to ourselves or an egg or anything."

"All right—call me a failure!" said Lou. "What can I do? I work hard and make good money, but the whole thing, practically, is taxed away for defense and old age pensions. And if it wasn't taxed away, where you think we'd find a vacant room to rent? Iowa, maybe? Well, who wants to live on the outskirts of Chicago?"

Em put her arms around his neck. "Lou, hon, I'm not calling you a failure. The Lord knows you're not. You just haven't had a chance to be anything or have anything because Gramps and the rest of his generation won't leave and let somebody else take over."

"Yeah, yeah," said Lou gloomily. "You can't exactly blame 'em, though, can you? I mean, I wonder how quick we'll knock off the anti-gerasone when we get to Gramps' age."

"Sometimes I wish there wasn't any such thing as anti-gerasone!" said Emerald passionately. "Or I wish it was made out of something real expensive and hard-to-get instead of mud and dandelions. Sometimes I wish folks just up and died regular as clockwork, without anything to say about it, instead of deciding themselves how long they're going to stay around. There ought to be a law against selling the stuff to anybody over one hundred and fifty."

"Fat chance of that," said Lou, "with all the money and votes the old people've got." He looked at her closely. "You ready to up and die, Em?"

"Well, for heaven's sakes, what a thing to say to your wife. Hon! I'm not even one hundred yet." She ran her hands lightly over her firm, youthful figure, as though for confirmation. "The best years of my life are still ahead of me. But you can bet that when one hundred and fifty rolls around, old Em's going to pour her anti-gerasone down the sink, and quit taking up room, and she'll do it smiling."

"Sure, sure," said Lou, "you bet. That's what they all say. How many you heard of doing it?"

"There was that man in Delaware."

"Aren't you getting kind of tired of talking about him, Em? That was five months ago."

"All right, then—Gramma Winkler, right here in the same building."

"She got smeared by a subway."

"That's just the way she picked to go," said Em.

"Then what was she doing carrying a six-pack of anti-gerasone when she got it?"

Emerald shook her head wearily and covered her eyes. "I dunno, I dunno, I dunno. All I know is, something's just got to be done." She sighed. "Sometimes I wish they'd left a couple of diseases kicking around somewhere, so I could get one and go to bed for a little while. Too many people!"

she cried, and her words cackled and gabbled and died in a thousand asphalt-paved, skyscraper-walled courtyards.

Lou laid his hand on her shoulder tenderly. "Aw, hon, I hate to see you down in the dumps like this."

"If we just had a car, like the folks used to in the old days," said Em, "we could go for a drive, and get away from people for a little while. Gee—if *those* weren't the days!"

"Yeah," said Lou, "before they'd used up all the metal."

"We'd hop in, and Pop'd drive up to a filling station and say, 'Fillerup!' "

"That *was* the nuts, wasn't it—before they'd used up all the gasoline."

"And we'd go for a carefree ride in the country."

"Yeah—all seems like a fairyland now, doesn't it, Em? Hard to believe there really used to be all that space between cities."

"And when we got hungry," said Em, "we'd find ourselves a restaurant, and walk in, big as you please, and say, 'I'll have a steak and French-fries, I believe,' or 'How are the pork chops today?' " She licked her lips, and her eyes glistened.

"Yeah man!" growled Lou. "How'd you like a hamburger with the works, Em?"

"Mmmmmmmm."

"If anybody'd offered us processed seaweed in those days, we would have spit right in his eye, huh, Em?"

"Or processed sawdust," said Em.

Doggedly, Lou tried to find the cheery side of the situation.

"Well, anyway, they've got the stuff so it tastes a lot less like seaweed and sawdust than it did at first; and they say it's actually better for us than what we used to eat."

"I felt fine!" said Em fiercely.

Lou shrugged. "Well, you've got to realize, the world wouldn't be able to support twelve billion people if it wasn't for processed seaweed and sawdust. I mean, it's a wonderful thing, really. I guess. That's what they say."

"They say the first thing that pops into their heads," said Em. She closed her eyes. "Golly—remember shopping, Lou? Remember how the stores used to fight to get our folks to buy something? You didn't have to wait for somebody to die to get a bed or chairs or a stove or anything like that. Just went in—bing!—and bought whatever you wanted. Gee whiz, that was nice, before they used up all the raw materials. I was just a little kid then, but I can remember so plain."

Depressed, Lou walked listlessly to the balcony's edge, and looked up at the clean, cold, bright stars against the black velvet of infinity. "Remember when we used to be bugs on science fiction, Em? Flight seventeen, leaving for Mars, launching ramp twelve. 'Board! All non-technical personnel kindly remain in bunkers. Ten seconds . . . nine . . . eight . . . seven . . . six . . . five . . . four . . . three . . . two . . . *one! Main Stage! Barrrrrroooom!*"

"Why worry about what was going on on Earth?" said Em, looking up at the stars with him. "In another few years, we'd all be shooting through space to start life all over again on a new planet."

Lou sighed. "Only it turns out you need something about twice the size of the Empire State Building to get one lousy colonist to Mars. And for another couple of trillion bucks he could take his wife and dog. *That's* the way to lick overpopulation—*emigrate!*"

"Lou—?"

"Hmmm?"

"When's the Five-Hundred-Mile Speedway Race?"

"Uh—Memorial Day, May thirtieth."

She bit her lip. "Was that awful of me to ask?"

"Not very, I guess. Everybody in the apartment's looked it up to make sure."

"I don't want to be awful," said Em, "but you've just got to talk over these things now and then, and get them out of your system."

"Sure you do. Feel better?"

"Yes—and I'm not going to lose my temper anymore, and I'm going to be just as nice to him as I know how."

"That's my Em."

They squared their shoulders, smiled bravely, and went back inside.

Gramps Schwartz, his chin resting on his hands, his hands on the crook of his cane, was staring irascibly at the five-foot television screen that dominated the room. On the screen, a news commentator was summarizing the day's happenings. Every thirty seconds or so, Gramps would jab the floor with his cane-tip and shout, "Hell! We did that a hundred years ago!"

Emerald and Lou, coming in from the balcony, were obliged to take seats in the back row, behind Lou's father and mother, brother and sister-in-law, son and daughter-in-law, grandson and wife, granddaughter and husband, great-grandson and wife, nephew and wife, grandnephew and wife, great-grandniece and husband, great-grandnephew and wife, and, of course, Gramps, who was in front of everybody. All, save Gramps, who was somewhat withered and bent, seemed by pre-anti-gerasone standards, to be about the same age—to be somewhere in their late twenties or early thirties.

*"Meanwhile,"* the commentator was saying, *"Council Bluffs, Iowa, was still threatened by stark tragedy. But two hundred weary rescue workers have refused to give up hope, and continue to dig in an effort to save Elbert Haggedorn, one hundred and eighty-three, who has been wedged for two days in a . . ."*

"I wish he'd get something more cheerful," Emerald whispered to Lou.

"Silence!" cried Gramps. "Next one shoots off his big bazoo while the TV's on is gonna find hisself cut off without a dollar"—and here his voice suddenly softened and sweetened—"when they wave that checkered flag at the Indianapolis Speedway, and old Gramps gets ready for the Big Trip Up Yonder." He sniffed sentimentally, while his heirs concentrated desperately on not making the slightest sound. For them, the poignancy of the prospective Big Trip had been dulled somewhat by its having been mentioned by Gramps about once a day for fifty years.

*"Dr. Brainard Keyes Bullard,"* said the commentator, *"President of Wyandotte College, said in an address to-night that most of the world's ills can be traced to the fact that Man's knowledge of himself has not kept pace with his knowledge of the physical world."*

"Hell!" said Gramps. "We said that a hundred years ago!"

*"In Chicago tonight,"* said the commentator, *"a special celebration is taking place in the Chicago Lying-in Hospi-*

*tal. The guest of honor is Lowell W. Hitz, age zero. Hitz, born this morning, is the twenty-five-millionth child to be born in the hospital."* The commentator faded, and was replaced on the screen by young Hitz, who squalled furiously.

"Hell," whispered Lou to Emerald, "we said that a hundred years ago."

"I heard that!" shouted Gramps. He snapped off the television set, and his petrified descendants stared silently at the screen. "You, there, boy—"

"I didn't mean anything by it, sir," said Lou.

"Get me my will. You know where it is. You kids *all* know where it is. Fetch, boy!"

Lou nodded dully, and found himself going down the hall, picking his way over bedding to Gramps's room, the only private room in the Schwartz apartment. The other rooms were the bathroom, the living room, and the wide, windowless hallway, which was originally intended to serve as a dining area, and which had a kitchenette in one end. Six mattresses and four sleeping bags were dispersed in the hallway and living room, and the daybed, in the living room, accommodated the eleventh couple, the favorites of the moment.

On Gramps's bureau was his will, smeared, dog-eared, perforated, and blotched with hundreds of additions, deletions, accusations, conditions, warnings, advice, and homely philosophy. The document was, Lou reflected, a fifty-year diary, all jammed onto two sheets—a garbled, illegible log of day after day of strife. This day, Lou would be disinherited for the eleventh time, and it would take him perhaps six months of impeccable behavior to regain the promise of a share in the estate.

"Boy!" called Gramps.

"Coming, sir." Lou hurried back into the living room, and handed Gramps the will.

"Pen!" said Gramps.

He was instantly offered eleven pens, one from each couple.

"Not *that* leaky thing," he said, brushing Lou's pen aside. "Ah, there's a nice one. Good boy, Willy." He accepted Willy's pen. That was the tip they'd all been waiting for. Willy, then, Lou's father, was the new favorite.

Willy, who looked almost as young as Lou, though one hundred and forty-two, did a poor job of concealing his pleasure. He glanced shyly at the daybed, which would become his, and from which Lou and Emerald would have to move back into the hall, back to the worst spot of all by the bathroom door.

Gramps missed none of the high drama he'd authored, and he gave his own familiar role everything he had. Frowning and running his finger along each line, as though he were seeing the will for the first time, he read aloud in a deep, portentous monotone, like a bass tone on a cathedral organ:

"I, Harold D. Schwartz, residing in Building 257 of Alden Village, New York City, do hereby make, publish, and declare this to be my last Will and Testament, hereby revoking any and all former wills and codicils by me at any time heretofore made." He blew his nose importantly, and went on, not missing a word, and repeating many for emphasis—repeating in particular his ever-more-elaborate specifications for a funeral.

At the end of these specifications, Gramps was so choked with emotion that Lou thought he might forget why he'd gotten out the will in the first place. But Gramps heroically brought his powerful emotions under control, and, after erasing for a full minute, he began to write and speak at the same time. Lou could have spoken his lines for him, he'd heard them so often.

"I have had many heartbreaks ere leaving this vale of tears for a better land," Gramps said and wrote. "But the deepest hurt of all has been dealt me by—" He looked around the group, trying to remember who the malefactor was.

Everyone looked helpfully at Lou, who held up his hand resignedly.

Gramps nodded, remembering, and completed the sentence: "my great-grandson, Louis J. Schwartz."

"Grandson, sir," said Lou.

"Don't quibble. You're in deep enough now, young man," said Gramps, but he changed the trifle. And from there he went without a misstep through the phrasing of the disinheritance, causes for which were disrespectfulness and quibbling.

In the paragraph following, the paragraph that had belonged to everyone in the room at one time or another, Lou's name was scratched out and Willy's substituted as heir to the apartment and, the biggest plum of all, the double bed in the private bedroom. "So!" said Gramps, beaming. He erased the date at the foot of the will, and substituted a new one, including the time of day. "Well— time to watch the McGarvey Family." The McGarvey Family was a television serial that Gramps had been following since he was sixty, or for one hundred and twelve years. "I can't wait to see what's going to happen next," he said.

Lou detached himself from the group and lay down on his bed of pain by the bathroom door. He wished Em would join him, and he wondered where she was.

He dozed for a few moments, until he was disturbed by someone's stepping over him to get into the bathroom. A moment later, he heard a faint gurgling sound, as though something were being poured down the washbasin drain. Suddenly, it entered his mind that Em had cracked up, and that she was in there doing something drastic about Gramps.

"Em—!" he whispered through the panel. There was no reply, and Lou pressed against the door. The worn lock, whose bolt barely engaged its socket, held for a second, then let the door swing inward.

"Morty!" gasped Lou.

Lou's great-grandnephew, Mortimer, who had just married and brought his wife home to the Schwartz menage, looked at Lou with consternation and surprise. Morty kicked the door shut, but not before Lou had glimpsed what was in his hand—Gramps's enormous economy-size bottle of anti-gerasone, which had been half-emptied, and which Morty was refilling to the top with tap water.

A moment later, Morty came out, glared defiantly at Lou, and brushed past him wordlessly to rejoin his pretty bride.

Shocked, Lou didn't know what on earth to do. He couldn't let Gramps take the mousetrapped anti-gerasone; but if he warned Gramps about it, Gramps would certainly make life in the apartment, which was merely insufferable now, harrowing.

Lou glanced into the living room, and saw that the Schwartzes, Emerald among them, were momentarily at rest, relishing the botches that McGarveys had made of *their* lives. Stealthily, he went into the bathroom, locked the door as well as he could, and began to pour the contents of Gramps's bottle down the drain. He was going to refill it with full-strength anti-gerasone from the twenty-two smaller bottles on the shelf. The bottle contained a half-gallon, and its neck was small, so it seemed to Lou that the emptying would take forever. And the almost imperceptible smell of anti-gerasone, like Worcestershire sauce, now seemed to Lou, in his nervousness, to be pouring out into the rest of the apartment through the keyhole and under the door.

*"Gloog-gloog-gloog-gloog-"* went the bottle monotonously. Suddenly, up came the sound of music from the living room, and there were murmurs and the scraping of chair legs on the floor. *"Thus ends,"* said the television announcer, *"the 29,121st chapter in the life of your neighbors and mine, the McGarveys."* Footsteps were coming down the hall. There was a knock on the bathroom door.

"Just a sec," called Lou cheerily. Desperately, he shook the big bottle, trying to speed up the flow. His palms slipped on the wet glass, and the heavy bottle smashed to splinters on the tile floor.

The door sprung open, and Gramps, dumbfounded, stared at the mess.

Lou grinned engagingly through his nausea, and, for want of anything remotely resembling a thought, he waited for Gramps to speak.

"Well, boy," said Gramps at last, "looks like you've got a little tidying up to do."

And that was all he said. He turned around, elbowed his way through the crowd, and locked himself in his bedroom.

The Schwartzes contemplated Lou in incredulous silence for a moment longer, and then hurried back to the living room, as though some of his horrible guilt would taint them, too, if they looked too long. Morty stayed behind long enough to give Lou a quizzical, annoyed glance. Then he, too, went into the living room, leaving only Emerald standing in the doorway.

Tears streamed over her cheeks. "Oh, you poor lamb —please don't look so awful. It was my fault. I put you up to this."

"No," said Lou, finding his voice, "really you didn't. Honest, Em, I was just—"

"You don't have to explain anything to me, hon. I'm on your side no matter what." She kissed him on his cheek, and whispered in his ear. "It wouldn't have been murder, hon. It wouldn't have killed him. It wasn't such a terrible thing to do. It just would have fixed him up so he'd be able to go any time God decided He wanted him."

"What's gonna happen next, Em?" said Lou hollowly. "What's he gonna do?"

Lou and Emerald stayed fearfully awake almost all night, waiting to see what Gramps was going to do. But not a sound came from the sacred bedroom. At two hours before dawn, the pair dropped off to sleep.

At six o'clock they arose again, for it was time for their generation to eat breakfast in the kitchenette. No one spoke to them. They had twenty minutes in which to eat, but their reflexes were so dulled by the bad night that they had hardly swallowed two mouthfuls of egg-type processed seaweed before it was time to surrender their places to their son's generation.

Then, as was the custom for whomever had been most recently disinherited, they began preparing Gramps' breakfast, which would presently be served to him in bed, on a tray. They tried to be cheerful about it. The toughest part of the job was having to handle the honest-to-God eggs and bacon and oleomargarine on which Gramps spent almost all of the income from his fortune.

"Well," said Emerald, "I'm not going to get all panicky until I'm sure there's something to be panicky about."

"Maybe he doesn't know what it was I busted," said Lou hopefully.

"Probably thinks it was your watch crystal," said Eddie their son, who was toying apathetically with his buckwheat-type processed sawdust cakes.

"Don't get sarcastic with your father," said Em, "and don't talk with your mouth full, either."

"I'd like to see anybody take a mouthful of this stuff

and *not* say something," said Eddie, who was seventy-three. He glanced at the clock. "It's time to take Gramps his breakfast, you know."

"Yeah, it is, isn't it," said Lou weakly. He shrugged. "Let's have the tray, Em."

"We'll both go."

Walking slowly, smiling bravely, they found a large semicircle of long-faced Schwartzes standing around the bedroom door.

Em knocked. "Gramps," she said brightly, "breakfast is ready."

There was no reply, and she knocked again, harder.

The door swung open before her fist. In the middle of the room, the soft, deep, wide, canopied bed, the symbol of the sweet by-and-by to every Schwartz, was empty.

A sense of death, as unfamiliar to the Schwartzes as Zoroastrianism or the causes of the Sepoy Mutiny, stilled every voice and slowed every heart. Awed, the heirs began to search gingerly under the furniture and behind the drapes for all that was mortal of Gramps, father of the race.

But Gramps had left not his earthly husk but a note, which Lou finally found on the dresser, under a paper-weight which was a treasured souvenir from the 2000 World's Fair. Unsteadily, Lou read it aloud:

" 'Somebody who I have sheltered and protected and taught the best I know how all these years last night turned on me like a mad dog and diluted my anti-gerasone, or tried to. I am no longer a young man. I can no longer bear the crushing burden of life as I once could. So, after last night's bitter experience, I say goodbye. The cares of this world will soon drop away like a cloak of thorns, and I shall know peace. By the time you find this, I will be gone.' "

"Gosh," said Willy brokenly, "he didn't even get to see how the Five-Hundred-Mile Speedway Race was going to come out."

"Or the World's Series," said Eddie.

"Or whether Mrs. McGarvey got her eyesight back," said Morty.

"There's more," said Lou, and he began reading aloud again: " 'I, Harold D. Schwartz . . . do hereby make, publish and declare this to be my last Will and Testament, hereby revoking any and all former wills and codicils by me at any time heretofore made.' "

"No!" cried Willy. "Not another one!"

" 'I do stipulate,' " read Lou, " 'that all of my property, of whatsoever kind and nature, not be divided, but do devise and bequeath it to be held in common by my issue, without regard for generation, equally, share and share alike.' "

"Issue?" said Emerald.

Lou included the multitude in a sweep of his hand. "It means we all own the whole damn shootin' match."

All eyes turned instantly to the bed.

"Share and share alike?" said Morty.

"Actually," said Willy, who was the oldest person present, "it's just like the old system, where the oldest people head up things with their headquarters in here, and—"

"I like *that!*" said Em. "Lou owns as much of it as you do, and I say it ought to be for the oldest one who's still working. You can snooze around here all day, waiting for your pension check, and poor Lou stumbles in here after work, all tuckered out, and—"

"How about letting somebody who's never had any privacy get a little crack at it?" said Eddie hotly. "Hell, you old people had plenty of privacy back when you were kids. I was born and raised in the middle of the goddam barracks in the hall! How about—"

"Yeah?" said Morty. "Sure, you've all had it pretty tough, and my heart bleeds for you. But try honeymooning in the hall for a real kick."

"Silence!" shouted Willy imperiously. "The next person who opens his mouth spends the next six months by the bathroom. Now clear out of my room. I want to think."

A vase shattered against the wall, inches above his head. In the next moment, a free-for-all was underway, with each couple battling to eject every other couple from the room. Fighting coalitions formed and dissolved with the lightning changes of the tactical situation. Em and Lou were thrown into the hall, where they organized others in the same situation, and stormed back into the room.

After two hours of struggle, with nothing like a decision in sight, the cops broke in.

For the next half-hour, patrol wagons and ambulances hauled away Schwartzes, and then the apartment was still and spacious.

An hour later, films of the last stages of the riot were being televised to 500,000,000 delighted viewers on the Eastern Seaboard.

In the stillness of the three-room Schwartz apartment on the 76th floor of Building 257, the television set had been left on. Once more the air was filled with the cries and grunts and crashes of the fray, coming harmlessly now from the loudspeaker.

The battle also appeared on the screen of the television set in the police station, where the Schwartzes and their captors watched with professional interest.

Em and Lou were in adjacent four-by-eight cells, and were stretched out peacefully on their cots.

"Em——" called Lou through the partition, "you got a washbasin all your own too?"

"Sure. Washbasin, bed, light—the works. Ha! And we thought Gramps's room was something. How long's this been going on?" She held out her hand. "For the first time in forty years, hon, I haven't got the shakes."

"Cross your fingers," said Lou, "the lawyer's going to try to get us a year."

"Gee," said Em dreamily, "I wonder what kind of wires you'd have to pull to get solitary?"

"All right, pipe down," said the turnkey, "or I'll toss the whole kit and caboodle of you right out. And first one who lets on to anybody outside how good jail is ain't never getting back in!"

The prisoners instantly fell silent.

The living room of the Schwartz apartment darkened for a moment, as the riot scene faded, and then the face of the announcer appeared, like the sun coming from behind a cloud. *"And now, friends," he said, "I have a special message from the makers of anti-gerasone, a message for all you folks over one hundred and fifty. Are you hampered socially by wrinkles, by stiffness of joints and discoloration or loss of hair, all because these things came upon you before anti-gearsone was developed? Well, if you are, you need no longer suffer, need no longer feel different and out of things.*

*"After years of research, medical science has now developed* super-*anti-gerasone! In weeks, yes weeks, you can look, feel, and act as young as your great-great-grandchildren! Wouldn't you pay $5,000 to be indistinguishable from everybody else? Well, you don't have to. Safe, tested super-anti-gerasone costs you only dollars a day. The average cost of regaining all the sparkle and attractiveness of youth is less than fifty dollars.*

*"Write now for your free trial carton. Just put your name and address on a dollar postcard, and mail it to 'Super,' Box 500,000, Schenectady, N. Y. Have you got that? I'll repeat it.* 'Super' *Box . . ."* Underlining the announcer's words was the scratching of Gramps's fountain pen, the one Willy had given him the night before. He had come in a few minutes previous from the Idle Hour Tavern, which commanded a view of Building 257 across the square of asphalt known as the Alden Village Green. He had called a cleaning woman to come straighten the place up, and had hired the best lawyer in town to get his descendants a conviction. Gramps had then moved the daybed before the television screen so that he could watch from a reclining position. It was something he'd dreamed of doing for years.

"Schen-*ec*-ta-dy," mouthed Gramps. "Got it." His face had changed remarkably. His facial muscles seemed to have relaxed, revealing kindness and equanimity under what had been taut, bad-tempered lines. It was almost as though his trial package of *Super*-anti-gerasone had already arrived. When something amused him on television, he smiled easily, rather than barely managing to lengthen the thin line of his mouth a millimeter. Life was good. He could hardly wait to see what was going to happen next.

Sarah Orne Jewett

# A WHITE HERON

*At what point does an individual realize the importance of the environment? Quite possibly, at some insignificant moment which only later does he understand fully.*

---

## I

The woods were already filled with shadows one June evening, just before eight o'clock, though a bright sunset still glimmered faintly among the trunks of the trees. A little girl was driving home her cow, a plodding, dilatory, provoking creature in her behavior, but a valued companion for all that. They were going away from whatever light there was, and striking deep into the woods, but their feet were familiar with the path, and it was no matter whether their eyes could see it or not.

There was hardly a night the summer through when the old cow could be found waiting at the pasture bars; on the contrary, it was her greatest pleasure to hide herself away among the huckleberry bushes, and though she wore a loud bell she had made the discovery that if one stood perfectly still it would not ring. So Sylvia had to hunt for her until she found her, and call Co'! Co'! with never an answering Moo, until her childish patience was quite spent. If the creature had not given good milk and plenty of it, the case would have seemed very different to her owners. Besides, Sylvia had all the time there was, and very little use to make of it.

Sometimes in pleasant weather it was a consolation to look upon the cow's pranks as an intelligent attempt to play hide and seek, and as the child had no playmates she lent herself to this amusement with a good deal of zest. Though this chase had been so long that the wary animal herself had given an unusual signal of her whereabouts, Sylvia had only laughed when she came upon Mistress Moolly at the swampside, and urged her affectionately homeward with a twig of birch leaves. The old cow was not inclined to wander farther; she even turned in the right direction for once as they left the pasture, and stepped along the road at a good pace. She was quite ready to be milked now, and seldom stopped to browse. Sylvia wondered what her grandmother would say because they were so late. It was a great while since she had left home at half-past five o'clock, but everybody knew the difficulty of making this errand a short one. Mrs. Tilley had chased the hornéd torment too many summer evenings herself to blame any one else for lingering, and was only thankful as she waited that she had Sylvia, nowadays, to give such valuable assistance. The good woman suspected that Sylvia loitered occasionally on her own account; there never was such a child for straying about out-of-doors since the world was made! Everybody said that it was a good change for a little maid who had tried to grow for eight years in a crowded manufacturing town, but as for Sylvia herself, it seemed as if she never had been alive at all before she came to live at the farm. She thought often with wistful compassion of a wretched geranium that belonged to a town neighbor.

" 'Afraid of folks,' " old Mrs. Tilley said to herself, with a smile, after she made the unlikely choice of Sylvia from her daughter's houseful of children, and was returning to the farm. " 'Afraid of folks,' they said! I guess she won't be troubled no great with 'em up to the old place!" When they reached the door of the lonely house and stopped to unlock it, and the cat came to purr loudly, and rub against them, a deserted pussy, indeed, but fat with young robins, Sylvia whispered that this was a beautiful place to live in, and she never should wish to go home.

The companions followed the shady woodroad, the cow taking slow steps and the child very fast ones. The cow stopped long at the brook to drink, as if the pasture were not half a swamp, and Sylvia stood still and waited, letting her bare feet cool themselves in the shoal water, while the great twilight moths struck softly against her. She waded on through the brook as the cow moved away, and listened to the thrushes with a heart that beat fast with pleasure. There was a stirring in the great boughs overhead. They were full of little birds and beasts that seemed to be wide awake, and going about their world, or else saying good night to each other in sleepy twitters. Sylvia herself felt sleepy as she walked along. However, it was not much farther to the house, and the air was soft and sweet. She was not often in the woods so late as this, and it made her feel as if she were a part of the gray shadows and the moving leaves. She was just thinking how long it seemed since she first came to the farm a year ago, and wondering if everything went on in the noisy town just the same as when she was there; the thought of the great red-faced boy who used to chase and frighten her made her hurry along the path to escape from the shadow of the trees.

Suddenly this little woods-girl is horror-stricken to hear a clear whistle not very far away. Not a bird's-whistle, which would have a sort of friendliness, but a boy's whistle, determined, and somewhat aggressive. Sylvia left the cow to whatever sad fate might await her, and stepped discreetly aside into the bushes, but she was just too late. The enemy had discovered her, and called out in a very cheerful and persuasive tone, "Halloa, little girl, how far is it to the road?" and trembling Sylvia answered almost inaudibly, "A good ways."

She did not dare to look boldly at the tall young man, who carried a gun over his shoulder, but she came out of her bush and again followed the cow, while he walked alongside.

"I have been hunting for some birds," the stranger said kindly, "and I have lost my way, and need a friend very much. Don't be afraid," he added gallantly. "Speak up and tell me what your name is, and whether you think I can spend the night at your house, and go out gunning early in the morning."

Sylvia was more alarmed than before. Would not her grandmother consider her much to blame? But who could have foreseen such an accident as this? It did not seem to be her fault, and she hung her head as if the stem of it were broken, but managed to answer "Sylvy," with much effort when her companion again asked her name.

Mrs. Tilley was standing in the doorway when the trio came into view. The cow gave a loud moo by way of explanation.

"Yes, you'd better speak up for yourself, you old trial! Where'd she tucked herself away this time, Sylvy?" But Sylvia kept an awed silence; she knew by instinct that her grandmother did not comprehend the gravity of the situation. She must be mistaking the stranger for one of the farmer-lads of the region.

The young man stood his gun beside the door, and dropped a lumpy game-bag beside it; then he bade Mrs. Tilley good evening, and repeated his wayfarer's story, and asked if he could have a night's lodging.

"Put me anywhere you like," he said. "I must be off early in the morning, before day; but I am very hungry, indeed. You can give me some milk at any rate, that's plain."

"Dear sakes, yes," responded the hostess, whose long-slumbering hospitality seemed to be easily awakened. "You might fare better if you went out to the main road a mile or so, but you're welcome to what we've got. I'll milk right off, and you make yourself at home. You can sleep on husks or feathers," she proffered graciously. "I raised them all myself. There's good pasturing for geese just below here toward the ma'sh. Now step round and set a plate for the gentleman, Sylvy!" And Sylvia promptly stepped. She was glad to have something to do, and she was hungry herself.

It was a surprise to find so clean and comfortable a little dwelling in this New England wilderness. The young man had known the horrors of its most primitive housekeeping, and the dreary squalor of that level of society which does not rebel at the companionship of hens. This was the best thrift of an old-fashioned farmstead, though on such a small scale that it seemed like a hermitage. He listened eagerly to the old woman's quaint talk, he watched Sylvia's pale face and shining gray eyes with ever growing enthusiasm, and insisted that this was the best supper he had eaten for a month, and afterward the new-made friends sat down in the doorway together while the moon came up.

Soon it would be berry-time, and Sylvia was a great help at picking. The cow was a good milker, though a plaguy thing to keep track of, the hostess gossiped frankly, adding presently that she had buried four children, so Sylvia's mother, and a son (who might be dead) in California were all the children she had left. "Dan, my boy, was a great hand to go gunning," she explained sadly. "I never wanted for pa'tridges or gray squer'ls while he was to home. He's been a great wand'rer, I expect, and he's no hand to write letters. There, I don't blame him, I'd ha' seen the world myself if it had been so I could."

"Sylvy takes after him," the grandmother continued affectionately, after a minute's pause. "There ain't a foot o' ground she don't know her way over, and the wild creaturs counts her one o 'themselves. Squer'ls she'll tame to come an' feed right out o' her hands, and all sorts o' birds. Last winter she got the jaybirds to bangeing here, and I believe she'd 'a' scanted herself of her own meals to have plenty to throw out amongst 'em, if I hadn't kep' watch. Anything but crows, I tell her, I'm willin' to help support—though Dan he had a tamed one o' them that did seem to have reason same as folks. It was round here a good spell after he went away. Dan an' his father they didn't hitch—but he never held up his head ag'n after Dan had dared him an' gone off."

The guest did not notice this hint of family sorrows in his eager interest in something else.

"So Sylvy knows all about birds, does she?" he exclaimed, as he looked around at the little girl who sat, very demure but increasingly sleepy, in the moonlight. "I am making a collection of birds myself. I have been at it ever since I was a boy." (Mrs. Tilly smiled.) "There are two or three very rare ones I have been hunting for these five years. I mean to get them on my own ground if they can be found."

"Do you cage 'em up?" asked Mrs. Tilley doubtfully, in response to this enthusiastic announcement.

"Oh no, they're stuffed and preserved, dozens and dozens of them," said the ornithologist, "and I have shot or snared every one myself. I caught a glimpse of a white heron a few miles from here on Saturday, and I have followed it in this direction. They have never been found in this district at all. The little white heron, it is," and he turned again to look at Sylvia with the hope of discovering that the rare bird was one of her acquaintances.

But Sylvia was watching a hop-toad in the narrow footpath.

"You would know the heron if you saw it," the stranger continued eagerly. "A queer tall white bird with soft feathers and long thin legs. And it would have a nest perhaps in the top of a high tree, made of sticks, something like a hawk's nest."

Sylvia's heart gave a wild beat; she knew that strange white bird, and had once stolen softly near where it stood in some bright green swamp grass, away over at the other side of the woods. There was an open place where the sunshine always seemed strangely yellow and hot, where tall, nodding rushes grew, and her grandmother had warned her that she might sink in the soft black mud underneath and never be heard of more. Not far beyond were the salt marshes just this side of the sea itself, which Sylvia wondered and dreamed much about, but never had seen, whose great voice could sometimes be heard above the noise of the woods on stormy nights.

"I can't think of anything I should like so much as to find that heron's nest," the handsome stranger was saying. "I would give ten dollars to anybody who could show it to me," he added desperately, "and I mean to spend my whole vacation hunting for it if need be. Perhaps it was only migrating, or had been chased out of its own region by some bird of prey."

Mrs. Tilley gave amazed attention to all this, but Sylvia still watched the toad, not divining, as she might have done at some calmer time, that the creature wished to get to its hole under the doorstep, and was much hindered by the unusual spectators at that hour of the evening. No amount of thought, that night, could decide how many wished-for treasures the ten dollars, so lightly spoken of, would buy.

The next day the young sportsman hovered about the woods, and Sylvia kept him company, having lost her first fear of the friendly lad, who proved to be most kind and sympathetic. He told her many things about the birds and what they knew and where they lived and what they did with themselves. And he gave her a jackknife, which she

thought as great a treasure as if she were a desert-islander.
All day long he did not once make her troubled or afraid
except when he brought down some unsuspecting singing
creature from its bough. Sylvia would have liked him vastly
better without his gun; she could not understand why he
killed the very birds he seemed to like so much. But as the
day waned, Sylvia still watched the young man with loving
admiration. She had never seen anybody so charming and
delightful; the woman's heart, asleep in the child, was
vaguely thrilled by a dream of love. Some premonition of
that great power stirred and swayed these young creatures
who traversed the solemn woodlands with soft-footed silent
care. They stopped to listen to a bird's song; they pressed
forward again eagerly, parting the branches—speaking to
each other rarely and in whispers; the young man going
first and Sylvia following, fascinated, a few steps behind,
with her gray eyes dark with excitement.

She grieved because the longed-for white heron was elusive, but she did not lead the guest, she only followed, and
there was no such thing as speaking first. The sound of her
own unquestioned voice would have terrified her—it was
hard enough to answer yes or no when there was need of
that. At last evening began to fall, and they drove the cow
home together, and Sylvia smiled with pleasure when they
came to the place where she heard the whistle and was
afraid only the night before.

## II

Half a mile from home, at the farther edge of the woods,
where the land was highest, a great pine-tree stood, the last
of its generation. Whether it was left for a boundary mark,
or for what reason, no one could say; the woodchoppers
who had felled its mates were dead and gone long ago, and
a whole forest of sturdy trees, pines and oaks and maples,
had grown again. But the stately head of this old pine towered above them all and made a landmark for sea and shore
miles and miles away. Sylvia knew it well. She had always
believed that whoever climbed to the top of it could see the
ocean; and the little girl had often laid her hand on the
great rough trunk and looked up wistfully at those dark
boughs that the wind always stirred, no matter how hot and

still the air might be below. Now she thought of the tree
with a new excitement, for why, if one climbed it at break
of day, could not one see all the world, and easily discover
from whence the white heron flew, and mark the place,
and find the hidden nest?

What a spirit of adventure, what wild ambition! What
fancied triumph and delight and glory for the later morning
when she could make known the secret! It was almost too
real and too great for the childish heart to bear.

All night the door of the little house stood open and the
whippoorwills came and sang upon the very step. The
young sportsman and his old hostess were sound asleep, but
Sylvia's great design kept her broad awake and watching.
She forgot to think of sleep. The short summer night
seemed as long as the winter darkness, and at last when the
whippoorwills ceased, and she was afraid the morning
would after all come too soon, she stole out of the house
and followed the pasture path through the woods, hastening
toward the open ground beyond, listening with a sense of
comfort and companionship to the drowsy twitter of a half-
awakened bird, whose perch she had jarred in passing.
Alas, if the great wave of human interest which flooded
for the first time this dull little life should sweep away the
satisfactions of an existence heart to heart with nature and
the dumb life of the forest!

There was the huge tree asleep yet in the paling moonlight, and small and silly Sylvia began with utmost bravery
to mount to the top of it, with tingling, eager blood coursing
the channels of her whole frame, with her bare feet and fingers, that pinched and held like bird's claws to the monstrous ladder reaching up, up, almost to the sky itself. First
she must mount the white oak tree that grew alongside,
where she was almost lost among the dark branches and the
green leaves heavy and wet with dew; a bird fluttered off its
nest, and a red squirrel ran to and fro and scolded pettishly
at the harmless housebreaker. Sylvia felt her way easily.
She had often climbed there, and knew that higher still one
of the oak's upper branches chafed against the pine trunk,
just where its lower boughs were set close together. There,
when she made the dangerous pass from one tree to the
other, the great enterprise would really begin.

She crept out along the swaying oak limb at last, and

took the daring step across into the old pine-tree. The way was harder than she thought; she must reach far and hold fast, the sharp dry twigs caught and held her and scratched her like angry talons, the pitch made her thin little fingers clumsy and stiff as she went around and around the tree's great stem, higher and higher upward. The sparrows and robins in the woods below were beginning to wake and twitter to the dawn, yet it seemed much lighter there aloft in the pine-tree, and the child knew she must hurry if her project were to be of any use.

The tree seemed to lengthen itself out as she went up, and to reach farther and farther upward. It was like a great main-mast to the voyaging earth; it must truly have been amazed that morning through all its ponderous frame as it felt this determined spark of human spirit wending its way from higher branch to branch. Who knows how steadily the least twigs held themselves to advantage this light, weak creature on her way! The old pine must have loved his new dependent. More than all the hawks, and bats, and moths, and even the sweet voiced thrushes, was the brave, beating heart of the solitary gray-eyed child. And the tree stood still and frowned away the winds that June morning while the dawn grew bright in the east.

Sylvia's face was like a pale star, if one had seen it from the ground, when the last thorny bough was past, and she stood trembling and tired but wholly triumphant, high in the treetop. Yes, there was the sea with the dawning sun making a golden dazzle over it, and toward that glorious east flew two hawks with slow-moving pinions. How low they looked in the air from that height when one had only seen them before far up, and dark against the blue sky. Their gray feathers were as soft as moths; they seemed only a little way from the tree, and Sylvia felt as if she too could go flying away among the clouds. Westward, the woodlands and farms reached miles and miles into the distance; here and there were church steeples, and white villages, truly it was a vast and awesome world!

The birds sang louder and louder. At last the sun came up bewilderingly bright. Sylvia could see the white sails of ships out at sea, and the clouds that were purple and rose-colored and yellow at first began to fade away. Where was the white heron's nest in the sea of green branches, and was

this wonderful sight and pageant of the world the only reward for having climbed to such a giddy height? Now look
down again, Sylvia, where the green marsh is set among the
shining birches and dark hemlocks; there where you saw the
white heron once you will see him again; look, look! a white
spot of him like a single floating feather comes up from the
dead hemlock and grows larger, and rises, and comes close
at last, and goes by the landmark pine with steady sweep of
wing and outstretched slender neck and crested head. And
wait! wait! do not move a foot or a finger, little girl, do not
send an arrow of light and consciousness from your two
eager eyes, for the heron has perched on a pine bough not
far beyond yours, and cries back to his mate on the nest
and plumes his feathers for the new day!

The child gives a long sigh a minute later when a company of shouting cat-birds comes also to the tree, and vexed
by their fluttering and lawlessness the solemn heron goes
away. She knows his secret now, the wild, light, slender bird
that floats and wavers, and goes back like an arrow presently to his home in the green world beneath. Then Sylvia,
well satisfied, makes her perilous way down again, not daring to look far below the branch she stands on, ready to cry
sometimes because her fingers ache and her lamed feet slip.
Wondering over and over again what the stranger would
say to her, and what he would think when she told him how
to find his way straight to the heron's nest.

"Sylvy, Sylvy!" called the busy old grandmother again
and again, but nobody answered, and the small husk bed
was empty and Sylvia had disappeared.

The guest waked from a dream, and remembering his
day's pleasure hurried to dress himself that might it sooner
begin. He was sure from the way the shy little girl looked
once or twice yesterday that she had at least seen the white
heron, and now she must really be made to tell. Here she
comes now, paler than ever, and her worn old frock is torn
and tattered, and smeared with pine pitch. The grandmother and the sportsman stand in the door together and
question her, and the splendid moment has come to speak
of the dead hemlock-tree by the green marsh.

But Sylvia does not speak after all, though the old grandmother fretfully rebukes her, and the young man's kind,

appealing eyes are looking straight in her own. He can make them rich with money; he has promised it, and they are poor now. He is so well worth making happy, and he waits to hear the story she can tell.

No, she must keep silence! What is it that suddenly forbids her and makes her dumb? Has she been nine years growing and now, when the great world for the first time puts out a hand to her, must she thrust it aside for a bird's sake? The murmur of the pine's green branches is in her ears, she remembers how the white heron came flying through the golden air and how they watched the sea and the morning together, and Sylvia cannot speak; she cannot tell the heron's secret and give its life away.

Dear loyalty, that suffered a sharp pang as the guest went away disappointed later in the day, that could have served and followed him and loved him as a dog loves! Many a night Sylvia heard the echo of his whistle haunting the pasture path as she came home with the loitering cow. She forgot even her sorrow at the sharp report of his gun and the sight of thrushes and sparrows dropping silent to the ground, their songs hushed and their pretty feathers stained and wet with blood. Were the birds better friends than their hunter might have been—who can tell? Whatever treasures were lost to her, woodlands and summertime, remember! Bring your gifts and graces and tell your secrets to this lonely country child!

Frank Herbert

# THE MARY CELESTE MOVE

*We allow our cars to fill the air with noxious gases; we allow the destruction of our forests for roads; we allow our roads to become wider and wider for faster and faster travel. Where are we driving ourselves?*

———◆━●━●◆———

Martin Fisk's car, a year-old 1997 Buick with triple turbines and *jato* boosters, flashed off the freeway, found a space between a giant mobile refueling tanker and a commuter bus, darted through and surged into the first of the eight right-hand lanes in time to make the turnoff marked "NEW PENTAGON ONLY—Reduce Speed to 75."

Fisk glanced at his surface/air rate-of-travel mixer, saw he was down to 80 miles per hour, close enough to legal speed, and worked his way through the press of morning traffic into the second lane in plenty of time to join the cars diverging onto the fifth-level ramp.

At the last minute, a big official limousine with a two-star general's decal-flag on its forward curve cut in front of him and he had to reduce speed to 50, hearing the drag-bar rasping behind him as his lane frantically matched speed. The shadow of a traffic copter passed over the roadway and Fisk thought: *Hope that general's driver loses his license!*

By this time he was into the sweeping curve-around that would drop him to the fifth level. Speed here was a monitored 55. The roadway entered the building and Fisk

145

brought his R-O-T up to the stated speed, watching for the code of his off-slot: BR71D$_a$. It loomed ahead, a flashing mnemonic blinker in brilliant green.

Fisk dropped behind an in-building shuttle, squeezed into the right-hand lane, slapped the turn-off alert that set all his rim lights blinking and activated the automatics. His machine caught the signal from the roadway, went on automatic and swerved into the off-slot still at 55.

Fisk released his control bar.

Drag hooks underneath the Buick snagged the catch ribbands of the slot, jerked his car to a stop that sent him surging against the harness.

The exit-warning wall ahead of him flashed a big red "7 SECONDS! 7 SECONDS!"

*Plenty of time,* he thought.

He yanked his briefcase out of its dashboard carrier with his right hand while unsnapping his safety harness with his left and hitting the door actuator with his knee. He was out onto the pedestrian ramp with three seconds to spare. The warning wall lifted; his car jerked forward into the down-elevator rack to be stored in a coded pile far below. His personal I-D signal to the computer-monitored system later would restore the car to him all checked and serviced and ready for the high-risk evening race out of the city.

Fisk glanced at his wrist watch—four minutes until his appointment with William Merill, the President's liaison officer on the Internal Control Board and Fisk's boss. Adopting the common impersonal discourtesy, Fisk joined the press of people hurrying along the ramp.

*Some day,* he thought, *I'll get a nice safe and sane job on one of the ocean hydroponic stations where all I have to do is watch gauges and there's nothing faster than a 40 mph pedestrian ramp.* He fished a green pill out of his coat pocket, gulped it, hoped he wouldn't have to take another before his blood pressure began its downslant to normal.

By this time he was into the pneumatic lift capsule that would take him up in an individual curve to easy walking distance from his destination. He locked his arms on the brace bars. The door thumped closed. There was a distant hiss, a feeling of smooth downward pressure that evened off. He stared at the familiar blank tan of the opposite wall.

Presently the pressure slackened, the capsule glided to a stop, its door swung open.

Fisk stepped out into the wide hall, avoided the guide-lanes for the high-speed ramp and dodged through thinning lines of people hurrying to work around him.

Within seconds he was into Merill's office and facing the WAC secretary, a well-endowed brunette with an air of brisk efficiency. She looked up from her desk as he entered.

"Oh, Mr. Fisk," she said, "how nice that you're a minute early. Mr. Merill's already here. You can have nine minutes. I hope that'll be enough. He has a very full schedule today and the Safety Council subcommittee session with the President this afternoon." She already was up and holding the inner door open for him, saying: "Wouldn't it be wonderful if we could invent a forty-eight hour day?"

*We already have,* he thought. *We just compressed it into the old twenty-four-hour model.*

"Mr. Fisk is here," she said, announcing him as she stepped out of his way.

Fisk was through to the inner sanctum then, wondering why his mind was filled with the sudden realization that he had driven out of his apartment's garage lift one hundred miles away only thirty-two minutes before. He heard the WAC secretary close the door behind him.

Merill, a wiry redhead with an air of darting tension, pale freckled skin and narrow face, sat at a desk directly opposite the door. He looked up, fixed his green eyes on Fisk, said: "Come on in and sit down, Marty, but make it snappy."

Fisk crossed the office. It was an irregular space of six sides about forty feet across at its widest point. Merill sat with his back to the narrowest of the walls and with the widest wall at an angle to his right. A computer-actuated map of the United States covered that surface, its color-intensity lines of red, blue and purple showing traffic density on the great expressway arteries that crisscrossed the nation. The ceiling was a similar map, this one showing the entire western hemisphere and confined to the Prime-1 arteries of twenty lanes or greater.

Fisk dropped into the chair across the desk from Merill, pushed a lock of dark hair back from his forehead, feeling the nervous perspiration there. *Blast it!* he thought. *"I'll have to take another pill!*

"Well?" Merill said.

"It's all here," Fisk said, slapping the briefcase onto Merill's desk. "Ten days, forty thousand miles of travel and eighteen personal interviews plus fifty-one other interviews and reports from my assistants."

"You know the President's worried about this," Merill said. "I hope you have it in some kind of order so I can present it to him this afternoon."

"It's in order," Fisk said. "But you're not going to like it."

"Yeah, well I was prepared for that," Merill said. "I don't like much of what comes across this desk." He glanced up suddenly at a strip of yellow that appeared on the overhead map indicating a partial blockage on the intercontinental throughway near Caracas. His right hand hovered over an intercom button, poised there as the yellow was replaced by red then blue shading into purple.

"Fourth problem in that area in two days," Merill said, removing his hand from the button. "Have to work a talk with Mendoza into this morning's schedule. Okay." He turned back to Fisk. "Give me your economy model brief rundown. What's got into these kooks who're moving all over the landscape?"

"I've about twenty interlocking factors to reinforce my original hunch," Fisk said. "The Psych Department confirms it. The question is whether this thing'll settle into some kind of steady pattern and even out. You might caution the President, off the record, that there are heavy political implications in this. Touchy ones if this leaks out the wrong way."

Merill pushed a recording button on his desk, said: "Okay, Marty, put the rest on the record. Recap and summate. I'll listen to it for review while I'm reading your report."

Fisk nodded. "Right." He pulled sheaves of papers in file folders out of the briefcase, lined them up in front of him. "We had the original report, of course, that people were making bold moves from one end of the country to the other in higher than usual numbers from unlikely starting places to unlikelier destinations. And these people turned out to be mostly mild, timid types instead of bold pioneers who'd pulled up their roots in the spirit of adventure."

"Are the psych profiles in your report?" Merill asked. "I'm going to have a time convincing the President unless I have all the evidence."

"Right here," Fisk said, tapping one of the folders. "I also have photostats of billings from the mobile refueling tankers and mobile food canteens to show that the people in these reports are actually the ones we've analyzed."

"Weird," Merill said. He glanced at another brief flicker of yellow on the overhead map near Seattle, returned his attention to Fisk.

"State and federal income-tax reports are here," Fisk said, touching another of the folders. "And, oh yes, car ownership breakdowns by area. I also have data on drivers' license transfers, bank and loan company records to show the business transactions involved in these moves. You know, some of these kooks sold profitable businesses at a loss and took up different trades at their new locations. Others took new jobs at lower pay. Some big industries are worried about this. They've lost key people for reasons that don't make sense. And the Welfare Department figures that . . ."

"Yeah, but what's this about car ownership breakdowns?" Merill asked.

*Trust him to dive right through to the sensitive area,* Fisk thought. He said: "There's a steep decline in car ownership among these people."

"Do the Detroit people suspect?" Merill asked.

"I covered my tracks best I could," Fisk said, "but there're bound to be some rumbles when their investigators interview the same people I did."

"We'd better invite them to review our findings," Merill said. "There're some big political contributors in that area. What's the pattern on communities chosen by these kooks?"

"Pretty indicative," Fisk said. "Most of the areas receiving a big influx are what our highway engineers irreverently call 'headwater swamps'—meaning areas where the highway feeder routes thin out and make it easy to leave the expressways."

"For example?"

"Oh . . . New York, San Francisco, Seattle, Los Angeles."

"That all?"

"No. There've been some significant population increases in areas where highway construction slowed traffic. There've been waves into Bangor, Maine . . . Blaine, Washington . . . and, my God! Calexico, California! They were hit on two consecutive weekends by one hundred and seventy of these weird newcomers."

In a tired voice, Merill said, "I suppose the concentration pattern's consistent?"

"Right down the line. They're all of middle age or past, drove well preserved older cars, are afraid to travel by air, are reluctant to explain why they moved such long distances. The complexion of entire areas in these headwater regions is being changed. There's sameness to them—people all conservative, timid . . . you know the pattern."

"I'm afraid I do. Bound to have political repercussions, too. Congressional representation from these areas will change to fit the new pattern, sure as hell. That's what you meant, wasn't it?"

"Yes." Fisk saw that he only had a few minutes more, began to feel his nervousness mount. He wondered if he'd dare gulp a pill in front of Merill, decided against it, said: "And you'd better look into the insurance angle. Costs are going up and people are beginning to complain. I saw a report on my desk when I checked in last night. These kooks were almost to a man low-risk drivers. As they get entirely out of the market, that throws a bigger load onto the others."

"I'll have the possibility of a subsidy investigated," Merill said. "Anything else? You're running out of time."

*Running out of time,* Fisk thought. *The story of our lives.* He touched another of the folders, said, "Here are the missing persons reports. There's a graph curve in them to fit this theory. I also have divorce records that are worth reviewing—wives who refused to join their husbands in one of these moves, that sort of thing."

"Husband moved and the wife refused to join him, eh?"

"That's the usual pattern. There are a couple of them, though, where the wife moved and refused to come back. Desertion charged . . . very indicative."

"Yeah, I was afraid of that," Merill said. "Okay, I'll review this when . . ."

"One thing more, Chief," Fisk said. "The telegrams and moving company records." He touched a thicker folder on the right. "I had photocopies made because few people would believe them without seeing them."

"Yeah?"

"The moving company gets an order from, say, Bangor, to move household belongings there from, for example, Tulsa, Oklahoma. The request contains a plea to feed the cat, the dog, the parrot or whatever. The movers go to the address and they find a hungry dog or cat in the house —or even a dead one on some occasions. One mover found a bowl of dead goldfish."

"So?"

"These houses fit right into the pattern," Fisk said. "The moving men find dinners that've been left cooking, plates on the table—all kinds of signs that people left and intended to come back . . . but didn't. They've got a name for this kind of thing in the moving industry. They call it the 'Mary Celeste' move after the story of the sailing ship that . . ."

"I know the story," Merill said in a sour voice.

Merill passed a hand wearily across his face, dropped the hand to the desk with a thump. "Okay, Marty, it fits," he said. "These characters go out for a Saturday or Sunday afternoon drive. They take a wrong turn onto a one-way access ramp and get trapped onto one of the highspeed expressways. They've never driven over 150 before in their lives and the expressway carrier beam forces them up to 280 or 300 and they panic, lock onto the automatic and then they're afraid to touch the controls until they reach a region where the automatics slow them for diverging traffic. And after that you're lucky if you can ever get them into something with wheels on it again."

"They sell their cars," Fisk said. "They stick to local tube and surface transportation. Used car buyers have come to spot these people, call them 'Panics.' A kook with out-of-state licenses drives in all glassy-eyed and trembling, asks: 'How much you give me for my car?' The dealer makes a killing, of course."

"Of course," Merill said. "Well, we've got to keep this

under wraps at least until after Congress passes the appropriation for the new trans-Huron expressway. After that . . ." He shrugged. "I don't know, but we'll think of something." He waved a hand to dismiss Fisk, bent to a report-corder that folded out of the desk and said, "Stay where I can get you in a hurry, Marty."

Within seconds, Fisk was out in the hallway facing the guidelanes to the high-speed ramp that would carry him to his own office. A man bumped into him and Fisk found that he was standing on the office lip reluctant to move out into the whizzing throngs of the corridor.

*No,* he thought, *I'm not reluctant. I'm afraid.*

He was honest enough with himself, though, to realize that he wasn't afraid of the high-speed ramp. It was what the ramp signified, where it could carry him.

*I wonder what my car would bring?* he asked himself. And he thought: *Would my wife move?* He dried his sweating palm on his sleeve before taking another green pill from his pocket and gulping it. Then he stepped out into the hall.

Saki (H. H. Munro)
# THE TOYS OF PEACE

> *In seeking solutions to our environmental prob-*
> *lems, we must be willing to accept failure—in the*
> *hope that each failure can lead to a fresh effort,*
> *a new beginning which may not come too late.*

———————◆•◉•◆———————

"Harvey," said Eleanor Bope, handing her brother a cutting from a London morning paper[1] of the 19th of March,
"just read this about children's toys, please; it exactly carries out some of our ideas about influence and upbringing."

"In the view of the National Peace Council," ran the extract, "there are grave objections to presenting our boys
with regiments of fighting men, batteries of guns, and
squadrons of 'Dreadnoughts.' Boys, the Council admits,
naturally love fighting and all the panoply of war . . . but
that is no reason for encouraging, and perhaps giving per-
manent form to, their primitive instincts. At the Children's
Welfare Exhibition, which opens at Olympia in three
weeks' time, the Peace Council will make an alternative
suggestion to parents in the shape of an exhibition of 'peace
toys.' In front of a specially painted representation of the
Peace Palace at The Hague will be grouped, not miniature
soldiers but miniature civilians, not guns but ploughs and
the tools of industry. . . . It is hoped that manufacturers
may take a hint from the exhibit, which will bear fruit in
the toy shops."

---

[1] An actual extract from a London paper of March 1914.

"The idea is certainly an interesting and very well-meaning one," said Harvey; "whether it would succeed well in practice—"

"We must try," interrupted his sister; "you are coming down to us at Easter, and you always bring the boys some toys, so that will be an excellent opportunity for you to inaugurate the new experiment. Go about in the shops and buy any little toys and models that have special bearing on civilian life in its more peaceful aspects. Of course you must explain the toys to the children and interest them in the new idea. I regret to say that the 'Siege of Adrianople' toy, that their Aunt Susan sent them, didn't need any explanation; they knew all the uniforms and flags, and even the names of the respective commanders, and when I heard them one day using what seemed to be the most objectionable language they said it was Bulgarian words of command; of course it *may* have been, but at any rate I took the toy away from them. Now I shall expect your Easter gifts to give quite a new impulse and direction to the children's minds; Eric is not eleven yet, and Bertie is only nine-and-a-half, so they are really at a most impressionable age."

"There is primitive instinct to be taken into consideration, you know," said Harvey doubtfully, "and hereditary tendencies as well. One of their great-uncles fought in the most intolerant fashion at Inkerman—he was specially mentioned in dispatches, I believe—and their great-grandfather smashed all his Whig neighbors' hothouses when the great Reform Bill was passed. Still, as you say, they are at an impressionable age. I will do my best."

On Easter Saturday Harvey Bope unpacked a large, promising-looking red cardboard box under the expectant eyes of his nephews. "Your uncle has brought you the newest thing in toys," Eleanor had said impressively, and youthful anticipation had been anxiously divided between Albanian soldiery and a Somali camel-corps. Eric was hotly in favor of the latter contingency. "There would be Arabs on horseback," he whispered; "the Albanians have got jolly uniforms, and they fight all day long, and all night too, when there's a moon, but the country's rocky, so they've got no cavalry."

A quantity of crinkly paper shavings was the first thing

that met the view when the lid was removed; the most exciting toys always began like that. Harvey pushed back the top layer and drew forth a square, rather featureless building.

"It's a fort!" exclaimed Bertie.

"It isn't, it's the palace of the Mpret of Albania," said Eric, immensely proud of his knowledge of the exotic title; "it's got no windows, you see, so that passers-by can't fire in at the Royal Family."

"It's a municipal dust-bin," said Harvey hurriedly; "you see all the refuse and litter of a town is collected there, instead of lying about and injuring the health of the citizens."

In an awful silence he disinterred a little lead figure of a man in black clothes.

"That," he said, "is a distinguished civilian, John Stuart Mill. He was an authority on political economy."

"Why?" asked Bertie.

"Well, he wanted to be; he thought it was a useful thing to be."

Bertie gave an expressive grunt, which conveyed his opinion that there was no accounting for tastes.

Another square building came out, this time with windows and chimneys.

"A model of the Manchester branch of the Young Women's Christian Association," said Harvey.

"Are there any lions?" asked Eric hopefully. He had been reading Roman history and thought that where you found Christians you might reasonably expect to find a few lions.

"There are no lions," said Harvey. "Here is another civilian, Robert Raikes, the founder of Sunday schools, and here is a model of a municipal wash-house. These little round things are loaves baked in a sanitary bakehouse. That lead figure is a sanitary inspector, this one is a district councillor, and this one is an official of the Local Government Board."

"What does he do?" asked Eric wearily.

"He sees to things connected with his Department," said Harvey. "This box with a slit in it is a ballot-box. Votes are put into it at election times."

"What is put into it at other times?" asked Bertie.

"Nothing. And here are some tools of industry, a wheelbarrow and a hoe, and I think these are meant for hop-poles. This is a model beehive, and that is a ventilator, for ventilating sewers. This seems to be another municipal dust-bin—no, it is a model of a school of art and a public library. This little lead figure is Mrs. Hemans, a poetess, and this is Rowland Hill, who introduced the system of penny postage. This is Sir John Herschel, the eminent astrologer."

"Are we to play with these civilian figures?" asked Eric.

"Of course," said Harvey, "these are toys; they are meant to be played with."

"But how?"

It was rather a poser. "You might make two of them contest a seat in Parliament," said Harvey, "and have an election—"

"With rotten eggs, and free fights, and ever so many broken heads!" exclaimed Eric.

"And noses all bleeding and everybody drunk as can be," echoed Bertie, who had carefully studied one of Hogarth's pictures.

"Nothing of the kind," said Harvey, "nothing in the least like that. Votes will be put in the ballot-box, and the Mayor will count them—the district councillor will do for the Mayor—and he will say which has received the most votes, and then the two candidates will thank him for presiding, and each will say that the contest has been conducted throughout in the pleasantest and most straightforward fashion, and they part with expressions of mutual esteem. There's a jolly game for you boys to play. I never had such toys when I was young."

"I don't think we'll play with them just now," said Eric, with an entire absence of the enthusiasm that his uncle had shown; "I think perhaps we ought to do a little of our holiday task. It's history this time; we've got to learn up something about the Bourbon period in France."

"The Bourbon period," said Harvey, with some disapproval in his voice.

"We've got to know something about Louis the Fourteenth," continued Eric; "I've learned the names of all the principal battles already."

This would never do. "There were, of course, some battles fought during his reign," said Harvey, "but I fancy the accounts of them were much exaggerated; news was very unreliable in those days, and there were practically no war correspondents, so generals and commanders could magnify every little skirmish they engaged in till they reached the proportions of decisive battles. Louis was really famous, now, as a landscape gardener; the way he laid out Versailles was so much admired that it was copied all over Europe."

"Do you know anything about Madame Du Barry?" asked Eric; "didn't she have her head chopped off?"

"She was another great lover of gardening," said Harvey evasively; "in fact, I believe the well-known rose Du Barry was named after her, and now I think you had better play for a little and leave your lessons till later."

Harvey retreated to the library and spent some thirty or forty minutes in wondering whether it would be possible to compile a history, for use in elementary schools, in which there should be no prominent mention of battles, massacres, murderous intrigues, and violent deaths. The York and Lancaster period and the Napoleonic era would, he admitted to himself, present considerable difficulties, and the Thirty Years' War would entail something of a gap if you left it out altogether. Still, it would be something gained if, at a highly impressionable age, children could be got to fix their attention on the invention of calico printing instead of the Spanish Armada or the Battle of Waterloo.

It was time, he thought, to go back to the boys' room, and see how they were getting on with their peace toys. As he stood outside the door he could hear Eric's voice raised in command; Bertie chimed in now and again with a helpful suggestion.

"That is Louis the Fourteenth," Eric was saying, "that one in knee-breeches, that Uncle said invented Sunday schools. It isn't a bit like him, but it'll have to do."

"We'll give him a purple coat from my paintbox by and by," said Bertie.

"Yes, an' red heels. That is Madame de Maintenon, that one he called Mrs. Hemans. She begs Louis not to go on this expedition, but he turns a deaf ear. He takes Marshal Saxe with him, and we must pretend that they have thousands of men with them. The watchword is *Qui vive?* and the answer is *L'état c'est moi*—that was one of his favorite remarks, you know. They land at Manchester in the dead of night, and a Jacobite conspirator gives them the keys of the fortress."

Peeping in through the doorway Harvey observed that the municipal dust-bin had been pierced with holes to accommodate the muzzles of imaginary cannon, and now represented the principal fortified position in Manchester; John Stuart Mill had been dipped in red ink, and apparently stood for Marshal Saxe.

"Louis orders his troops to surround the Young Women's Christian Association and seize the lot of them. 'Once back at the Louvre and the girls are mine,' he exclaims. We must use Mrs. Hemans again for one of the girls; she says 'Never,' and stabs Marshal Saxe to the heart."

"He bleeds dreadfully," exclaimed Bertie, splashing red ink liberally over the façade of the Association building.

"The soldiers rush in and avenge his death with the utmost savagery. A hundred girls are killed"—here Bertie emptied the remainder of the red ink over the devoted building—"and the surviving five hundred are dragged off to the French ships. 'I have lost a Marshal,' says Louis, 'but I do not go back empty-handed.' "

Harvey stole away from the room, and sought out his sister.

"Eleanor," he said, "the experiment—"

"Yes?"

"Has failed. We have begun too late."

J. G. Ballard

# THE SUBLIMINAL MAN

*We are all consumers, and each of us is influenced by advertising. But we must ask ourselves: What are we buying along with the new (!), the improved (!)? Where are we heading in our quest for economic growth?*

◆━━◆●◆━━◆

"The signs, Doctor! Have you seen the signs?"

Frowning with annoyance, Dr. Franklin quickened his pace and hurried down the hospital steps toward the line of parked cars. Over his shoulder he caught a glimpse of a man in ragged sandals and lime-stained jeans waving to him from the far side of the drive, then break into a run when he saw Franklin try to evade him.

"Dr. Franklin! The signs!"

Head down, Franklin swerved around an elderly couple approaching the out-patients department. His car was over a hundred yards away. Too tired to start running himself, he waited for the young man to catch him up.

"All right, Hathaway, what is it this time?" he snapped irritably. "I'm getting sick of you hanging around here all day."

Hathaway lurched to a halt in front of him, uncut black hair like an awning over his eyes. He brushed it back with a claw-like hand and turned on a wild smile, obviously glad to see Franklin and oblivious of the latter's hostility.

"I've been trying to reach you at night, Doctor, but your wife always puts the phone down on me," he explained without a hint of rancor, as if well-used to this kind of snub. "And I didn't want to look for you inside the Clinic." They were standing by a privet hedge that shielded them from the lower windows of the main administrative block, but Franklin's regular rendezvous with Hathaway and his strange messianic cries had already been the subject of amused comment.

Franklin began to say: "I appreciate that—" but Hathaway brushed this aside. "Forget it, Doctor, there are more important things happening now. They've started to build the first big signs! Over a hundred feet high, on the traffic islands just outside town. They'll soon have all the approach roads covered. When they do we might as well stop thinking."

"Your trouble is that you're thinking too much," Franklin told him. "You've been rambling about these signs for weeks now. Tell me, have you actually seen one signalling?"

Hathaway tore a handful of leaves from the hedge, exasperated by this irrelevancy. "Of course I haven't, that's the whole point, Doctor." He dropped his voice as a group of nurses walked past, watching him uneasily out of the corners of their eyes. "The construction gangs were out again last night, laying huge power cables. You'll see them on the way home. Everything's nearly ready now."

"They're traffic signs," Franklin explained patiently. "The flyover has just been completed. Hathaway, for God's sake relax. Try to think of Dora and the child."

"I *am* thinking of them!" Hathaway's voice rose to a controlled scream. "Those cables were 40,000-volt lines, Doctor, with terrific switch-gear. The trucks were loaded with enormous metal scaffolds. Tomorrow they'll start lifting them up all over the city, they'll block off half the sky! What do you think Dora will be like after six months of that? We've got to stop them, Doctor, they're trying to transistorize our brains!"

Embarrassed by Hathaway's high-pitched shouting, Franklin had momentarily lost his sense of direction and helplessly searched the sea of cars for his own. "Hathaway, I can't waste any more time talking to you. Believe me, you need skilled help, these obsessions are beginning to master you."

Hathaway started to protest, and Franklin raised his

right hand firmly. "Listen. For the last time, if you can show me one of these new signs, and prove that it's transmitting subliminal commands, I'll go to the police with you. But you haven't got a shred of evidence, and you know it. Subliminal advertising was banned thirty years ago, and the laws have never been repealed. Anyway, the technique was unsatisfactory; any success it had was marginal. Your idea of a huge conspiracy with all these thousands of giant signs everywhere is preposterous."

"All right, Doctor." Hathaway leaned against the bonnet of one of the cars. His moods seemed to switch abruptly from one level to the next. He watched Franklin amiably. "What's the matter—lost your car?"

"All your damned shouting has confused me." Franklin pulled out his ignition key and read the number off the tag: "NYN 299-566-367-21—can you see it?"

Hathaway leaned around lazily, one sandal up on the bonnet, surveying the square of a thousand or so cars facing them. "Difficult, isn't it, when they're all identical, even the same color? Thirty years ago there were about ten different makes, each in a dozen colors."

Franklin spotted his car, began to walk toward it. "Sixty years ago there were a hundred makes. What of it? The economies of standardization are obviously bought at a price."

Hathaway drummed his palm lightly on the roofs. "But these cars aren't all that cheap, Doctor. In fact, comparing them on an average income basis with those of thirty years ago they're about forty percent more expensive. With only one make being produced you'd expect a substantial reduction in price, not an increase."

"Maybe," Franklin said, opening his door. "But mechanically the cars of today are far more sophisticated. They're lighter, more durable, safer to drive."

Hathaway shook his head sceptically. "They *bore* me. The same model, same styling, same color, year after year. It's a sort of communism." He rubbed a greasy finger over the windshield. "This is a new one again, isn't it, Doctor? Where's the old one—you only had it for three months?"

"I traded it in," Franklin told him, starting the engine. "If you ever had any money you'd realize that it's the most

economical way of owning a car. You don't keep driving
the same one until it falls apart. It's the same with everything else—television sets, washing machines, refrigerators.
But you aren't faced with the problem—you haven't got
any."

Hathaway ignored the gibe and leaned his elbow on
Franklin's window. "Not a bad idea, either, Doctor. It
gives me time to think. I'm not working a twelve-hour
day to pay for a lot of things I'm too busy to use before
they're obsolete."

He waved as Franklin reversed the car out of its line,
then shouted into the wake of exhaust: "Drive with your
eyes closed, Doctor!"

On the way home Franklin kept carefully to the slowest
of the four-speed lanes. As usual after his discussions with
Hathaway he felt vaguely depressed. He realized that
unconsciously he envied Hathaway's footloose existence.
Despite the grimy cold-water apartment in the shadow and
roar of the flyover, despite his nagging wife and their sick
child, and the endless altercations with the landlord and
the supermarket credit manager, Hathaway still retained
his freedom intact. Spared any responsibilities, he could
resist the smallest encroachment upon him by the rest of
society, if only by generating obsessive fantasies, such as
his latest one about subliminal advertising.

The ability to react to stimuli, even irrationally, was a
valid criterion of freedom. By contrast, what freedom
Franklin possessed was peripheral, sharply demarked by
the manifold responsibilities in the center of his life—the
three mortgages on his home, the mandatory rounds of
cocktail and TV parties, the private consultancy occupying
most of Saturday which paid the instalments on the multitude of household gadgets, clothes and past holidays.
About the only time he had to himself was driving to and
from work.

But at least the roads were magnificent. Whatever other
criticisms might be leveled at the present society, it certainly knew how to build roads. Eight-, ten- and twelve-lane
expressways interlaced across the continent, plunging from
overhead causeways into the giant car parks in the center
of the cities, or dividing into the great suburban arteries

with their multiacre parking aprons around the marketing centers. Together the roadways and car parks covered more than a third of the country's entire area, and in the neighborhood of the cities the proportion was higher. The old cities were surrounded by the vast, dazzling abstract sculptures of the clover-leaves and flyovers, but even so the congestion was unremitting.

The ten-mile journey to his home in fact covered over twenty-five miles and took him twice as long as it had done before the construction of the expressway, the additional miles contained within the three- giant cloverleaves. New cities were springing from the motels, cafés and car marts around the highways. At the slightest hint of an intersection a shanty town of shacks and filling stations sprawled away among the forest of electric signs and route indicators, many of them substantial cities.

All around him cars bulleted along, streaming toward the suburbs. Relaxed by the smooth motion of the car, Franklin edged outward into the next speed-lane. As he accelerated from 40 to 50 mph a strident ear-jarring noise drummed out from his tires, shaking the chassis of the car. Ostensibly an aid to lane discipline, the surface of the road was covered with a mesh of small rubber studs, spaced progressively further apart in each of the lanes so that the tire hum resonated exactly on 40, 50, 60, and 70 mph. Driving at an intermediate speed for more than a few seconds became physiologically painful, and soon resulted in damage to the car and tires.

When the studs wore out they were replaced by slightly different patterns, matching those on the latest tires, so that regular tire changes were necessary, increasing the safety and efficiency of the expressway. It also increased the revenues of the car and tire manufacturers, for most cars over six months old soon fell to pieces under the steady battering, but this was regarded as a desirable end, the greater turnover reducing the unit price and making necessary more frequent model changes, as well as ridding the roads of dangerous vehicles.

A quarter of a mile ahead, at the approach to the first of the clover-leaves, the traffic stream was slowing, huge police signs signaling "Lanes Closed Ahead" and "Drop Speed by 10 mph." Franklin tried to return to the previous lane, but the cars were jammed bumper to bumper. As the chassis began to shudder and vibrate, jarring his spine, he clamped his teeth and tried to restrain himself from sounding the horn. Other drivers were less self-controlled, and everywhere engines were plunging and snarling, horns blaring. Road taxes were now so high, up to 30 percent of income (by contrast, income taxes were a bare 2 percent) that any delay on the expressways called for an immediate government inquiry, and the major departments of state were concerned with the administration of the road systems.

Nearer the clover-leaf the lanes had been closed to allow a gang of construction workers to erect a massive metal sign on one of the traffic islands. The palisaded area swarmed with engineers and surveyors and Franklin assumed that this was the sign Hathaway had seen unloaded the previous night. His apartment was in one of the gimcrack buildings in the settlement that straggled away around a nearby flyover, a low-rent area inhabited by service station personnel, waitresses and other migrant labor.

The sign was enormous, at least a hundred feet high, fitted with heavy concave grilles similar to radar bowls. Rooted in a series of concrete caissons, it reared high into the air above the approach roads, visible for miles. Franklin craned up at the grilles, tracing the power cables from the transformers up into the intricate mesh of metal coils that covered their surface. A line of red aircraft-warning beacons was already alight along the top strut, and Franklin assumed that the sign was part of the ground approach system of the city airport ten miles to the east.

Three minutes later, as he accelerated down the two-mile link of straight highway to the next clover-leaf, he saw the second of the giant signs looming up into the sky before him.

Changing down into the 40 mph lane, Franklin uneasily watched the great bulk of the second sign recede in his rearview mirror. Although there were no graphic symbols among the wire coils covering the grilles, Hathaway's warnings still sounded in his ears. Without knowing why, he felt sure that the signs were not part of the airport approach system. Neither of them was in line with the principal airlanes. To justify the expense of siting them in the center of the expressway—the second sign required elaborate angled buttresses to support it on the narrow island—obviously meant that their role related in some way to the traffic streams.

Two hundred yards away was a roadside auto-mart, and Franklin abruptly remembered that he needed some cigarettes. Swinging the car down the entrance ramp, he joined the queue slowly passing the self-service dispenser at the far end of the rank. The auto-mart was packed with cars, each of the five purchasing ranks lined with tired-looking men hunched over their wheels.

Inserting his coins (paper money was no longer in circulation, unmanageable by the automats) he took a carton from the dispenser. This was the only brand of cigarettes available—in fact there was only one brand of everything—though giant economy packs were an alternative. Moving off, he opened the dashboard locker.

Inside, still sealed in their wrappers, were three other cartons.

A strong fish-like smell pervaded the house when he reached home, steaming out from the oven in the kitchen. Sniffing it uneagerly, Franklin took off his coat and hat, and found his wife crouched over the TV set in the lounge. An announcer was dictating a stream of numbers, and Judith scribbled them down on a pad, occasionally cursing under her breath. "What a muddle!" she snapped finally. "He was talking so quickly I took only a few things down."

"Probably deliberate," Franklin commented. "New panel game?"

Judith kissed him on the cheek, discreetly hiding the ashtray loaded with cigarette butts and chocolate wrappings. "Hullo, darling, sorry not to have a drink ready for you. They've started this series of Spot Bargains. They give you a selection of things on which you get a ninety percent trade-in discount at the local stores, if you're in the right area and have the right serial numbers. It's all terribly complicated."

"Sounds good, though. What have you got?"

Judith peered at her checklist. "Well, as far as I can

see the only thing is the infra-red barbecue spit. But we have to be there before eight o'clock tonight. It's seven-thirty already."

"Then that's out. I'm tired, angel, I need something to eat." When Judith started to protest he added firmly: "Look, I don't want a new infra-red barbecue spit; we've only had this one for two months. Damn it, it's not even a different model."

"But, darling, don't you see, it makes it cheaper if you keep buying new ones. We'll have to trade ours in at the end of the year anyway, we signed the contract, and this way we save at least twenty dollars. These Spot Bargains aren't just a gimmick, you know. I've been glued to that set all day." A note of irritation had crept into her voice, but Franklin sat his ground, doggedly ignoring the clock.

"Right, we lose twenty dollars. It's worth it." Before she could remonstrate he said, "Judith, please, you probably took the wrong number down anyway." As she shrugged and went over to the bar he called, "Make it a stiff one. I see we have health foods on the menu."

"They're good for you, darling. You know you can't live on ordinary foods all the time. They don't contain any proteins or vitamins. You're always saying we ought to be like people in the old days and eat nothing but health foods."

"I would, but they smell so awful." Franklin lay back, nose in the glass of whiskey, gazing at the darkened skyline outside.

A quarter of a mile away, gleaming out above the roof of the neighborhood supermarket, were the five red beacon lights. Now and then, as the headlamps of the Spot Bargainers swung up across the face of the building, he could see the square massive bulk of the giant sign clearly silhouetted against the evening sky.

"Judith!" He went into the kitchen and took her over to the window. "That sign, just behind the supermarket. When did they put it up?"

"I don't know." Judith peered at him curiously. "Why are you so worried, Robert? Isn't it something to do with the airport?"

Franklin stared thoughtfully at the dark hull of the sign. "So everyone probably thinks."

Carefully he poured his whiskey into the sink.

After parking his car on the supermarket apron at seven o'clock the next morning, Franklin carefully emptied his pockets and stacked the coins in the dashboard locker. The supermarket was already busy with early morning shoppers and the line of thirty turnstiles clicked and slammed. Since the introduction of the "twenty-four-hour spending day" the shopping complex was never closed. The bulk of the shoppers were discount buyers, housewives contracted to make huge volume purchases of food, clothing and appliances against substantial overall price cuts, and forced to drive around all day from supermarket to supermarket, frantically trying to keep pace with their purchase schedules and grappling with the added incentives inserted to keep the schemes alive.

Many of the women had teamed up, and as Franklin walked over to the entrance a pack of them charged toward their cars, stuffing their pay slips into their bags and gesticulating at each other. A moment later their cars roared off in a convoy to the next marketing zone.

A large neon sign over the entrance listed the latest discount—a mere 5 percent—calculated on the volume of turnover. The highest discounts, sometimes up to 25 percent, were earned in the housing estates where junior white-collar workers lived. There, spending had a strong social incentive, and the desire to be the highest spender in the neighborhood was given moral reinforcement by the system of listing all the names and their accumulating cash totals on a huge electric sign in the supermarket foyers. The higher the spender, the greater his contribution to the discounts enjoyed by others. The lowest spenders were regarded as social criminals, free-riding on the backs of others.

Luckily this system had yet to be adopted in Franklin's neighborhood. Not because the professional men and their wives were able to exercise more discretion, but because their higher incomes allowed them to contract into more expensive discount schemes operated by the big department stores in the city.

Ten yards from the entrance Franklin paused, looking up at the huge metal sign mounted in an enclosure at the edge of the car park. Unlike the other signs and hoardings that proliferated everywhere, no attempt had been made to decorate it, or disguise the gaunt bare rectangle of riveted steel mesh. Power lines wound down its sides, and the concrete surface of the car park was crossed by a long scar where a cable had been sunk.

Franklin strolled along, then fifty feet from the sign stopped and turned, realizing that he would be late for the hospital and needed a new carton of cigarettes. A dim but powerful humming emanated from the transformers below the sign, fading as he retraced his steps to the supermarket.

Going over to the automats in the foyer, he felt for his change, then whistled sharply when he remembered why he had deliberately emptied his pockets.

"The cunning thing!" he said, loud enough for two shoppers to stare at him. Reluctant to look directly at the sign, he watched its reflection in one of the glass door-panes, so that any subliminal message would be reversed.

Almost certainly he had received two distinct signals—"Keep Away" and "Buy Cigarettes." The people who normally parked their cars along the perimeter of the apron were avoiding the area under the enclosure, the cars describing a loose semicircle fifty feet around it.

He turned to the janitor sweeping out the foyer. "What's that sign for?"

The man leaned on his broom, gazing dully at the sign. "Dunno," he said, "must be something to do with the airport." He had an almost fresh cigarette in his mouth, but his right hand reached unconsciously to his hip pocket and pulled out a pack. He drummed the second cigarette absently on his thumbnail as Franklin walked away.

Everyone entering the supermarket was buying cigarettes.

Cruising quietly along the 40 mph lane, Franklin began to take a closer interest in the landscape around him. Usually he was either too tired or too preoccupied to do more than think about his driving, but now he examined the expressway methodically, scanning the roadside cafés for any smaller versions of the new signs. A host of neon displays covered the doorways and windows, but most of them seemed innocuous, and he turned his attention to the larger billboards erected along the open stretches of the expressway. Many of these were as high as four-story houses, elaborate three-dimensional devices in which giant glossy-skinned housewives with electric eyes and teeth jerked and postured around their ideal kitchens, neon flashes exploding from their smiles.

The areas on either side of the expressway were waste-land, continuous junkyards filled with cars and trucks, washing machines and refrigerators, all perfectly workable but jettisoned by the economic pressure of the succeeding waves of discount models. Their intact chrome hardly tarnished, the mounds of metal shells and cabinets glittered in the sunlight. Nearer the city the billboards were sufficiently close together to hide them, but now and then, as he slowed to approach one of the flyovers, Franklin caught a glimpse of the huge pyramids of metal, gleaming silently like the refuse grounds of some forgotten El Dorado.

That evening Hathaway was waiting for him as he came down the hospital steps. Franklin waved him across the court, then led the way quickly to his car.

"What's the matter, Doctor?" Hathaway asked as Franklin wound up the windows and glanced around the lines of parked cars. "Is someone after you?"

Franklin laughed somberly. "I don't know. I hope not, but if what you say is right, I suppose there is."

Hathaway leaned back with a chuckle, propping one knee up on the dashboard. "So you've seen something, Doctor, after all."

"Well, I'm not sure yet, but there's just a chance you may be right. This morning at the Fairlawne super-market—" He broke off, uneasily remembering the huge blank sign and the abrupt way in which he had turned back to the supermarket as he approached it, then described his encounter.

Hathaway nodded slowly. "I've seen the sign there. It's big, but not as big as some that are going up. They're building them everywhere now. All over the city. What are you going to do, Doctor?"

Franklin gripped the wheel tightly. Hathaway's thinly veiled amusement irritated him. "Nothing, of course. Damn it, it may be just auto-suggestion, you've probably got me imagining—"

Hathaway sat up with a jerk, his face mottled and savage. "Don't be absurd, Doctor! If you can't believe your own senses what chance have you left? They're invading your brain; if you don't defend yourself they'll take it over completely! We've got to act now, before we're all paralyzed."

Wearily Franklin raised one hand to restrain him. "Just a minute. Assuming that these signs *are* going up everywhere, what would be their object? Apart from wasting the enormous amount of capital invested in all the other millions of signs and billboards, the amounts of discretionary spending power still available must be infinitesimal. Some of the present mortgage and discount schemes reach half a century ahead, so there can't be much slack left to take up. A big trade war would be disastrous."

"Quite right, Doctor," Hathaway rejoined evenly, "but you're forgetting one thing. What would supply that extra spending power? A big increase in production. Already they've started to raise the working day from twelve hours to fourteen. In some of the appliances plants around the city Sunday working is being introduced as a norm. Can you visualize it, Doctor—a seven-day week, everyone with at least three jobs."

Franklin shook his head. "People won't stand for it."

"They will. Within the last twenty-five years the gross national product has risen by fifty percent, but so have the average hours worked. Ultimately we'll all be working and spending twenty-four hours a day, seven days a week. No one will dare refuse. Think what a slump would mean —millions of lay-offs, people with time on their hands and nothing to spend it on. Real leisure, not just time spent buying things." He seized Franklin by the shoulder. "Well, Doctor, are you going to join me?"

Franklin freed himself. Half a mile away, partly hidden by the four-story bulk of the Pathology Department, was the upper half of one of the giant signs, workmen still crawling across its girders. The airlines over the city had deliberately been routed away from the hospital, and the sign obviously had no connection with approaching aircraft.

"Isn't there a prohibition on subliminal living? How can the unions accept it?"

"The fear of a slump. You know the new economic dogmas. Unless output rises by a steady inflationary 5 percent the economy is stagnating. Ten years ago increased efficiency alone would raise output, but the advantages there are minimal now and only one thing is left. More work. Increased consumption and subliminal advertising will provide the spur."

"What are you planning to do?"

"I can't tell you, Doctor, unless you accept equal responsibility for it."

"Sounds rather Quixotic," Franklin commented. "Tilting at windmills. You won't be able to chop those things down with an axe."

"I won't try." Hathaway suddenly gave up and opened the door. "Don't wait too long to make up your mind, Doctor. By then it may not be yours to make up." With a wave he was gone.

On the way home Franklin's scepticism returned. The idea of the conspiracy was preposterous, and the economic arguments were too plausible. As usual, though, there had been a hook in the soft bait Hathaway dangled before him—Sunday working. His own consultancy had been extended into Sunday morning with his appointment as visiting factory doctor to one of the automobile plants that had started Sunday shifts. But instead of resenting this incursion into his already meager hours of leisure he had been glad. For one frightening reason—he needed the extra income.

Looking out over the lines of scurrying cars, he noticed that at least a dozen of the great signs had been erected along the expressway. As Hathaway had said, more were going up everywhere, rearing over the supermarkets in the housing developments like rusty metal sails.

Judith was in the kitchen when he reached home, watching the TV program on the hand-set over the cooker. Franklin climbed past a big cardboard carton, its seals still unbroken, which blocked the doorway, and kissed her on the cheek as she scribbled numbers down on her pad. The pleasant odor of pot-roast chicken—or, rather, a gelatine dummy of a chicken fully flavored and free of any toxic or nutritional properties—mollified his irritation at finding her still playing the Spot Bargains.

He tapped the carton with his foot. "What's this?"

"No idea, darling, something's always coming these days, I can't keep up with it all." She peered through the glass door at the chicken—an economy twelve-pounder, the size of a turkey, with stylized legs and wings and an enormous breast, most of which would be discarded at the end of the meal (there were no dogs or cats these days, the crumbs from the rich man's table saw to that) and then glanced at him pointedly.

"You look rather worried, Robert. Bad day?"

Franklin murmured noncommittally. The hours spent trying to detect false clues in the faces of the Spot Bargain announcers had sharpened Judith's perceptions, and he felt a pang of sympathy for the legion of husbands similarly outmatched.

"Have you been talking to that crazy beatnik again?"

"Hathaway? As a matter of fact I have. He's not all that crazy." He stepped backward into the carton, almost spilling his drink. "Well, what is this thing? As I'll be working for the next fifty Sundays to pay for it I'd like to find out."

He searched the sides, finally located the label. *"A TV set?* Judith, do we need another one? We've already got three. Lounge, dining room, and the hand-set. What's the fourth for?"

"The guest room, dear, don't get so excited. We can't leave a hand-set in the guest room, it's rude. I'm trying to economize, but four TV sets is the bare minimum. All the magazines say so."

*"And* three radios?" Franklin stared irritably at the carton. "If we do invite a guest here how much time is he going to spend alone in his room watching television? Judith, we've got to call a halt. It's not as if these things were free, or even cheap. Anyway, television is a total

waste of time. There's only one program. It's ridiculous to have four sets."

"Robert, there are *four* channels."

"But only the commercials are different." Before Judith could reply the telephone rang. Franklin lifted the kitchen receiver, listened to the gabble of noise that poured from it. At first he wondered whether this was some off-beat prestige commercial, then realized it was Hathaway in a manic swing.

"Hathaway!" he shouted back. "Relax, man! What's the matter now?"

"—Doctor, you'll have to believe me this time. I tell you I got on to one of the islands with a stroboscope; they've got hundreds of high-speed shutters blasting away like machine-guns straight into people's faces and they can't see a thing, it's fantastic! The next big campaign's going to be cars and TV sets, they're trying to swing a two-month model change—can you imagine it, Doctor, a new car every two months? God Almighty, it's just—"

Franklin waited impatiently as the five-second commercial break cut in (all telephone calls were free, the length of the commercial extending with range—for long-distance calls the ratio of commercial to conversation was as high as 10:1, the participants desperately trying to get a word in edgeways between the interminable interruptions), but just before it ended he abruptly put the telephone down, then removed the receiver from the cradle.

Judith came over and took his arm. "Robert, what's the matter? You look terribly strained."

Franklin picked up his drink and walked through into the lounge. "It's just Hathaway. As you say, I'm getting a little too involved with him. He's starting to prey on my mind."

He looked at the dark outline of the sign over the supermarket, its red warning lights glowing in the night sky. Blank and nameless, like an area forever closed-off in an insane mind, what frightened him was its total anonymity.

"Yet I'm not sure," he muttered. "So much of what Hathaway says makes sense. These subliminal techniques are the sort of last-ditch attempt you'd expect from an overcapitalized industrial system."

He waited for Judith to reply, then looked up at her.

She stood in the center of the carpet, hands folded limply, her sharp, intelligent face curiously dull and blunted. He followed her gaze out over the rooftops, then with an effort turned his head and quickly switched on the TV set.

"Come on," he said grimly. "Let's watch television. God, we're going to need that fourth set."

A week later Franklin began to compile his inventory. He saw nothing more of Hathaway; as he left the hospital in the evening the familiar scruffy figure was absent. When the first of the explosions sounded dimly around the city and he read of the attempts to sabotage the giant signs he automatically assumed that Hathaway was responsible, but later he heard on a newscast that the detonations had been set off by construction workers excavating foundations.

More of the signs appeared over the rooftops, isolated on the palisaded islands near the suburban shopping centers. Already there were over thirty on the ten-mile route from the hospital, standing shoulder to shoulder over the speeding cars like giant dominoes. Franklin had given up his attempt to avoid looking at them, but the slim possibility that the explosions might be Hathaway's counterattack kept his suspicions alive.

He began his inventory after hearing the newscast, discovered that in the previous fortnight he and Judith had traded in their

> Car (previous model 2 months old)
> 2 TV sets (4 months)
> Power mower (7 months)
> Electric cooker (5 months)
> Hair dryer (4 months)
> Refrigerator (3 months)
> 2 radios (7 months)
> Record player (5 months)
> Cocktail bar (8 months)

Half these purchases had been made by himself, but exactly when he could never recall realizing at the time. The car, for example, he had left in the garage near the hospital to be greased; that evening he had signed for the new model as he sat at its wheel, accepting the salesman's assurance that the depreciation on the two-month trade-in was virtually less than the cost of the grease-job. Ten minutes later, as he sped along the expressway, he suddenly realized that he had bought a new car. Similarly, the TV sets had been replaced by identical models after developing the same irritating interference pattern (curiously, the new sets also displayed the pattern, but as the salesman assured them, this promptly vanished two days later.)

*Not once had he actually decided of his own volition that he wanted something and then gone out to a store and bought it!*

He carried the inventory around with him, adding to it as necessary, quietly and without protest analyzing these new sales techniques, wondering whether total capitulation might be the only way of defeating them. As long as he kept up even a token resistance, the inflationary growth curve would show a controlled annual 10 percent climb. With that resistance removed, however, it would begin to rocket upward out of control. . . .

Then, driving home from the hospital two months later, he saw one of the signs for the first time.

He was in the 40 mph lane, unable to keep up with the flood of new cars, had just passed the second of the three clover-leaves when the traffic half a mile away began to slow down. Hundreds of cars had driven up on to the grass verge, and a large crowd was gathering around one of the signs. Two small black figures were climbing up the metal face, and a series of huge grid-like patterns of light flashed on and off, illuminating the evening air. The patterns were random and broken, as if the sign was being tested for the first time.

Relieved that Hathaway's suspicions had been completely groundless, Franklin turned off onto the soft shoulder, then walked forward through the spectators as the lights blinked and stuttered in their faces. Below, behind the steel palisades around the island, was a large group of police and engineers, craning up at the men scaling the sign a hundred feet over their heads.

Suddenly Franklin stopped, the sense of relief fading instantly. With a jolt he saw that several of the police on the ground were armed with shot-guns, and that the two policemen climbing the sign carried submachine-guns slung over their shoulders. They were converging on a third figure, crouched by a switchbox on the penultimate tier, a ragged bearded man in a grimy shirt, a bare knee poking through his jeans.

Hathaway!

Franklin hurried toward the island, the sign hissing and spluttering, fuses blowing by the dozen.

Then the flicker of lights cleared and steadied, blazing out continuously, and together the crowd looked up at the decks of brilliant letters. The phrases, and every combination of them possible, were entirely familiar, and Franklin knew that he had been reading them unconsciously in his mind for weeks as he passed up and down the expressway.

BUY NOW BUY NOW BUY NOW BUY NOW
BUY NOW NEW CAR NOW NEW CAR NOW
NEW CAR NOW YES YES YES YES YES YES
YES YES YES YES YES

Sirens blaring, two patrol cars swung up onto the verge through the crowd and plunged across the damp grass. Police spilled from its doors, batons in their hands, and quickly began to force back the crowd. Franklin held his ground as they approached, started to say: "Officer, I know the man—" but the policeman punched him in the chest with the flat of his hand. Winded, he stumbled back among the cars, leaned helplessly against a fender as the police began to break the windshields, the hapless drivers protesting angrily, those further back rushing for their vehicles.

The noise fell away abruptly when one of the submachine-guns fired a brief roaring burst, then rose in a massive gasp of horror as Hathaway, arms outstretched, let out a cry of triumph and pain, and jumped.

"But, Robert, what does it really matter?" Judith asked as Franklin sat inertly in the lounge the next morning. "I know it's tragic for his wife and daughter, but Hathaway was in the grip of an obsession. If he hated advertising signs so much why didn't he dynamite those we *can* see, instead of worrying so much about those we can't?"

Franklin stared at the TV screen, hoping the program would distract him.

"Hathaway was *right*," he said simply.

"Was he? Advertising is here to stay. We've no real freedom of choice, anyway. We can't spend more than we can afford, the finance companies soon clamp down."

"You accept that?" Franklin went over to the window. A quarter of a mile away, in the center of the estate, another of the signs was being erected. It was due east from them, and in the early morning light the shadows of its rectangular superstructure fell across the garden, reaching almost to the steps of the French windows at his feet. As a concession to the neighborhood, and perhaps to allay any suspicions while it was being erected by an appeal to petty snobbery the lower sections had been encased in mock-Tudor paneling.

Franklin stared at it numbly, counting the half-dozen police lounging by their patrol cars as the construction gang unloaded prefabricated grilles from a couple of trucks. Then he looked at the sign by the supermarket, trying to repress his memories of Hathaway and the pathetic attempts the man had made to convince Franklin and gain his help.

He was still standing there an hour later when Judith came in, putting on her hat and coat, ready to visit the supermarket.

Franklin followed her to the door. "I'll drive you down there, Judith," he said in a flat dead voice. "I have to see about booking a new car. The next models are coming out at the end of the month. With luck we'll get one of the early deliveries."

They walked out into the trim drive, the shadows of the great signs swinging across the quiet neighborhood as the day progressed, sweeping over the heads of the people on their way to the supermarket like the dark blades of enormous scythes.

Steven Schrader

# THE COHEN DOG EXCLUSION ACT

*Smog and smaze, incinerators and automobiles
are not the only urban environmental problems.
For some, a stroll down city streets raises a disturbing question: Is man's best friend still man's
best friend?*

---

The doctors at the institute are pleased with my progress.
The medication has calmed me. They're talking of letting
me go home weekends. Only I have no place to go. Which
is disgraceful. You'd think the city would have paid my
rent or would at least find me a place to live now that I'm
ready to be released. After all, I've done great service for
them, been personally responsible for vast improvements.
Perhaps I overdid certain aspects of my plan, but, looking
back, I see no way to have effected change without radical,
even bizarre acts. I sacrificed my freedom in a worthy
cause. The administration, of course, is not interested in
such heroism. They are internationalists. Speak of overpopulation or ecology and they will immediately hold a
dinner for your cause; apply for a permit for a peace
demonstration and you will receive one before you complete your application. But try something closer to home,
try to improve the quality of city life, and see how quickly
obstacles are placed before you, how soon politics enters.
Such is democracy. Heads of state, like everyone else, are
interested in their own welfare. The people can go to hell.

Well, great ideas like mine are simple and become obvious after their fulfillment. But if you are the first to follow an idea through you know perfectly well what happens. You will be called dangerous, thrown in jail or, like I was, locked up in Long Island like a madman. But at least I have my achievement to comfort me—the Cohen Dog Exclusion Act passed by the City Council. My only regret is that it was not called the Seymour Cohen Dog Exclusion Act. For I am sure other Cohens are right now pretending they are responsible, scrambling for the honor, assuming the credit, while I rot in Long Island unable to set the record straight.

The dogs were disturbing me greatly. I wrote letters to all the heads of departments. From some I received replies. Thank you for your interest. We will look into the matter you have complained about and let you know if anything definite comes of our investigation or if you can be of further help to us. Please do not contact us again unless we request you to. Official city business requires so much time and effort that second letters on unsolicited matters assume an untenable burden on our limited staff. Sincerely yours, Commissioner Plotz.

Conditions grew worse. Wherever you looked there was dog shit. In the morning young ladies who had moved to the renovated brownstones on my block walked their German shepherds on the sidewalk, in the curb, and the center of the street. Some of the dogs were unleashed, all of them sniffing away, peeing and shitting. The owners gossiped to one another, and some men, I'm sure, bought dogs for the sole purpose of meeting girls. I thought of it myself, could imagine smooth conversations with them while our dogs took craps at our feet. But I'm not a hypocrite. I can't hide my feelings. I don't understand how people can chat casually while their dogs shit all around them.

The block began to have an odor, perhaps a city-wide odor—the collective smell of dog shit—but it seemed that my block had its own particular smell, that our dogs ate one brand of dog food or suffered from one type of anxiety which resulted in a sweet, cloying, musty odor.

I approached people on the block. First, Woofer, the psychiatrist, who was dragged in his gray, baggy, innocuous suit up the middle of the block every morning by his German shepherd.

"How can you stand it?" I asked. "Your dog shitting away. Turds all over. Isn't it disgusting? Suppose I were to do that?"

"You've got a shit hang-up," he said. "Anal oriented. Relax. Give away your coin collection. Accept your own shit and the shit of animals."

"Never. There must be an alternate solution. A place to take them. Up on a roof. Toilets. A dog pissoir."

Woofer laughed. He was carried away by his brute.

I approached several of the girl owners, but they blushed and refused to answer. One in a yellow sweater and leather skirt, thin with pointy boobs, set her beast on me.

"Attack, Ringo," she ordered and I dashed up the street, just managing to close the door on him.

Every day I stepped in dog shit. I dreamed of it. At work I was preoccupied by it. One morning as the coffee break was over and I was on my way to the bathroom to delay the boredom of work a little longer I thought of the solution. I would piss on the floor like a dog. I pictured everyone doing it. We'd need an attendant with a mop and pail.

"Here, boy," we'd shout, and a man in a white uniform and hat would come running.

I finally did go to the bathroom. The office wasn't the place. The street was better, more dramatic. Everyone would see. I thought of stickers and buttons. A huge campaign. Rallies in Madison Square Garden.

The next morning I went out at eight, the height of dog activity. They were promenading, shitting, pissing, barking, frolicking, chasing balls and sticks. I went to a tree in the middle of the block, loosened my pants, let them fall with my underwear, and squatted. A girl nearby gasped.

"Come away, Fang," she called.

Heads poked out of windows, shouting, "Stop it, pervert."

A little girl giggled. "Mommy, the man's making do-do."

I took my time, squatting above the earth.

A squad car turned down the block, arriving as quickly as if I had shot a policeman. Both officers jumped out of the car. The girl who'd seen me first sobbingly told what had happened. Woofer was there, too. "Anal neurosis," he told the police and shook his head.

The cops walked over. I was just tucking my shirt in.

They both had moustaches and long sideburns. I could tell they'd taken human relations courses.

"Did you do that?" one cop asked politely, his hand indicating my shit.

"I don't deny it."

"Uh, huh. Well, it's against the law, mister. I'm going to write out a summons." He looked at his partner. "What should I put down? Littering, causing a public disturbance, obscenity?"

"Put 'em all down," the other cop said.

He filled out the ticket and handed it to me.

"Don't do it again. You'll get in trouble."

At court I passed out Xeroxed statements explaining my position. I had prepared it secretly on my job. IF DOGS WHY NOT MEN?

The courtroom was packed. The judge looked like Woofer, but more impressive in robes. Underneath, though, I knew his suit was baggy.

"Seymour, you have committed an outrage on the people," he said.

I handed him a Xeroxed sheet.

"Damn it, you're mad. You're going to be locked up next time."

He fined me and banged the gavel.

Spectators began shouting and fighting. Outside on the steps people came up to me.

"We're with you," they shouted. They elected me chairman.

The next morning my street was filled with newspaper reporters and television cameramen. A dozen of my group stationed themselves at trees, squatted, and began shitting. Squad cars pulled up from all over. Flashbulbs popped.

"Get Cohen," the captain said. They handcuffed me and pushed me into a squad car. At Bellevue Woofer filled out the papers.

"You can't stop us," I shouted. "It's out of control."

"Anal paranoid," he yelled back.

I read about it at the hospital library in the back issues of *The Times*. Two days after my arrest *The Times* did an exposé of dog shit, pointing to a high correlation with cancer, asthma, and crime. A Central Park Shit-In drew four thousand participants. Civil strife grew. Both sides wore buttons. One showed a man shitting. The other the silhouette of a Scotty.

The movement to outlaw dogs was gaining, and the Mayor came to see me in the hospital. He resembled Woofer, though he was taller and more handsome. His suit fit well, but there was still something baggy about it.

"My career's at stake," he said. "You're the only one who can save me, Cohen. Recant and I won't have to take a stand. I'll appoint you to the U.N. Anything."

I barked at him, pulled up my hospital gown, and started to shit.

He resigned before the bill was passed.

The police are rounding up dogs as best they can. A thousand trainees have been added to the force. Of course it's an impossible task. Dogs will always be hidden by addict owners. But at least they will remain indoors. Dog shit in the city is at an end. I can't wait to get out and see for myself.

Isaac Asimov

# IT'S SUCH A BEAUTIFUL DAY

> *Solutions to our environmental problems are as complex as our relations with the environment. Some interest, some understanding, and some awareness may, however, start us in the right direction.*

On April 12, 2117, the field-modulator brake-valve in the Door belonging to Mrs. Richard Hanshaw depolarized for reasons unknown. As a result, Mrs. Hanshaw's day was completely upset and her son, Richard, Jr., first developed his strange neurosis.

It was not the type of thing you would find listed as a neurosis in the usual textbooks and certainly young Richard behaved, in most respects, just as a well-brought-up twelve-year-old in prosperous circumstances ought to behave.

And yet from April 12 on, Richard Hanshaw, Jr., could only with regret ever persuade himself to go through a Door.

Of all this, on April 12, Mrs. Hanshaw had no premonition. She woke in the morning (an ordinary morning) as her mekkano slithered gently into her room, with a cup of coffee on a small tray. Mrs. Hanshaw was planning a visit to New York in the afternoon and she had several things to do first that could not quite be trusted to a mekkano, so after one or two sips, she stepped out of bed.

The mekkano backed away, moving silently along the diamagnetic field that kept its oblong body half an inch above the floor, and moved back to the kitchen, where its simple computer was quite adequate to set the proper controls on the various kitchen appliances in order that an appropriate breakfast might be prepared.

Mrs. Hanshaw, having bestowed the usual sentimental glance upon the cubograph of her dead husband, passed through the stages of her morning ritual with a certain contentment. She could hear her son across the hall clattering through his, but she knew she need not interfere with him. The mekkano was well adjusted to see to it, as a matter of course, that he was showered, that he had on a change of clothing, and that he would eat a nourishing breakfast. The tergo-shower she had had installed the year before made the morning wash and dry so quick and pleasant that, really, she felt certain Dickie would wash even without supervision.

On a morning like this, when she was busy, it would certainly not be necessary for her to do more than deposit a casual peck on the boy's cheek before he left. She heard the soft chime the mekkano sounded to indicate approaching school time and she floated down the force-lift to the lower floor (her hair-style for the day only sketchily designed, as yet) in order to perform that motherly duty.

She found Richard standing at the door, with his textreels and pocket projector dangling by their strap and a frown on his face.

"Say, Mom," he said, looking up, "I dialed the school's co-ords but nothing happens."

She said, almost automatically, "Nonsense, Dickie. I never heard of such a thing."

"Well, you try."

Mrs. Hanshaw tried a number of times. Strange, the school door was always set for general reception. She tried other coordinates. Her friends' Doors might not be set for reception, but there would be a signal at least, and then she could explain.

But nothing happened at all. The Door remained an inactive gray barrier despite all her manipulations. It was obvious that the Door was out of order—and only five months after its annual fall inspection by the company.

She was quite angry about it.

It *would* happen on a day when she had much planned. She thought petulantly of the fact that a month earlier she had decided against installing a subsidiary Door on the ground that it was an unnecessary expense. How was she to know that Doors were getting to be so *shoddy?*

She stepped to the visiphone while the anger still burned in her and said to Richard, "You just go down the road, Dickie, and use the Williamsons' Door."

Ironically, in view of later developments, Richard balked. "Aw, gee, Mom, I'll get dirty. Can't I stay home till the Door is fixed?"

And, as ironically, Mrs. Hanshaw insisted. With her finger on the combination board of the phone, she said, "You won't get dirty if you put flexies on your shoes, and don't forget to brush yourself well before you go into their house."

"But, golly—"

"No back-talk, Dickie. You've got to be in school. Just let me see you walk out of here. And quickly, or you'll be late."

The mekkano, an advanced model and very responsive, was already standing before Richard with flexies in one appendage.

Richard pulled the transparent plastic shields over his shoes and moved down the hall with visible reluctance. "I don't even know how to work this thing, Mom."

"You just push that button," Mrs. Hanshaw called. "The red button. Where it says 'For Emergency Use.' And don't dawdle. Do you want the mekkano to go along with you?"

"Gosh, no," he called back, morosely, "what do you think I am? A baby? Gosh!" His muttering was cut off by a slam.

With flying fingers, Mrs. Hanshaw punched the appropriate combination on the phone board and thought of the things she intended saying to the company about this.

Joe Bloom, a reasonably young man, who had gone through technology school with added training in force-field mechanics, was at the Hanshaw residence in less than half an hour. He was really quite competent, though Mrs. Hanshaw regarded his youth with deep suspicion.

She opened the movable house-panel when he first signaled and her sight of him was as he stood there, brushing at himself vigorously to remove the dust of the open air. He took off his flexies and dropped them where he stood. Mrs. Hanshaw closed the house-panel against the flash of raw sunlight that had entered. She found herself irrationally hoping that the step-by-step trip from the public Door had been an unpleasant one. Or perhaps that the public Door itself had been out of order and the youth had had to lug his tools even farther than the necessary two hundred yards. She wanted the Company, or its representative at least, to suffer a bit. It would teach them what broken Doors meant.

But he seemed cheerful and unperturbed as he said, "Good morning, ma'am. I came to see about your Door."

"I'm glad someone did," said Mrs. Hanshaw, ungraciously. "My day is quite ruined."

"Sorry, ma'am. What seems to be the trouble?"

"It just won't work. Nothing at all happens when you adjust co-ords," said Mrs. Hanshaw. "There was no warning at all. I had to send my son out to the neighbors through that—that thing."

She pointed to the entrance through which the repairman had come.

He smiled and spoke out of the conscious wisdom of his own specialized training in Doors. "That's a door, too, ma'am. You don't give that kind a capital letter when you write it. It's a hand-door, sort of. It used to be the only kind once."

"Well, at least it works. My boy's had to go out in the dirt and germs."

"It's not bad outside today, ma'am," he said, with the connoisseur-like air of one whose profession forced him into the open nearly every day. "Sometimes it *is* real unpleasant. But I guess you want I should fix this here Door, ma'am, so I'll get on with it."

He sat down on the floor, opened the large tool case he had brought in with him and in half a minute, by use of a point-demagnetizer, he had the control panel removed and a set of intricate vitals exposed.

He whistled to himself as he placed the fine electrodes of the field-analyzer on numerous points, studying the shifting needles on the dials. Mrs. Hanshaw watched him, arms folded.

Finally, he said, "Well, here's something," and with a deft twist, he disengaged the brake-valve.

He tapped it with a fingernail and said, "This here brake-valve is depolarized, ma'am. There's your whole trouble." He ran his finger along the little pigeonholes in his tool case and lifted out a duplicate of the object he had taken from the door mechanism. "These things just go all of a sudden. Can't predict it."

He put the control panel back and stood up. "It'll work now, ma'am."

He punched a reference combination, blanked it, then punched another. Each time, the dull gray of the Door gave way to a deep, velvety blackness. He said, "Will you sign here, ma'am? And put down your charge number, too, please? Thank you, ma'am."

He punched a new combination, that of his home factory, and with a polite touch of finger to forehead, he stepped through the Door. As his body entered the blackness, it cut off sharply. Less and less of him was visible and the tip of his tool case was the last thing that showed. A second after he had passed through completely, the Door turned back to dull gray.

Half an hour later, when Mrs. Hanshaw had finally completed her interrupted preparations and was fuming over the misfortune of the morning, the phone buzzed annoyingly and her real troubles began.

Miss Elizabeth Robbins was distressed. Little Dick Hanshaw had always been a good pupil. She hated to report him like this. And yet, she told herself, his actions were certainly queer. And she would talk to his mother, not to the principal.

She slipped out to the phone during the morning study period, leaving a student in charge. She made her connection and found herself staring at Mrs. Hanshaw's handsome and somewhat formidable head.

Miss Robbins quailed, but it was too late to turn back. She said, diffidently, "Mrs. Hanshaw, I'm Miss Robbins." She ended on a rising note.

Mrs. Hanshaw looked blank, then said, "Richard's teacher?" That, too, ended on a rising note.

"That's right. I called you, Mrs. Hanshaw," Miss Robbins plunged right into it, "to tell you that Dick was quite late to school this morning."

"He *was?* But that couldn't be. I saw him leave."

Miss Robbins looked astonished. She said, "You mean you saw him use the Door?"

Mrs. Hanshaw said quickly, "Well, no. Our Door was temporarily out of order. I sent him to a neighbor and he used that Door."

"Are you sure?"

"Of course I'm sure. I wouldn't lie to you."

"No, no, Mrs. Hanshaw. I wasn't implying that at all. I meant are you sure he found the way to the neighbor? He might have got lost."

"Ridiculous. We have the proper maps, and I'm sure Richard knows the location of every house in District A-3." Then, with the quiet pride of one who knows what is her due, she added, "Not that he ever needs to know, of course. The co-ords are all that are necessary at any time."

Miss Robbins, who came from a family that had always had to economize rigidly on the use of its Doors (the price of power being what it was) and who had therefore run errands on foot until quite an advanced age, resented the pride. She said, quite clearly, "Well, I'm afraid, Mrs. Hanshaw, that Dick did not use the neighbor's Door. He was over an hour late to school and the condition of his flexies made it quite obvious that he tramped cross-country. They were *muddy.*"

"*Muddy?*" Mrs. Hanshaw repeated the emphasis on the word. "What did he say? What was his excuse?"

Miss Robbins couldn't help but feel a little glad at the discomfiture of the other woman. She said, "He wouldn't talk about it. Frankly, Mrs. Hanshaw, he seems ill. That's why I called you. Perhaps you might want to have a doctor look at him."

"Is he running a temperature?" The mother's voice went shrill.

"Oh, no. I don't mean physically ill. It's just his attitude and the look in his eyes." She hesitated, then said with every attempt at delicacy, "I thought perhaps a routine checkup with a psychic probe—"

She didn't finish. Mrs. Hanshaw, in a chilled voice and with what was as close to a snort as her breeding would permit, said, "Are you implying that Richard is *neurotic?*"

"Oh, no, Mrs. Hanshaw, but—"

"It certainly sounded so. The idea! He has always been perfectly healthy. I'll take this up with him when he gets home. I'm sure there's a perfectly normal explanation which he'll give to *me*."

The connection broke abruptly, and Miss Robbins felt hurt and uncommonly foolish. After all she had only tried to help, to fulfill what she considered an obligation to her students.

She hurried back to the classroom with a glance at the metal face of the wall clock. The study period was drawing to an end. English Composition next.

But her mind wasn't completely on English Composition. Automatically, she called the students to have them read selections from their literary creations. And occasionally she punched one of those selections on tape and ran it through the small vocalizer to show the students how English *should* be read.

The vocalizer's mechanical voice, as always, dripped perfection, but, again as always, lacked character. Sometimes, she wondered if it was wise to try to train the students into a speech that was divorced from individuality and geared only to a mass-average accent and intonation.

Today, however, she had no thought for that. It was Richard Hanshaw she watched. He sat quietly in his seat, quite obviously indifferent to his surroundings. He was lost deep in himself and just not the same boy he had been. It was obvious to her that he had had some unusual experience that morning and, really, she was right to call his mother, although perhaps she ought not to have made the remark about the probe. Still it was quite the thing these days. All sorts of people got probed. There wasn't any disgrace attached to it. Or there shouldn't be, anyway.

She called on Richard, finally. She had to call twice, before he responded and rose to his feet.

The general subject assigned had been: "If you had your choice of traveling on some ancient vehicle, which would you choose, and why?" Miss Robbins tried to use the topic every semester. It was a good one because it carried a sense of history with it. It forced the youngster to think about the manner of living of people in past ages.

She listened while Richard Hanshaw read in a low voice.

"If I had my choice of ancient vehicles," he said, pronouncing the "h" in vehicles, "I would choose the stratoliner. It travels slow like all vehicles but it is clean. Because it travels in the stratosphere, it must be all enclosed so that you are not likely to catch disease. You can see the stars if it is night time almost as good as in a planetarium. If you look down you can see the Earth like a map or maybe see clouds—" He went on for several hundred more words.

She said brightly when he had finished reading, "It's pronounced vee-ick-ulls, Richard. No 'h.' Accent on the first syllable. And you don't say 'travels slow' or 'see good.' What do you say, class?"

There was a small chorus of responses and she went on, "That's right. Now what is the difference between an adjective and an adverb? Who can tell me?"

And so it went. Lunch passed. Some pupils stayed to eat; some went home. Richard stayed. Miss Robbins noted that, as usually he didn't.

The afternoon passed, too, and then there was the final bell and the usual upsurging hum as twenty-five boys and girls rattled their belongings together and took their leisurely place in line.

Miss Robbins clapped her hands together. "Quickly, children. Come, Zelda, take your place."

"I dropped my tape-punch, Miss Robbins," shrilled the girl, defensively.

"Well, pick it up, pick it up. Now children, be brisk, be brisk."

She pushed the button that slid a section of the wall into a recess and revealed the gray blankness of a large Door. It was not the usual Door that the occasional student used in going home for lunch, but an advanced model that was one of the prides of this well-to-do private school.

In addition to its double width, it possessed a large and impressively gear-filled "automatic serial finder" which was capable of adjusting the door for a number of different coordinates at automatic intervals.

At the beginning of the semester, Miss Robbins always had to spend an afternoon with the mechanic, adjusting the device for the coordinates of the homes of the new class. But then, thank goodness, it rarely needed attention for the remainder of the term.

The class lined up alphabetically, first girls, then boys. The door went velvety black and Hester Adams waved her hand and stepped through. "By-y-y—"

The "bye" was cut off in the middle, as it almost always was.

The door went gray, then black again, and Theresa Cantrocchi went through. Gray, black, Zelda Charlowicz. Gray, black, Patricia Coombs. Gray, black, Sara May Evans.

The line grew smaller as the Door swallowed them one by one, depositing each in her home. Of course, an occasional mother forgot to leave the house Door on special reception at the appropriate time and then the school Door remained gray. Automatically, after a minute-long wait, the Door went on to the next combination in line and the pupil in question had to wait till it was all over, after which a phone call to the forgetful parent would set things right. This was always bad for the pupils involved, especially the sensitive ones who took seriously the implication that they were little thought of at home. Miss Robbins always tried to impress this on visiting parents, but it happened at least once every semester just the same.

The girls were all through now. John Abramowitz stepped through and then Edwin Byrne—

Of course, another trouble, and a more frequent one was the boy or girl who got into line out of place. They *would* do it despite the teacher's sharpest watch, particularly at the beginning of the term when the proper order was less familiar to them.

When that happened, children would be popping into the wrong houses by the half-dozen and would have to be sent back. It always meant a mix-up that took minutes to straighten out and parents were invariably irate.

Miss Robbins was suddenly aware that the line had

stopped. She spoke sharply to the boy at the head of the line.

"Step through, Samuel. What are you waiting for?"

Samuel Jones raised a complacent countenance and said, "It's not my combination, Miss Robbins."

"Well, whose is it?" She looked impatiently down the line of five remaining boys. "Who was out of place?"

"It's Dick Hanshaw's, Miss Robbins."

"Where is he?"

Another boy answered, with the rather repulsive tone of self-righteousness all children automatically assume in reporting the deviations of their friends to elders in authority, "He went through the fire door, Miss Robbins."

"What?"

The schoolroom Door had passed on to another combination and Samuel Jones passed through. One by one, the rest followed.

Miss Robbins was alone in the classroom. She stepped to the fire door. It was a small affair, manually operated, and hidden behind a bend in the wall so that it would not break up the uniform structure of the room.

She opened it a crack. It was there as a means of escape from the building in case of fire, a device which was enforced by an anachronistic law that did not take into account the modern methods of automatic fire-fighting that all public buildings used. There was nothing outside, but the—outside. The sunlight was harsh and a dusty wind was blowing.

Miss Robbins closed the door. She was glad she had called Mrs. Hanshaw. She had done her duty. More than ever, it was obvious that something was wrong with Richard. She suppressed the impulse to phone again.

Mrs. Hanshaw did not go to New York that day. She remained home in a mixture of anxiety and an irrational anger, the latter directed against the impudent Miss Robbins.

Some fifteen minutes before school's end, her anxiety drove her to the Door. Last year she had had it equipped with an automatic device which activated it to the school's coordinates at five of three and kept it so, barring manual adjustment, until Richard arrived.

Her eyes were fixed on the Door's dismal gray (why couldn't an inactive force-field be any other color, something more lively and cheerful?) and waited. Her hands felt cold as she squeezed them together.

The Door turned black at the precise second but nothing happened. The minutes passed and Richard was late. Then quite late. Then very late.

It was quarter of four and she was distracted. Normally, she would have phoned the school, but she couldn't, she couldn't. Not after that teacher had deliberately cast doubts on Richard's mental well-being. How could she?

Mrs. Hanshaw moved about restlessly, lighting a cigarette with fumbling fingers, then smudging it out. Could it be something quite normal? Could Richard be staying after school for some reason? Surely he would have told her in advance. A gleam of light struck her; he knew she was planning to go to New York and might not be back till late in the evening—

No, he would surely have told her. Why fool herself?

Her pride was breaking. She would have to call the school, or even (she closed her eyes and teardrops squeezed through between the lashes) the police.

And when she opened her eyes, Richard stood before her, eyes on the ground and his whole bearing that of someone waiting for a blow to fall.

"Hello, Mom."

Mrs. Hanshaw's anxiety transmuted itself instantly (in a manner known only to mothers) into anger. "Where have you been, Richard?"

And then, before she could go further into the refrain concerning careless, unthinking sons and broken-hearted mothers, she took note of his appearance in greater detail, and gasped in utter horror.

She said, "You've been in the open."

Her son looked down at his dusty shoes (minus flexies), at the dirt marks that streaked his lower arms and at the small, but definite tear in his shirt. He said, "Gosh, Mom, I just thought I'd—" and he faded out.

She said, "Was there anything wrong with the school Door?"

"No, Mom."

"Do you realize I've been worried sick about you?" She

waited vainly for an answer. "Well, I'll talk to you afterward, young man. First, you're taking a bath, and every stitch of your clothing is being thrown out. Mekkano!"

But the mekkano had already reacted properly to the phrase "taking a bath" and was off to the bathroom in its silent glide.

"You take your shoes off right here," said Mrs. Hanshaw, "then march after mekkano."

Richard did as he was told with a resignation that placed him beyond futile protest.

Mrs. Hanshaw picked up the soiled shoes between thumb and forefinger and dropped them down the disposal chute which hummed in faint dismay at the unexpected load. She dusted her hands carefully on a tissue which she allowed to float down the chute after the shoes.

She did not join Richard at dinner but let him eat in the worse-than-lack-of-company of the mekkano. This, she thought, would be an active sign of her displeasure and would do more than any amount of scolding or punishment to make him realize that he had done wrong. Richard, she frequently told herself, was a sensitive boy.

But she went up to see him at bedtime.

She smiled at him and spoke softly. She thought that would be the best way. After all, he had been punished already.

She said, "What happened today, Dickie-boy?" She had called him that when he was a baby and just the sound of the name softened her nearly to tears.

But he only looked away and his voice was stubborn and cold. "I just don't like to go through those darn Doors, Mom."

"But why ever not?"

He shuffled his hands over the filmy sheet (fresh, clean, antiseptic and, of course, disposable after each use) and said, "I just don't like them."

"But then how do you expect to go to school, Dickie?"

"I'll get up early," he mumbled.

"But there's nothing wrong with Doors."

"Don't like 'em." He never once looked up at her.

She said, despairingly, "Oh, well, you have a good sleep and tomorrow morning, you'll feel much better."

She kissed him and left the room, automatically passing

her hand through the photo-cell beam and in that manner dimming the room-lights.

But she had trouble sleeping herself that night. Why should Dickie dislike Doors so suddenly? They had never bothered him before. To be sure, the Door had broken down in the morning but that should make him appreciate them all the more.

Dickie was behaving so unreasonably.

Unreasonably? That reminded her of Miss Robbins and her diagnosis and Mrs. Hanshaw's soft jaw set in the darkness and privacy of her bedroom. Nonsense! The boy was upset and a night's sleep was all the therapy he needed.

But the next morning when she arose, her son was not in the house. The mekkano could not speak but it could answer questions with gestures of its appendages equivalent to a yes or no, and it did not take Mrs. Hanshaw more than half a minute to ascertain that the boy had arisen thirty minutes earlier than usual, skimped his shower, and darted out of the house.

But not by way of the Door.

Out the other way—through the door. Small "d."

Mrs. Hanshaw's visiphone signaled genteelly at 3:10 P.M. that day. Mrs. Hanshaw guessed the caller and having activated the receiver, saw that she had guessed correctly. A quick glance in the mirror to see that she was properly calm after a day of abstracted concern and worry and then she keyed in her own transmission.

"Yes, Miss Robbins," she said coldly.

Richard's teacher was a bit breathless. She said, "Mrs. Hanshaw, Richard has deliberately left through the fire door although I told him to use the regular Door. I do not know where he went."

Mrs. Hanshaw said, carefully, "He left to come home."

Miss Robbins looked dismayed, "Do you approve of this?"

Pale-faced, Mrs. Hanshaw set about putting the teacher in her place. "I don't think it is up to you to criticize. If my son does not choose to use the Door, it is his affair and mine. I don't think there is any school ruling that would force him to use the Door, is there?" Her bearing quite plainly intimated that if there were she would see to it that it was changed.

Miss Robbins flushed and had time for one quick remark before contact was broken. She said, "I'd have him probed. I really would."

Mrs. Hanshaw remained standing before the quartzinium plate, staring blindly at its blank face. Her sense of family placed her for a few moments quite firmly on Richard's side. Why *did* he have to use the Door if he chose not to? And then she settled down to wait and pride battled the gnawing anxiety that something after all was wrong with Richard.

He came home with a look of defiance on his face, but his mother, with a strenuous effort at self-control, met him as though nothing were out of the ordinary.

For weeks, she followed that policy. It's nothing, she told herself. It's a vagary. He'll grow out of it.

It grew into an almost normal state of affairs. Then, too, every once in a while, perhaps three days in a row, she would come down to breakfast to find Richard waiting sullenly at the Door, then using it when school time came. She always refrained from commenting on the matter.

Always, when he did that, and especially when he followed it up by arriving home via the Door, her heart grew warm and she thought, "Well, it's over." But always with the passing of one day, two or three, he would return like an addict to his drug and drift silently out by the door— small "d"—before she woke.

And each time she thought despairingly of psychiatrists and probes, and each time the vision of Miss Robbins' low-bred satisfaction at (possibly) learning of it, stopped her, although she was scarcely aware that that was the true motive.

Meanwhile, she lived with it and made the best of it. The mekkano was instructed to wait at the door—small "d"—with a Tergo kit and a change of clothing. Richard washed and changed without resistance. His underthings, socks and flexies were disposable in any case, and Mrs. Hanshaw bore uncomplainingly the expense of daily disposal of shirts. Trousers she finally allowed to go a week before disposal on condition of rigorous nightly cleansing.

One day she suggested that Richard accompany her on a trip to New York. It was more a vague desire to keep him in sight than part of any purposeful plan. He did not object. He was even happy. He stepped right through the Door, unconcerned. He didn't hesitate. He even lacked the look of resentment he wore on those mornings he used the Door to go to school.

Mrs. Hanshaw rejoiced. This could be a way of weaning him back into Door usage, and she racked her ingenuity for excuses to make trips with Richard. She even raised her power bill to quite unheard-of heights by suggesting, and going through with, a trip to Canton for the day in order to witness a Chinese festival.

That was on a Sunday, and the next morning Richard marched directly to the hole in the wall he always used. Mrs. Hanshaw, having wakened particularly early, witnessed that. For once, badgered past endurance, she called after him plaintively, "Why not the Door, Dickie?"

He said, briefly, "It's all right for Canton," and stepped out of the house.

So that plan ended in failure. And then, one day, Richard came home soaking wet. The mekkano hovered about him uncertainly and Mrs. Hanshaw, just returned from a four-hour visit with her sister in Iowa, cried, "Richard Hanshaw!"

He said, hang-dog fashion, "It started raining. All of a sudden, it started raining."

For a moment, the word didn't register with her. Her own school days and her studies of geography were twenty years in the past. And then she remembered and caught the vision of water pouring recklessly and endlessly down from the sky—a mad cascade of water with no tap to turn off, no button to push, no contact to break.

She said, "And you stayed out in it?"

He said, "Well, gee, Mom, I came home fast as I could. I didn't know it was going to rain."

Mrs. Hanshaw had nothing to say. She was appalled and the sensation filled her too full for words to find a place.

Two days later, Richard found himself with a running nose, and a dry, scratchy throat. Mrs. Hanshaw had to admit that the virus of disease had found a lodging in her house, as though it were a miserable hovel of the Iron Age.

It was over that that her stubbornness and pride broke and she admitted to herself that, after all, Richard had to have psychiatric help.

Mrs. Hanshaw chose a psychiatrist with care. Her first impulse was to find one at a distance. For a while, she considered stepping directly into the San Francisco Medical Center and choosing one at random.

And then it occurred to her that by doing that she would become merely an anonymous consultant. She would have no way of obtaining any greater consideration for herself than would be forthcoming to any public-Door user of the city slums. Now if she remained in her own community, her word would carry weight——

She consulted the district map. It was one of that excellent series prepared by Doors, Inc., and distributed free of charge to their clients. Mrs. Hanshaw couldn't quite suppress that little thrill of civic pride as she unfolded the map. It wasn't a fine-print directory of Door coordinates only. It was an actual map, with each house carefully located.

And why not? District A-3 was a name of moment in the world, a badge of aristocracy. It was the first community on the planet to have been established on a completely Doored basis. The first, the largest, the wealthiest, the best-known. It needed no factories, no stores. It didn't even need roads. Each house was a little secluded castle, the Door of which had entry anywhere the world over where other Doors existed.

Carefully, she followed down the keyed listing of the five thousand families of District A-3. She knew it included several psychiatrists. The learned professions were well represented in A-3.

Doctor Hamilton Sloane was the second name she arrived at and her finger lingered upon the map. His office was scarcely two miles from the Hanshaw residence. She liked his name. The fact that he lived in A-3 was evidence of worth. And he was a neighbor, practically a neighbor. He would understand that it was a matter of urgency—and confidential.

Firmly, she put in a call to his office to make an appointment.

Doctor Hamilton Sloane was a comparatively young man, not quite forty. He was of good family and he had indeed heard of Mrs. Hanshaw.

He listened to her quietly and then said, "And this all began with the Door breakdown."

"That's right, Doctor."

"Does he show any fear of the Doors?"

"Of course not. What an idea!" She was plainly startled.

"It's possible, Mrs. Hanshaw, it's possible. After all, when you stop to think of how a Door works it is rather a frightening thing, really. You step into a Door, and for an instant your atoms are converted into field-energies, transmitted to another part of space and reconverted into matter. For that instant you're not alive."

"I'm sure no one thinks of such things."

"But your son may. He witnessed the breakdown of the Door. He may be saying to himself, 'What if the Door breaks down just as I'm halfway through?' "

"But that's nonsense. He still uses the Door. He's even been to Canton with me; Canton, China. And as I told you, he uses it for school about once or twice a week."

"Freely? Cheerfully?"

"Well," said Mrs. Hanshaw, reluctantly, "he does seem a bit put out by it. But really, Doctor, there isn't much use talking about it, is there? If you would do a quick probe, see where the trouble was," and she finished on a bright note, "why, that would be all. I'm sure it's quite a minor thing."

Dr. Sloane sighed. He detested the word "probe" and there was scarcely any word he heard oftener.

"Mrs. Hanshaw," he said patiently, "there is no such thing as a quick probe. Now I know the mag-strips are full of it and it's a rage in some circles, but it's much over-rated."

"Are you serious?"

"Quite. The probe is very complicated and the theory is that it traces mental circuits. You see, the cells of the brains are interconnected in a large variety of ways. Some of those interconnected paths are more used than others. They represent habits of thought, both conscious and un-conscious. Theory has it that these paths in any given brain can be used to diagnose mental ills early and with certainty."

"Well, then?"

"But subjection to the probe is quite a fearful thing, especially to a child. It's a traumatic experience. It takes over an hour. And even then, the results must be sent to the Central Psychoanalytical Bureau for analysis, and that could take weeks. And on top of all that, Mrs. Hanshaw, there are many psychiatrists who think the theory of probe-analyses to be most uncertain."

Mrs. Hanshaw compressed her lips. "You mean nothing can be done."

Dr. Sloane smiled. "Not at all. There were psychiatrists for centuries before there were probes. I suggest that you let me talk to the boy."

"Talk to him? Is that all?"

"I'll come to you for background information when necessary, but the essential thing, I think, is to talk to the boy."

"Really, Dr. Sloane, I doubt if he'll discuss the matter with you. He won't talk to me about it and I'm his mother."

"That often happens," the psychiatrist assured her. "A child will sometimes talk more readily to a stranger. In any case, I cannot take the case otherwise."

Mrs. Hanshaw rose, not at all pleased. "When can you come, Doctor?"

"What about this coming Saturday? The boy won't be in school. Will you be busy?"

"We will be ready."

She made a dignified exit. Dr. Sloane accompanied her through the small reception room to his office Door and waited while she punched the coordinates of her house. He watched her pass through. She became a half-woman, a quarter-woman, an isolated elbow and foot, a nothing.

It *was* frightening.

Did a Door ever break down during passage, leaving half a body here and half there? He had never heard of such a case, but he imagined it could happen.

He returned to his desk and looked up the time of his next appointment. It was obvious to him that Mrs. Hanshaw was annoyed and disappointed at not having arranged for a psychic probe treatment.

Why, for God's sake? Why should a thing like the probe, an obvious piece of quackery in his own opinion, get such a hold on the general public? It must be part of this general trend toward machines. Anything man can do, machines can do better. Machines! More machines! Machines for anything and everything! O tempora! O mores!

Oh, hell!

His resentment of the probe was beginning to bother him. Was it a fear of technological unemployment, a basic insecurity on his part, a mechanophobia, if that was the word—

He made a mental note to discuss this with his own analyst.

Dr. Sloane had to feel his way. The boy wasn't a patient who had come to him, more or less anxious to talk, more or less anxious to be helped.

Under the circumstances it would have been best to keep his first meeting with Richard short and noncommittal. It would have been sufficient merely to establish himself as something less than a total stranger. The next time he would be someone Richard had seen before. The time after he would be an acquaintance, and after that a friend of the family.

Unfortunately, Mrs. Hanshaw was not likely to accept a long-drawn-out process. She would go searching for a probe and, of course, she would find it.

And harm the boy. He was certain of that.

It was for that reason he felt he must sacrifice a little of the proper caution and risk a small crisis.

An uncomfortable ten minutes had passed when he decided he must try. Mrs. Hanshaw was smiling in a rather rigid way, eyeing him narrowly, as though she expected verbal magic from him. Richard wriggled in his seat, unresponsive to Dr. Sloane's tentative comments, overcome with boredom and unable not to show it.

Dr. Sloane said, with casual suddenness, "Would you like to take a walk with me, Richard?"

The boy's eyes widened and he stopped wriggling. He looked directly at Dr. Sloane. "A walk, sir?"

"I mean, outside."

"Do you go—outside?"

"Sometimes. When I feel like it."

Richard was on his feet, holding down a squirming eagerness. "I didn't think anyone did."

"I do. And I like company."

The boy sat down, uncertainly. "Mom—?"

Mrs. Hanshaw had stiffened in her seat, her compressed lips radiating horror, but she managed to say, "Why certainly, Dickie. But watch yourself."

And she managed a quick and baleful glare at Dr. Sloane.

In one respect, Dr. Sloane had lied. He did *not* go outside "sometimes." He hadn't been in the open since early college days. True, he had been athletically inclined (still was to some extent) but in his time the indoor ultraviolet chambers, swimming pools and tennis courts had flourished. For those with the price, they were much more satisfactory than the outdoor equivalents, open to the elements as they were, could possibly be. There was no occasion to go outside.

So there was a crawling sensation about his skin when he felt wind touch it, and he put down his flexied shoes on bare grass with a gingerly movement.

"Hey, look at that." Richard was quite different now, laughing, his reserve broken down.

Dr. Sloane had time only to catch a flash of blue that ended in a tree. Leaves rustled and he lost it.

"What was it?"

"A bird," said Richard. "A blue kind of bird."

Dr. Sloane looked about him in amazement. The Hanshaw residence was on a rise of ground, and he could see for miles. The area was only lightly wooded and between clumps of trees, grass gleamed brightly in the sunlight.

Colors set in deeper green made red and yellow patterns. They were flowers. From the books he had viewed in the course of his lifetime and from the old video shows, he had learned enough so that all this had an eerie sort of familiarity.

And yet the grass was so trim, the flowers so patterned. Dimly, he realized he had been expecting something wilder. He said, "Who takes care of all this?"

Richard shrugged. "I dunno. Maybe the mekkanos do it."

"Mekkanos?"

"There's loads of them around. Sometimes they got a sort of atomic knife they hold near the ground. It cuts the grass. And they're always fooling around with the flowers and things. There's one of them over there."

It was a small object, half a mile away. Its metal skin cast back highlights as it moved slowly over the gleaming meadow, engaged in some sort of activity that Dr. Sloane could not identify.

Dr. Sloane was astonished. Here it was a perverse sort of estheticism, a kind of conspicuous consumption—

"What's that?" he asked suddenly.

Richard looked. He said, "That's a house. Belongs to the Froehlichs. Coordinates, A-3, 23, 461. That little pointy building over there is the public Door."

Dr. Sloane was staring at the house. Was that what it looked like from the outside? Somehow he had imagined something much more cubic, and taller.

"Come along," shouted Richard, running ahead.

Dr. Sloane followed more sedately. "Do you know all the houses about here?"

"Just about."

"Where is A-23, 26, 475?" It was his own house, of course.

Richard looked about. "Let's see. Oh, sure, I know where it is—you see that water there?"

"Water?" Dr. Sloane made out a line of silver curving across the green.

"Sure. Real water. Just sort of running over rocks and things. It keeps running all the time. You can get across it if you step on the rocks. It's called a river."

More like a creek, thought Dr. Sloane. He had studied geography, of course, but what passed for the subject these days was really economic and cultural geography. Physical geography was almost an extinct science except among specialists. Still, he knew what rivers and creeks were, in a theoretical sort of way.

Richard was still talking. "Well, just past the river, over that hill with the big clump of trees and down the other side a way is A-23, 26, 475. It's a light green house with a white roof."

"It is?" Dr. Sloane was genuinely astonished. He hadn't known it was green.

Some small animal disturbed the grass in its anxiety to avoid the oncoming feet. Richard looked after it and shrugged. "You can't catch them. I tried."

A butterfly flitted past, a wavering bit of yellow. Dr. Sloane's eyes followed it.

There was a low hum that lay over the fields, interspersed with an occasional harsh, calling sound, a rattle, a twittering, a chatter that rose, then fell. As his ear accustomed itself to listening, Dr. Sloane heard a thousand sounds, and none were man-made.

A shadow fell upon the scene, advancing toward him, covering him. It was suddenly cooler and he looked upward, startled.

Richard said, "It's just a cloud. It'll go away in a minute —looka these flowers. They're the kind that smell."

They were several hundred yards from the Hanshaw residence. The cloud passed and the sun shone once more. Dr. Sloane looked back and was appalled at the distance they had covered. If they moved out of sight of the house and if Richard ran off, would he be able to find his way back?

He pushed the thought away impatiently and looked out toward the line of water (nearer now) and past it to where his own house must be. He thought wonderingly: Light green?

He said, "You must be quite an explorer."

Richard said, with a shy pride, "When I go to school and come back, I always try to use a different route and see new things."

"But you don't go outside every morning, do you? Sometimes you use the Doors, I imagine."

"Oh, sure."

"Why is that, Richard?" Somehow, Dr. Sloane felt there might be significance in that point.

But Richard quashed him. With his eyebrows up and a look of astonishment on his face, he said, "Well, gosh, some mornings it rains and I *have* to use the Door. I hate that, but what can you do? About two weeks ago, I got caught in the rain and I—" he looked about him automatically, and his voice sank to a whisper "—caught a cold, and wasn't Mom upset, though."

Dr. Sloane sighed. "Shall we go back now?"

There was a quick disappointment on Richard's face. "Aw, what for?"

"You remind me that your mother must be waiting for us."

"I guess so." The boy turned reluctantly.

They walked slowly back. Richard was saying, chattily, "I wrote a composition at school once about how if I could go on some ancient vehicle" (he pronounced it with exaggerated care) "I'd go in a stratoliner and look at stars and clouds and things. Oh, boy, I was sure nuts."

"You'd pick something else now?"

"You bet. I'd go in an aut'm'bile, real slow. Then I'd see everything there was."

Mrs. Hanshaw seemed troubled, uncertain. "You don't think it's abnormal, then, Doctor?"

"Unusual, perhaps, but not abnormal. He likes the outside."

"But how can he? It's so dirty, so unpleasant."

"That's a matter of individual taste. A hundred years ago our ancestors were all outside most of the time. Even today, I dare say there are a million Africans who have never seen a Door."

"But Richard's always been taught to behave himself the way a decent person in District A-3 is supposed to behave," said Mrs. Hanshaw, fiercely. "Not like an African or— or an ancestor."

"That may be part of the trouble, Mrs. Hanshaw. He feels this urge to go outside and yet he feels it to be wrong. He's ashamed to talk about it to you or to his teacher. It forces him into sullen retreat and it could eventually be dangerous."

"Then how can we persuade him to stop?"

Dr. Sloane said, "Don't try. Channel the activity instead. The day your Door broke down, he was forced outside, found he liked it, and that set a pattern. He used the trip to school and back as an excuse to repeat that first exciting experience. Now suppose you agree to let him out of the house for two hours on Saturdays and Sundays. Suppose he gets it through his head that after all he can go outside without necessarily having to go anywhere in the process. Don't you think he'll be willing to use the Door to go to school and back thereafter? And don't you think that will stop the trouble he's now having with his teacher and probably with his fellow-pupils?"

"But then will matters remain so? Must they? Won't he ever be normal again?"

Dr. Sloane rose to his feet. "Mrs. Hanshaw, he's as normal as need be right now. Right now, he's tasting the joys of the forbidden. If you cooperate with him, show that you don't disapprove, it will lose some of its attraction right there. Then, as he grows older, he will become more aware of the expectations and demands of society. He will learn to conform. After all, there is a little of the rebel in all of us, but it generally dies down as we grow old and tired. Unless, that is, it is unreasonably suppressed and allowed to build up pressure. Don't do that. Richard will be all right."

He walked to the Door.

Mrs. Hanshaw said, "And you don't think a probe will be necessary, Doctor?"

He turned and said vehemently, "No, definitely not! There is nothing about the boy that requires it. Understand? Nothing."

His fingers hesitated an inch from the combination board and the expression on his face grew lowering.

"What's the matter, Dr. Sloane?" asked Mrs. Hanshaw.

But he didn't hear her because he was thinking of the Door and the psychic probe and all the rising, choking tide of machinery. There is a little of the rebel in all of us, he thought.

So he said in a soft voice, as his hand fell away from the board and his feet turned away from the Door, "You know, it's such a beautiful day that I think I'll walk."

William Saroyan

# THE HUMMINGBIRD THAT LIVED THROUGH WINTER

*Sometimes we are amazed that a small, a trivial act can start a chain of destruction. But a chain of life can be begun by a small act, as well. In this beautiful story, an old man and a young boy show us how.*

———————◆◆◆◆◆———————

Sometimes even instinct is overpowered by individuality—in creatures other than men, I mean. In men instinct is supposed to be controlled, but whether or not it ever actually is I leave to others. At any rate, the fundamental instinct of most—or all—creatures is to live. Each form of life has an instinctive technique of defense against other forms of life, as well as against the elements. What happens to hummingbirds is something I have never found out—from actual observation or from reading. They die, that's true. And they're born somehow or other, although I have never seen a hummingbird's egg, or a young hummingbird.

The mature hummingbird itself is so small that the egg must be magnificent, probably one of the most smiling little things in the world. Now, if hummingbirds come into the world through some other means than eggs, I ask the reader to forgive me. The only thing I know about Agass Agasig Agassig Agazig (well, the great American naturalist) is that he once studied turtle eggs, and in order to get the information he was seeking, had to find fresh ones. This caused an exciting adventure in Boston to a young fellow

207

who wrote about it six or seven years before I read it, when I was fourteen. I was fourteen in 1922, which goes to show you how unimportant the years are when you're dealing with eggs of any kind. I envy the people who study birds, and some day I hope to find out everything that's known about hummingbirds.

I've gathered from rumor that the hummingbird travels incredible distances on incredibly little energy—what carries him, then? Spirit? But the best things I know about hummingbirds are the things I've noticed about them myself: that they are on hand when the sun is out in earnest, when the blossoms are with us, and the smell of them everywhere. You can hardly go through the best kind of day without seeing a hummingbird suspended like a little miracle in a shaft of light or over a big flower or a cluster of little ones. Or turning like gay insanity and shooting straight as an arrow toward practically nothing, for no reason, or for the reason that it's alive. Now, how can creatures such as that—so delicately magnificent and mad —possibly find time for the routine business of begetting young? Or for the exercise of instinct in self-defense? Well, however it may be, let a good day come by the grace of God, and with it will come the hummingbirds.

As I started to say, however, it appears that sometimes even instinct fails to operate in a specie. Or species. Or whatever it is. Anyhow, when all of a kind of living thing turn and go somewhere, in order to stay alive, in order to escape cold or whatever it might be, sometimes, it appears, one of them does not go. Why he does not go I cannot say. He may be eccentric, or there may be exalted reasons— specific instead of abstract passion for another of its kind— perhaps dead—or for a place. Or it may be stupidity, or stubbornness. Who can ever know?

There was a hummingbird once which in the wintertime did not leave our neighborhood in Fresno, California.

I'll tell you about it.

Across the street lived old Dikran, who was almost blind. He was past eighty and his wife was only a few years younger. They had a little house that was as neat inside as it was ordinary outside—except for old Dikran's garden, which was the best thing of its kind in the world. Plants, bushes, trees—all strong, in sweet black moist earth whose guardian was old Dikran. All things from the sky loved this spot in our poor neighborhood, and old Dikran loved *them*.

One freezing Sunday, in the dead of winter, as I came home from Sunday School I saw old Dikran standing in the middle of the street trying to distinguish what was in his hand. Instead of going into our house to the fire, as I had wanted to do, I stood on the steps of the front porch and watched the old man. He would turn around and look upward at his trees and then back to the palm of his hand. He stood in the street at least two minutes and then at last he came to me. He held his hand out, and in Armenian he said, "What is this in my hand?"

I looked.

"It is a hummingbird," I said half in English and half in Armenian. Hummingbird I said in English because I didn't know its name in Armenian.

"What is that?" old Dikran asked.

"The little bird," I said. "You know. The one that comes in the summer and stands in the air and then shoots away. The one with the wings that beat so fast you can't see them. It's in your hand. It's dying."

"Come with me," the old man said. "I can't see, and the old lady's at church. I can feel its heart beating. Is it in a bad way? Look again, once."

I looked again. It was a sad thing to behold. This wonderful little creature of summertime in the big rough hand of the old peasant. Here it was in the cold of winter, absolutely helpless and pathetic, not suspended in a shaft of summer light, not the most alive thing in the world, but the most helpless and heartbreaking.

"It's dying," I said.

The old man lifted his hand to his mouth and blew warm breath on the little thing in his hand which he could not even see. "Stay now," he said in Armenian. "It is not long till summer. Stay, swift and lovely."

We went into the kitchen of his little house, and while he blew warm breath on the bird he told me what to do.

"Put a tablespoonful of honey over the gas fire and pour it into my hand, but be sure it is not too hot."

This was done.

After a moment the hummingbird began to show signs

of fresh life. The warmth of the room, the vapor of the warm honey—and, well, the will and love of the old man. Soon the old man could feel the change in his hand, and after a moment or two the hummingbird began to take little dabs of the honey.

"It will live," the old man announced. "Stay and watch."

The transformation was incredible. The old man kept his hand generously open, and I expected the helpless bird to shoot upward out of his hand, suspend itself in space, and scare the life out of me—which is exactly what happened. The new life of the little bird was magnificent. It spun about in the little kitchen, going to the window, coming back to the heat, suspending, circling as if it were summertime and it had never felt better in its whole life.

The old man sat on the plain chair, blind but attentive. He listened carefully and tried to see, but of course he couldn't. He kept asking about the bird, how it seemed to be, whether it showed signs of weakening again, what its spirit was, and whether or not it appeared to be restless; and I kept describing the bird to him.

When the bird was restless and wanted to go, the old man said, "Open the window and let it go."

"Will it live?" I asked.

"It is alive now and wants to go," he said. "Open the window."

I opened the window, the hummingbird stirred about here and there, feeling the cold from the outside, suspended itself in the area of the open window, stirring this way and that, and then it was gone.

"Close the window," the old man said.

We talked a minute or two and then I went home.

The old man claimed the hummingbird lived through that winter, but I never knew for sure. I saw hummingbirds again when summer came, but I couldn't tell one from the other.

One day in the summer I asked the old man.

"Did it live?"

"The little bird?" he said.

"Yes," I said. "That we gave the honey to. You remember. The little bird that was dying in the winter. Did it live?"

"Look about you," the old man said. "Do you see the bird?"

"I see humming*birds*," I said.

"Each of them is our bird," the old man said. "Each of them, each of them," he said swiftly and gently.